Praise for *The Lookback Window*

Named one of the best books of the year by
Vanity Fair, **Debutiful,** and *CrimeReads*

"Hertz has managed to tell a story of queer healing with all the narrative force of a thriller and the searing fury of an indictment. It's an achievement of language, of style, in which the process of finding one's way back to the world is considered at least in part as an act of learning to 'speak the unspeakable.' It's a matter, Hertz seems to say, of finding the right words. . . . At his best, Hertz sheds the trappings of traditional realism, adopting instead a swerving, almost psychedelic style that mirrors the abrupt and mercurial perceptions of a turbulent mind. He follows the worthy example of writers like Jean Rhys, Gary Indiana, and Denis Johnson."

—*The New York Times Book Review* (editors' choice)

"At turns poetic and chilling—and wholly, unapologetically queer—*The Lookback Window* . . . is brutally told. I had to look away, put the book down, take a deep breath often. But it proved impossible to ever stay away from."

—*Vanity Fair*

"[*The Lookback Window* is] a herald of disruption, transcendence, and resilience, and its momentum is unlikely to halt anytime soon."

—*BOMB*

"Hertz writes with a powerful blend of publicly experienced scene and deeply private interiority . . . [He] expertly presents both the rapturous facade of post-closet gay life and the cracks in its hastily constructed foundation."

—*Slant*

"Ca   tty recovery story that packs
a pu

—*Bay Area Reporter*

"Hertz's haunting debut gazes unwaveringly into the darkness—and unexpected light—of memory."

—*Electric Literature*

"The prose is remarkable, alternating from lush sensuality to unsparing brutality to quick cutting asides. This marks the arrival of a vital new talent."

—*Publishers Weekly*

"This forceful, necessary novel . . . depicts the often silent suffering and unfathomable effects of sexual abuse. Readers of Garth Greenwell or Eimear McBride will find it well worth diving into."

—*Library Journal*

"*The Lookback Window* will shake you to your core . . . Kyle Dillon Hertz's phenomenal prose is tender and powerful and provides moments of beauty and hope even in the darkest and more harrowing moments."

—*Debutiful*

"In its sensitive portrayal of the profoundly social nature of recovery and justice, *The Lookback Window* asks us to consider in all its complexity the question of how we might be able to make a better world together."

—*Interview*

"Kyle Dillon Hertz's searing debut novel puts a spotlight on male sexual abuse and a path toward healing. . . . *The Lookback Window* powerfully explores the lasting effects of childhood trauma."

—*Shondaland*

"*The Lookback Window* is a beautiful and heartbreaking tour de force. Hertz writes vengeance as salvation, refusal as a reclamation of humanity."

—Raven Leilani, *New York Times* bestselling author of *Luster*

THE LOOKBACK WINDOW

A NOVEL

KYLE DILLON HERTZ

SIMON & SCHUSTER PAPERBACKS

New York London Toronto Sydney New Delhi

YEARS
SIMON &
SCHUSTER
PAPERBACKS

An Imprint of Simon & Schuster, LLC
1230 Avenue of the Americas
New York, NY 10020

First Simon & Schuster trade paperback edition August 2024

SIMON & SCHUSTER PAPERBACKS and colophon are registered trademarks of Simon & Schuster, LLC

Simon & Schuster: Celebrating 100 Years of Publishing in 2024

For information about special discounts for bulk purchases, please contact Simon & Schuster Special Sales at 1-866-506-1949 or business@simonandschuster.com.

The Simon & Schuster Speakers Bureau can bring authors to your live event. For more information or to book an event, contact the Simon & Schuster Speakers Bureau at 1-866-248-3049 or visit our website at www.simonspeakers.com.

Interior design by Wendy Blum

Manufactured in the United States of America

10 9 8 7 6 5 4 3 2 1

Library of Congress Cataloging-in-Publication Data has been applied for.

ISBN 978-1-6680-0587-3
ISBN 978-1-6680-0588-0 (pbk)
ISBN 978-1-6680-0589-7 (ebook)

To John Freeman, Chris Parris-Lamb,
and Tim O'Connell

I've seen things you people wouldn't believe. Attack ships on fire off the shoulder of Orion. I watched C-beams glitter in the dark near the Tannhäuser Gate. All those moments will be lost in time, like tears in rain.

—Roy Batty, *Blade Runner*

I was one thing, now I'm being another.

—Lana Del Rey, "Happiness Is a Butterfly"

PARADISE

PARADISE

CHAPTER 1

I escaped to a resort of extraordinary beauty. This way when the news stories appeared, I'd be in such an otherworldly place I could act like I had only been dreaming. I pitched it as a vacation to Moans, a way to get away before our impending wedding. I showed him the site for The Monarchs, a luxurious oceanfront hotel in Florida, and we booked a room. Before we departed, I took a sedative to ease the journey, and I returned to consciousness outside the wooden gates.

Scores of palm trees concealed a pool, two hot tubs, and dozens of naked men. The owner stood with his hands on his hips and surveyed his territory, telling us that he had planted these trees forty years ago; he hadn't expected the foliage to grow so wildly, but with coastal life came onslaughts of rain and all that sustenance had shifted the foundations.

"Nothing can prevent the course of nature," he said, so I took off my clothes and wandered the property until I found a spot in the shade to be alone.

The world felt very far away. No matter how hard I studied the jacaranda petals, I couldn't shake the feeling that I didn't completely exist. I placed my feet on the hot stone patio and searched for three red items: *the second hand of the hot tub clock, the limp resort flag, the rusty fractured stones lifting from the earth.*

Sweat dragged down my chest as I followed a blue hummingbird to a feeder.

"Would you like a bottle of water?" a pool boy asked, watching me lean over the railing into the trees. "You don't have to drink like the birds."

We would stay for a week.

We kept to ourselves at first and spent afternoons by the pool, reading and lifting our sunglasses to flick our eyes at certain men's conversations, or when, despite the casual nudity, a man seemed particularly naked, even if he wore briefs or a cap. Moans belonged to that category. He wore navy trunks.

Piercings, tattoos, the way men walked up the pool steps, reaching for a towel before it was within their grasp: all contributed to a taxonomy. They were uninhibited, curious but ashamed, and some of them introduced themselves as Nudists while touching their chests as a priest might grasp his cross. Among them were men who had been denied what they wanted for half a century, men so old they felt unseen. Some questioned if they could be desired. Others knew. One idiot in his fifties flopped around on a floating pool chair, attempting to use his dick like bait and tackle.

Moans' thirty-four to my twenty-seven, and I was covered in tattoos and silent—the men even commented on this, like *you're a quiet one*, after they'd tried to get the meaning out of certain ink. I offered nothing. Mostly I kept to my novels.

I woke the second afternoon on a lounge chair to a pool boy handing out Popsicles on a silver platter, unwrapping the plastic to tease the guests with a purple tip. What simplicity, what luxury. I asked for a newspaper. There was the story of a man who had just taken his life after what happened to him as a child, his wife crying and screaming on the steps of a courthouse. A quote from a lawyer about the flood of cases to come. That was enough for me.

The third afternoon, I checked the closet and discovered a sampling of adult films above the safe. Skin flicks. Warped DVD cases, the plastic lifting and torn. They were dated, and I loved the anachronism. I held one in the air and said to Moans, "I honestly wouldn't know how to use this."

"You grew up with cassettes and VHS."

"I haven't used one in years." I opened the case and held the disc upside down, where my breath caught each scratch along its mirrored surface. We were naked, otherwise I would have wiped it off on my shirt. "Blow on it for luck?"

Moans pulled my wrist to his face and exhaled. He smelled like vodka, and my hair stood on end. I kneeled in front of the DVD player and pressed the Eject button. A tray slid out. I put the DVD in the slot and pushed it inside. The box gently whirred, and the blue screen switched to black. I really hadn't seen machinery like this in years. Nobody tells you that you will outgrow your own life as you live it. I didn't know how to say this exactly to Moans, so as I kneeled before him I said, "The world ends in a thousand ways."

Moans laughed and ran his finger along my chin, as if I were just talking drunk.

I sat on the floral quilt and waited for the show. Moans sat right behind me, his knees grazing my back. The title screen gave us options: *Arabian Nights, Treasure Island, Around the World in Eighty Days, Journey to the Center of the Earth.* I chose the last one, pressing the sticky remote twice.

"Why that one?" Moans asked.

"I can figure out all the others."

At first, on the small grainy television, a middle-aged man and a guy around my age receive a secret letter describing the entrance to a remarkable destination. The scene cuts to the boy carrying a torch through the wilderness, excited and terrified, turning to the older man to ask a question.

"I've seen enough."

"You don't want to know what happens next?"

Moans lay back on the edge of the bed as I turned onto my knees. I couldn't tell if he followed me or the film, if the cicadas called from outside the room or the jungle, if the laughter surrounded or came from us, or why as he lifted me onto his lap and covered my mouth with his palm the way he fucked me felt as if it had originated from somebody else. Moans fell asleep after he came inside me. The sun went down. For a while, I lay in the crook of his arm, and then, without disturbing him, I used my phone to light a path to the patio outside, a novel in hand, to read.

A guest from the adjacent room had done the same. He eyed me as I sat beside him, turning off the single overhead light in the umbrella. He untied his robe and let the wind blow it open. We whispered for a while with our novels spread-eagle on the glass table between us. The man had come to the coast to reset his mind to work on a play. As he told me this, he ran his fingers down my thigh. Pleasure is the only true escape, he said. I sensed the playwright believed what he was telling me, even though it sounded like the bullshit artists say before they suck your cock.

I stood.

The playwright drew his finger down my navel to the tattoo. "*Paradise?*"

"Yes," I said. "*Paradise.*"

"How was it?"

"You mean how is it?"

He looked at me the same way I looked at him. He wanted to believe me. The night encased us as the ocean breathed on our necks. We could hear the dying parties, and we kissed as a breeze guided my lips to his. I put my fingers in his hair and felt my dick hit the back of his throat. He stayed there, his core contracting, trying to be quiet as he choked and slobbered and worked until he retched. At the sound, a light turned on in the window above him. I watched a man lower his shaved head into a running sink. When he stood, water dripped from him like a melted silver crown. The man opened the window, saying, "I see you've met my husband."

With teary eyes, the playwright said, "We lost our youth."

"Where'd it go?"

"It was here until you arrived, and now the mosquitos are taking it from you as we speak."

"They don't bite me."

Now, the playwright became sad, as if I hadn't reached the age to stop believing my own lies.

"Who are you?" the husband asked.

"A neighbor," I said.

"Our neighbor without a name," the playwright said. The husband opened the patio door and stepped out fully clothed. We drank, they smoked, and neither kissed the other. They wanted me to spend the night, but I felt my time with them was over. I'd forgotten my key and had to climb through the open window and slipped into bed with Moans. He draped his arm over me and asked where I had been. I hesitated. He briefly opened his eyes and said, "You always look like you're gonna say something, but you never do." Within moments, he was asleep again, and I was alone as the birds began to sing.

At dawn, I had a cup of coffee by the pool. I waited for the *New York Times*, checking to see if more stories of the men were printed. A doctor who cried in the break room spoke about what happened to him as an Eagle Scout, how he learned what he could achieve under extraordinary pressure. A man whose grandmother used to creep down the stairs when everyone else in the house slept. A woman who never knew what had happened to her was haunted by nightmares. I could hardly admit to myself that this was why I was here. As the ink paper bled over my fingers, the guests drifted across the pool on neon floats. They crumpled their speedos and tossed them to the deck. I felt my skin start to burn. This was an invitation to get off the chair and spray sunscreen over my body, feel the spritz on my neck and my boyfriend's hands on my back, or even a stranger's, but the world in front of me fell flat. The more my skin burned, the less capable I became of disrupting the moment. The drifting strangers slowed. The wind died down. The sky was as blue as any other perfect conspiracy.

For years, I wondered if I was alive. I lived in the alleged world. I thirsted and hungered for and craved other people, who recognized I was there, but every now and then, often without notice, I disappeared deep into my body. I would enter a scene just like this, so cured of my own presence, with this heart buried deep inside the moment, that I could have been erased from it completely. Even light pain, the bright tight sensation spreading across my body, lifted right off my skin, disposed of as easily as clothing. I could dip my feet in the sparkling pool, lodge my head in the Atlantic, ride a stranger in the moonlight with his husband's hands guiding my lips to his lap, and still encounter a fundamental division.

I had been just a lonely kid looking for connection when I received a blinking message from a man on a site that no longer exists. He liked the way I looked, flashy and bright from holding up a camera to a thin mirror in my bedroom. I answered, I went to his house in a low end-of-summer fog, and he lifted a Zippo flame to a grape Swisher, exactly how he'd been taught when he was my age. He was adopted, and I was too, and I wondered if we could have been related. He told me that maybe he was a brother I never met and kissed me. We had what I thought was awkward teenage sex—blood the symptom of inexperience, pain the way of life. He was six inches taller than me, had a big dick, and kept a black Nikon near the bed that he used to take my picture. I had hair that swooped over my face, lips that pressed against my braces. He would kiss me full of smoke and tell me to name what I hated about being alive. He'd tell me stories of everything he'd done at my age. He posted the pictures he took of me online, pressed pills into my mouth, and found men who wanted to pay for a gray-eyed boy. I believed he was showing me the world at its truest, full of fire and longing, secrets and locked doors, and for years, despite what happened to me and the threats he made, I lied to keep him safe. I didn't know any better.

I was still in the initial phase of recovery. I didn't yet have the words for what happened to me. And years after just know that when I vanished, nothing could reach me. No glass pipe, no bloody punch could bring me back. I made myself invulnerable to physical pain. I tatted my throat and fingers and spine. Whatever strip of flesh a tattoo artist warned would hurt the most, I donated to their needles. I taught myself to feel nothing. With their hands on my throat, the artists wanted to know how I never flinched while a needle punctured thin veils of skin.

"Practice," I always said.

A clock lorded over the hot tub in the dead center of the resort. Beside it, there was a manual calendar. Nothing much happened there, but I liked to watch the staff remove the days of the week. You felt like the Fates were at work, or at least I did, drunk and high, high and drunk. We'd been there for four days when a pool boy I hadn't seen before slipped a Tuesday into his waistband. The pool boy asked me if I wanted a newspaper, which I accepted.

I held the *New York Times* on my lap, not quite ready to open it, my sweat dampening the paper until the ink bled over my dick and thighs. I needed to read the pages before I'd ruin them, but I knew the news could ruin me. So I waited. People splashed in the pool and sprayed sunscreen around me. The men lined up on blue lounge chairs, trying to position themselves for the best lot of sunlight as the shade retreated into the trees behind us. The man beside me had a face temporarily preserved in time, and to dismiss the chance of him talking to me I finally opened the paper.

In the Opinion section, a writer debated the law I was waiting for news on: the Child Victims Act. The law extended the statute of limitations for child victims of sexual assault. Victims used to only get five years after they turned eighteen to report the assault. Once they turned twenty-three, their case died. Most people didn't report. Even if they finally came to terms with what happened, it took years longer than this. That was what happened to me. I had always suspected that no one cared what happened to boys anyway. Since then, I had spent my energy on ensuring I never thought about what happened. I did everything I possibly could to escape. Because I didn't know how to live with it, and I didn't want to live in a world that was cool with letting that violence go unpunished.

The Child Victims Act permanently extended the statute of limitations for fresh child victims only. If you were like me, and the statute had been four years expired, there was a special provision. A lookback window, they called it, starting August 14, where I would have a one-year period to decide whether to bring a case. Once that year ended, my case would be permanently closed again. It wasn't a criminal case. This would be purely the chance at a civil lawsuit. Money. Even though I didn't want money for what happened, I kept having brief visions of justice, and maybe even a life of it. Maybe. The longer time passes, the less evidence exists. The more my memories warp. I knew all this was true. I knew the effects of what happened to me grew with time, but my recollection faded. I imagined all the men I knew who had been assaulted as kids shedding their lives of hiding, stepping out of the routine of survival to bang on the court doors. I dreamed of this freedom with equal parts desire and dread. When I tried to think about what happened, I needed to get high or get fucked, or let rage and abandonment consume my whole life.

The pool boy came over with a pot of iced coffee and martini glasses. He poured coffee into the glass and dropped a crushed blue pill in it.

"What is it?" I asked.

"A Fort Lauderdale Brew." He stirred the cocktail. "You look like you need it."

"What'll it do?"

"Make you feel good," he said, winking, as I drank mine, and he poured another for the next guy. I relaxed. I dropped the paper and waded into the pool. All the ink washed off. I wrapped my legs around someone and floated on the water as he ran his fingers over my body. I drifted between guys. The clouds swept across the sky. I kissed a few people, returned to my chair with a towel pulled over my body, and woke up during happy hour, when everybody was dressed in dinner clothes, and I was sprawled naked in the cool dusk. The playwright was above me, wiping drool from my face with the towel. He told me not to worry, the pool boys sprayed sunscreen on me while I slept. He told me that I had been having obviously good dreams, the towel falling and rising over my cock. I stood up and stretched, looking for Moans, when an iguana fell from a palm tree and somebody swept the frozen lizard into the bushes with his feet.

"Have you seen my boyfriend?" I asked the playwright, and he pointed at the gym. I ran to Moans, who had been wanting to see an iguana, but we hadn't yet come across one. He was running on the rickety treadmill. The loose belt forced him to speed up randomly. He was grinning.

"What?" Moans asked, darting theatrically.

"Iguanas are falling from the trees."

Moans jumped off the treadmill and we ran back to the pool, where the men continued dancing and laughing and drinking. We looked into the palm trees. Nothing collapsed.

"I have the worst timing," Moans said, grabbing a bag of chips and a seltzer from the table. "Why are you the only one naked?"

"I had a weird coffee."

Moans squinted at me like I was insane. He pressed his fingers into my sunburn and watched the white impression fade. The pink lights made it look worse. Awful music played over the speakers. We had a month until our wedding. However, we already wore our wedding rings since we couldn't afford engagement rings and everyone kept asking when we had gotten married. We didn't know better. Young love.

I walked over to the chair and grabbed the wet paper. The pages were lost words. I crumpled up what I hadn't been able to read. Moans took it from my hands and threw the paper away. I had a temporary urge to find another paper, but I was being swept away on the Fort Lauderdale Brew. Stars broke through the sky. I followed the moon. I tried to forget about everything. To survive, you lived through it, but you never looked back. I didn't want to throw away my relationship, my friends, my whole life, and I was afraid that's what the lookback window would bring, but I knew if I didn't try I would simply kill myself. So I quietly waited for the stories of what would happen when the law went into effect, and maybe, if I were lucky, a glimpse of my future would come with it.

CHAPTER 2

We had been at the resort for six days when I met the drunk. The rotating guests made it difficult to remember names. We knew each other by occupation. Clockwise, in the hot tub, we had Moans and me, the lawyer and the philanthropist, the doctor and the statistician, the firefighter and the drunk. When silence overwhelmed us the lawyer intervened, like when he raised his index finger toward Orion and informed us that the star to the right in Orion's Belt hovered closest to the equator. In olden times, sailors measured the distance between their position and the star to plot their routes. They stared for too long. I wasn't wearing my glasses. I examined the wrinkled skin around my wedding band. I could be silent forever. Mosquitos swarmed the drunk. He ducked under the water and resurfaced with a splash that prompted the lawyer to question where he was from.

"We just got off a cruise," the drunk said. "It never stops. We keep moving."

The air jets prevented us from hearing one another well. The palm trees rustled, and I took this moment to lift myself onto the ledge. The drunk stared. He followed two columns of text on my forearm. As I stretched my arms above my head, the ink morphed and twisted, unable to keep form as I moved. The tattoo artist placed words wherever they fit, like graffiti, overlapping phrases, vandalizing my body. It was possible to read a couple of lines on my arms, and if you really spent time close to my skin, you could make out the smaller words and phrases. Only a few sayings were absolutely clear: NO DEATH on my collarbone, FOREVER as the knucklebangers, and PARADISE, which you've already seen, of course. If you've seen me around, this is the one you know me by. I'd thought by covering myself this way I'd prevent certain men from ever being able to get what they wanted from me. The tattoos aged me, but they felt like armor.

"Did the neck hurt?" the drunk asked.

"No," I said, and covered my throat.

"He's delusional," Moans said, running a hand over his own unfinished half-sleeve of a palm tree on fire. "They hurt."

"It's meditative," I said.

"I always wanted one," the statistician said, "but I could never decide on what. It's too permanent."

"You got an earring." I pointed to his silver hoop. "And you're married. What about that?"

"An earring?" The statistician giggled and placed his hand on his husband. "*That's* not forever. Neither is marriage. I wish you could try it out. I could compile success rates."

"Tattoos or marriage?" the lawyer asked.

Everyone laughed, except for me and the drunk.

"I don't know what's worse," the philanthropist said, "getting stabbed with a needle or burned with a laser for the removal."

"You don't get burnt. Technically, you are exploded." The doctor relished his knowledge with wriggling fingers. "Every tattoo is a different color." The doctor pointed at the blue and black lettering on my arm. "Each color has a corresponding wave-length of light."

"Oh God," the statistician said.

"Try being married to a lawyer," the philanthropist said.

"The laser is beamed against the tattoo." The doctor's arm rose out of the water and grabbed mine. He clamped my wrist and with his right hand he stuck out his index finger and struck it against my skin. "The ink absorbs the force of the laser, which shatters the ink into tiny little bits that the immune system is then able to expel. *Boom*."

"But people get burns," Moans said.

"If the laser is beamed too long it'll burn."

"So choose your doctor wisely, folks," the lawyer said, "and call me if you get burned."

"You do injury cases?" the drunk asked.

"I was joking. You might want to wake up your partner there. Is this your first night?"

"We just got off a cruise," the drunk repeated. He had an old party boy tattoo. Blue stars. That's how you pick a gay alcoholic out of a crowd.

"Did yours hurt?" I asked.

"I thought it did," the drunk said.

"You get used to the pain."

"No. No. No, no, no. I thought I knew what pain was until I lost my arm."

The drunk lifted himself onto the ledge and sat opposite me. He revealed his left stump—an amputated limb and a trail of fleshy scars. We waited for the lawyer, who up until now had been the prosecutor of our privacy, to ask the drunk what happened. I needed the answer. I glanced at the lawyer: *do your fucking job!* The drunk looked at me, and I felt sick to my stomach. I slipped into the water and grabbed Moans' hand. A jet pounded into my back as the drunk walked away.

Now, we were seven—six, if you counted the incapacitated, retired firefighter. A dog barked.

"Hot damn," the firefighter said, scratching his white mustache as he pushed himself up. "I had the craziest dream." He looked at us as if he were completely lost. "Forget it. I need the dream back." He pulled himself out on the steel handrail, the elastic keychain around his ankle, and grabbed a rolled towel off a chair. I didn't see him again.

"On that note, we're turning in," the statistician said.

"We are? It's only one," the doctor said, but when he saw his naked husband dripping he followed him back to their room.

The lawyer yawned, and the philanthropist said, "Come on," and the couple retreated. The drunk returned with eight water bottles that dripped condensation into a little pool on the wooden deck, reflecting the smallest bit of blue light. Moans leaned into my ear and whispered, "That color is named madder blue. I know things too."

"What's the secret?" the drunk asked.

"No secret," I said. Moans cracked his back and said he'd leave the door unlocked. He grabbed a can of bug spray and spritzed himself as he went back. The air brightened, no longer blocked by all those bodies, and I could see clear to the floor.

"*Fan-dang-o*." The drunk read from my arm, then he wheezed. As the jets fizzled out and the timer chimed, moonlight polished his scars. "It's just us now. I'll show you mine if you show me yours."

"You go first."

"I fell asleep at the wheel on the 805. A bystander told the news they saw me do a triple axel through the windshield."

"But did you lose it right away?"

He zipped his lips. It was my turn. He said, "I want to know what they mean."

"They're the last words of a killer in a novel," I said. I held out my wrist and he underlined the word *boom.* "He's in the gas chamber. He abandoned somebody who got raped and he murdered a security guard during a robbery. It's about forgiveness. Humanity. Justice. He's thinking about his last breaths and telling jokes to God."

"You know what they call you here?"

"Tell me."

"The Paperboy." His face radiated with knowledge. "You're the one under the tree with ten different newspapers. What's the news, Paperboy?"

"Why drive so drunk?"

"Which time?"

I understood. "Did it hurt?"

"The sound was worse. They can't put you under when you're wasted. Want to know what it sounded like?"

"Yes," I said. "More than anything."

"Then give me something worth the trouble."

I needed to make sure we were alone. I left the tub to turn on the jets for two minutes. Only long enough to say my piece. Once the surface trembled, I stepped through and rested beside the drunk, and I tried to speak so that my voice wouldn't carry beyond his ear. I didn't think he truly wanted to know, I didn't think he'd remember, and I needed to push against the loneliness taking me away, like one of the mosquitos flapping against the current of the pool before it's sucked into the drain.

"Back home, they passed a law to allow kids who were sexually assaulted to sue their abusers. I got pimped out as a boy. Men your age rented me. It feels like a very different life, sometimes, when I don't feel like I'm still in it. Every day I get the papers, and I read about people I'll never know fighting over people like me. I read about all the potential cases, what others like me experienced, what they're going to do with the year. Some people even doubt the law should exist. Some people think men can't get raped. I am an idea who used to be a body."

"Shouldn't you be home, then?"

"I wanted to visit a place so beautiful that no matter what happened it didn't seem real. Get the news in heaven before I go back to hell. Maybe I got it backward."

"Yes," the drunk said. "Watch this."

The drunk lifted his stump, and the underwater light cast a shadow of his limb far across the wall behind us, cutting through the clock, so that, in the shadows, what he had lost had been returned to him in the dead of night.

"Don't move," he said. "I'll give you one last trick. Here's what it sounded like."

At first, nothing changed. We didn't budge. A mosquito landed on the water's surface. I stared into the drunk's black eyes as he parted his lips, but he didn't need to tell me to stay still. We didn't touch each other. The insects kept coming. I heard the electric buzzing as the mosquitoes feasted on him. He didn't bat them away. We stayed with each other while the saw descended in his memory.

When I got back to our suite, I searched the bedroom to wake Moans, but he wasn't inside. I found him outside, looking up into the trees. Moans called me over with a flick of his hand. Up in the trees, almost indivisible from the branches, he found his iguana. I kneeled on the stones. Moans lived up to his name.

The next afternoon Moans packed our bags. The hotel let us stay until we had to leave for our flight. Every second on the lounge chair felt necessary. The sun hit like a Fort Lauderdale Brew, which I thought was probably morphine. Moans started a memoir, prospecting the pages for something. He knew he wasn't going to finish. As we lay down, the lawyer handed me two pills. The doctor overheard and told us it was a beta blocker and warned that despite feeling normal, I would seem slow to other people if I mixed it with a benzo. I suspected people already thought this, and I swallowed both pills seconds after the warning. This had been a great lonely resort. I had the feeling the whole time I was out there like I was constantly going to miss my fate. I saw Moans neglect his phone to smile at strangers he would pretend to never have seen. We had until dusk to waste some time imagining what our lives would be like if we had spent our youths like this. Neither of us wanted to leave.

"Are you ready to go back?" Moans asked.

"Yes," I said.

CHAPTER 3

We returned home to the most romantic time in New York, the sweaty end of summer. I rode the subway with dark stains under my arms and a line down my back, as did everyone else, like the man next to me on the L who wiped his brow with his hand and ran his fingers over his hairy thighs below the hem of his shorts. He looked out the black windows and found my eyes in the reflection. As the train grew more crowded, stop by stop, he moved closer until both of our hands were holding on to the ceiling bar, our shirts lifting. He brushed a finger over the hair on my stomach, very lightly, looking elsewhere, lighting me up and getting me hard. He knew what he was doing. When he could feel my bulge on his leg, his palm fell against it. I wanted to stay still as he touched me, to get caught by strangers and have him hit me right across the face. I wish I could say this were the only moment where I wanted to drop to my knees and beg a stranger to place their hand on me for one more second. I felt like I would die the second he stopped touching me. We separated at the stop.

I exited the Union Square subway station under the low canopy of green boughs and passed lone men waiting at chess tables for any stranger to take the empty seat and make a move. I turned down University, where a guy rode a bike, his shirt unbuttoned, winging out behind him. We locked eyes and he disappeared. Summer meant everything to me in a way that I wouldn't understand for years. I could wear less clothes and long openly. I could watch a hundred men leave and dream of futures that I wouldn't have. My body constantly reminded me of its existence; this was nature's trick to staying in the moment.

I decided to walk to my therapy session.

As the victim of a crime, New York State paid for my therapy through a special grant to the Crime Victims Treatment Center. The office is five floors above Exchange Place with a view of Wall Street and a buzzer to enter. I told the security guard what I was there for, and he opened the turnstile for the elevator lobby, where I pressed the fifth floor and wondered if everyone else in the elevator on the way to work knew what the fifth floor meant. I pressed the buzzer, the door unlocked, and I ignored a mother and her son in the waiting room. The boy played video games on her phone and messily ate a bagel while she stared at a painting of a flower. I kept catching her look at the locked door, wondering if she too had people in the world who wanted her dead, if her ex-husband had already tried to kill her. Everything becomes what you fear. A flickering light becomes a sign from God that your death is coming on the elevator with a gun. That the man who trapped you would be waiting across Exchange Place to keep you quiet forever.

My therapist, Matan, retrieved me from the waiting room by walking just to where I could see him in the hallway. He had a buzzed head, big blue eyes, and a very soft manner. Tel Aviv to the Bronx to whichever suburb he now lived in where loafers were a thing. I always forgot that he wasn't taller than me until I walked behind him to the office, trying to avoid making the squeaking sound of basketball sneakers on laminated floors. The Center was very quiet, and a single utterance could make you feel like all the doors would open and a hundred social workers' eyes would be on you, although that would never happen. They were trained to make you feel safe, as unseen as possible in a watchful place.

Matan worked in the last office in the hall. He had a standing desk by the door and two navy armchairs set far enough apart that I could fully outstretch my legs without reaching him. Birds decorated the paintings and walls, a few humble plants lived, and he had a giant mason jar for drinking water, the closest anything he ever did that came to having sensuality, as the water spilled slightly down the side of his lips and he'd wipe it with his sleeve. He could see halfway up my thighs. I didn't want to fuck him. When he sat, he crossed his legs.

"I was worried about you last week," Matan said.

"Fuck Lauderdale. I should have told you."

"Were you able to relax?"

"Yes and no," I said. "I'm living a secret life, and it's tiring me out."

Across the hall, a social worker shut their door, and the sound transported me back thirteen years, to the inside of a dark and inescapable room that locked from the outside. I sensed the heat of a torch lighter and the taste of skin from a man's palm as he wrenched open my jaw to blow smoke into my mouth. I could feel the great warmth spreading across my lungs, a sudden film of sweat, the blood shooting up through my head like rain in reverse.

"Are you still here?" Matan asked, but he knew, leaning back with his knees parted and ankles crossed.

Matan held up his huge right palm, and I watched him as the past descended on me, feeling so heavy and beleaguered I could have fallen asleep. He put down his hand, uncrossed his ankles, and scooted back in his chair. The farther back he moved from me, the easier it was to breathe. I saw he was going to tell me to find things in the room, to return myself to the present, and I hated to hear him say anything so silly and effortless, as it confirmed my suspicions that I had beat my brain senseless and fried it from drugs, so I caught the green vines and book lettering and pen and walls, which freed me from the past long enough to sit up and take a deep breath. I nodded for him to continue.

"Remember?" Matan asked, and he raised his palm again. He referred to his thumb as the amygdala, the part of the brain responsible for storing memories and regulating fear. Or emotions. The other fingers were different parts of the brain. When a person encounters extraordinary violence at a young age, the mind doesn't have the language to store the experience. Without proper language, bits are stored randomly in the mind. He closed his fist tightly over his thumb. Each time you encounter pain, your mind displaces it. You disappear to survive. One moment you are moving forward in time, and the next you are staring, immobilized, at a bird feeder or the buildings outside Matan's, which begin to resemble those moments early in your life.

"I'm here," I said.

"You know what will happen in a week?"

"I know. I was trying to get away. I heard there is a flood coming."

"A flood?"

"Of cases." I swallowed. "A flood to ruin the peace."

"Do you have plans for when the law goes into effect?"

"Blow my brains out. Get curb stomped. Fuck a toaster."

Matan pretended to be shocked. "Should I ask again?"

"I'm going to pretend like it's any other day. I can't even tell you what I am afraid of." I started to tear up and knocked my elbow into the table. My arm went numb. I sat on my hand. "I have so much stuff I never used to have, but sometimes I get so angry thinking about what happened, I don't know what to do with it."

"I have said this before, but you are not trapped here. You are free to leave. The door is unlocked," Matan said. I looked at the door, but it felt too far away. I didn't leave, at first. I couldn't. At the time, I claimed I didn't dissociate. I never rose out of my body. I didn't see myself from above, which, no offense, sounded like bullshit. I just slipped into a world as flat as a painting, unable to differentiate my body from the couch from the city from the present or past, like all the world was a still life—that shit is the angle of death. Time ran out. Matan said he'd check in, to see if I was adjusting well to the new world, if I could handle it. I was absolutely not going to handle it well.

I left. A dozen pigeons lifted into the sky.

I would now need to choose. I would have to let the past infiltrate willingly, instead of unconsciously. I didn't like to touch that world. You wouldn't believe what I had done to stay alive.

I walked to meet Moans for dinner. The sidewalks overflowed with people toasting one another, walking crookedly into the open doors of a bar, single lighters passed around groups of cigarettes while a New York Ice Cream truck wailed down University Avenue. It was no longer the song of the fifties, but a trap remix, with bass drops and slurry drums. Some young skater fell down after a bad trick and a lost blond NYU student took a picture of a person bathing in the fountain. Nothing ever surprised you about Washington Square Park. You could sketch the Roti Cart, the college kids getting high in a place they had wanted to believe was their home, and night protests starting to gather late in the day. But every night, the sun would set and cast half the park in shadow, and a feeling of ruin settled quietly over us. You could as easily imagine the park populated as desolate, and when this moment came, as it did while I walked through it, for a moment the people stopped taking pictures of strangers and snapped a quick pic of the red sky over the arch that seemed to welcome a future that belonged to none of us.

I arrived at Elio's on West Tenth and asked for a window seat to people-watch. I counted the men who passed in front of the window in groups of four, knowing, statistically, one of them had been assaulted, and I wondered what each of them would choose. I saw Moans as he approached the restaurant waving his shirt hem, airing out his back. He took a napkin from his pocket and dabbed sweat off his neck. I could see him singing along to music in his headphones. He had a farmer's tan, and his lips moved just so. He stopped under a bodega's awning to let the song finish.

A minute later, he slid into his seat at our table, sitting down with his back to the AIDS memorial that resembled a crashed spaceship on the street. The server filled our water glasses to the brim. Moans dragged the glass by the stem and lowered his mouth to sip without spilling a drop.

"What?" Moans said. "Am I doing something funny?"

I mimicked him, lapping the water like a dog.

Moans dunked his nose in the glass, and then he dipped his chin. I ignored talking about next week and what it would bring. Why ruin a date? We were having such a good time. We had come such a long way, and I knew what happened when the past intruded. The server lit the candle on the table as the street darkened. I thought of everyone at the Center. We who'd overdosed or would again soon. We who failed spectacularly at suicide. Hospitalizations. We who married. Cheated, divorced, lied, and died. I had been trying, after everything, to be good. I did not go swinging a baseball bat through the streets. And now I had to decide whether or not to bring a case.

Our gold rings shimmered near the flickering votive. I knew what I had to do. I covered the candle with my hand and snuffed out the light.

THE GLASS
MOTHERFUCKER

CHAPTER 4

For the second week of August I had kept myself busy. I whittled down my body at the gym, told Moans I wanted to look hot in our wedding photos. It was my only job really, to look good. I was broke and wild, but I was handsome and young, so the relationship made sense to everyone. I ran. Miles and miles around Brooklyn and Manhattan. I ran as far away from home as I could to be forced to have a daunting return, cycling between running, jogging, and an exasperated walk. Upon returning, I'd hobble to the bathroom and run the hot water until the air was thick and I'd emptily zone out while the heat soothed my muscles. I wish I could say I busied myself with the wedding, although, if I'm being honest, Moans mostly handled things and asked for my final opinion. I didn't want anything special. Only a dark venue with my friends, molly and coke, no frills.

If anybody thought I was acting nervous, I could blame the upcoming wedding or the start of grad school in September, and nobody would question the running or sleeplessness or time I spent on my own as having anything to do with the lookback window opening. Even without those reasons, I know people wouldn't question me. I was the type of person who disappeared, who you thought had died already, whose absence was a normal part of life. Maybe my family, or Moans', believed these new normal benchmarks would cure me of whatever made me like this. I felt, at times, like I was being made into a person. Like, here is Dylan, and now let us train him, like a person. Here is school. Here is a wedding. Here is the future. Dylan, say Hi.

We had left our outfits to the last minute, and on the fourteenth Moans asked if I wanted to go looking. We had less than a week before the wedding, and I agreed to walk around SoHo. I threw on an olive T-shirt and denim shorts. Moans put on a very tight white tank that compressed his stomach and chest, and then he wore a bigger white shirt over it. I wanted to tell him he didn't need to wear the undershirt. He still couldn't bear the evidence of his body in pictures. I knew I shouldn't have said it, but I said, "You don't need to wear that."

"I'm going to see these pictures forever." Moans laced his shoes. "You know what this means."

"Not forever. Maybe fifty more years, if you're lucky."

"Forever," he said, seriously, before we left the apartment for the subway. "Every time I used to go to my grandparents' house, they'd point out their wedding picture to me. They'd say, *Oh, little old us*, and give each other a kiss. I want the pictures hanging where everyone can see them."

"For the dogs to see."

"Exactly."

"I don't think there's a single picture of myself I have ever looked at more than once."

"What about the ones from when I met you?"

"Okay, yes, but that's just because I don't look like that anymore. That's some random slut. Maybe that's the type of clothing I want to wear for the ceremony." I looked at him quickly before adding, "Not random," and then again before saying, "Or slut."

"Seven days out and you're still making little jokes."

"We cope differently."

"Cope?"

"You know what I mean," I said, and he relaxed. We scrolled through stores on our phones while the G took us to the L, showing each other shirts we liked, places we wanted to browse, outfits in the thousands that we wondered if we could splurge on. I didn't like to shop around, and he knew that. Despite the idea to cross the city, I thought we'd strike gold at our first stop. I knew what I liked and didn't want to fuck around. Moans, on the other hand, would hit every store if he could, holding up ugly thing after ugly thing until he returned to the very first spot, too. At Union Square, we transferred to the Q and exited at Canal Street, where we dodged people on our way to Howard Street to visit Opening Ceremony, a place a tourist brochure might describe as a three-floor eclectic American clothing store known for its mix of lowbrow and high-brow brands, or as I thought of it, a clothing store for people who liked to have sex after getting high in a downtown club.

As soon as we entered, we split ways across the room, each drawn to short-sleeve button-downs. Mine was a silk teal piece, bruised by colors resembling the outline of flowers. I tried it on in the dressing room, and the sleeves and hem had a squared-off look, a slightly oversized relaxed feeling. When I walked out to show Moans, he stepped out of his dressing room, wearing a metallic-blue shirt, cut a little softer than mine, reflecting light ever so slightly, as if he were glowing.

"I love it," I said.

"I do too," Moans said. "Did you check the price?"

I pulled up the tag and laughed.

"$1,138." He shook his head. "Of course you didn't look first."

"What about you?"

"You got me beat."

"I don't have cheap taste."

"It's not much cheaper."

"But I love it, too. I love the way you look."

We walked next to each other and looked in the mirror. A shop guy in a huge white shirt wearing platform sneakers looked at us and said, "Looks cunt." I imagined the lights low, the music playing, moving side to side a bit, as Moans stood there frozen, smiling all beatific and feeling rich. We each picked out shoes: green velvet sneakers for me, nineties black creepers for Moans. The shoes made him taller than me by an inch. Moans gave his credit card to the cashier. We looked like two guys on vacation, at a club in London, where we had planned to honeymoon. Two men who were living a different life than we were living now. The woman folded the clothes and placed a giant bag in my hands, which Moans took, proudly carrying the haul outside as we walked to Broadway for a car, giving me a kiss on the cheek as we stopped at the corner.

Moans called a car as taxis passed us, and when our driver pulled to the side of the avenue, we silently texted our families that we were finally all set. My parents were relieved, asking to see a picture, but I didn't want to hear them freak out about how underdressed we were. Moans' family would all just say okay, or "Great honey," or ask a hundred questions about what they were going to do in Brooklyn when they arrived next week. I texted my best friend James, who wrote back: *Fuck your outfit! I still need to figure out mine. You're just the sideshow for my big day.*

As the car crossed the Brooklyn Bridge, the driver turned the radio station to a news channel and my stomach dropped. The host was interviewing people who had launched their Child Victims Act cases. There was a lawyer who referred to the tide of justice as the silver water turned black beneath the bridge. A woman whose husband took his own life yesterday, wanting to forever avoid the truth, and as she yelled the host kept saying, "I'm sorry, but we can't hear you." A former priest who quit when he learned what his own parish had done. An Eagle Scout, a nail tech, a singer. A librarian, a comedian, a janitor.

Moans was so wrapped up in thinking about the wedding, he didn't hear a thing, and he still didn't know everything anyway. He didn't see my face reflected in the window. How it changed. He couldn't see the thousand ways the world vanished around us, the way I tried to envision myself speaking during these interviews. I pictured each man who had raped me paraded in front of the judge with a price tag attached. No money felt right. I couldn't accept each outcome. The driver kept looking at my fingers picking at the rubber on the window, my chest exploding, as I thought about the infinite space between my eyes and the world. He locked the doors again. He dropped us at home, where Empedocles and Voyager pawed at our knees. The day ended like any other. I went to bed and tried to sleep. My world began to collapse.

CHAPTER 5

After eight years together, Moans and I invited our whole world to the party. They each arrived in town with announcements of having been scammed by taxi drivers. They asked for advice, and they ignored everything we had told them. They stayed at luxurious Williamsburg hotels or found themselves in Bushwick motels or the real idiots found themselves in Times Square, where they texted us: *Can you buy shit from a guy whispering cokeandsmoke.*

Moans fucked me while our phones were buzzing with questions, each query a light passing briefly over the ceiling. I came over his chest while he came inside my ass. The sex felt like it used to, full of love and necessity and even a bit of longing. The feeling died as we replied to the texts we'd been ignoring. *Yes, that's Brooklyn. No registry, CASH ONLY.*

There was one final errand, so we showered and hopped in the car and drove to Harlem, where Moans had a friend who was running coke. Passing our first apartment in Morningside Heights, we slowed down to detour, leaning toward the front to peer up at that fourth-floor walk-up, which had a tree outside the window full of nocturnal birds that had refused to let us sleep. Moans drove single-handed, one hand on my knee.

When we arrived at his friend's place, she ran down to us, the amber-and-black city glistening behind her, and slipped into the back seat. She dropped off ten vials of coke, yellow bags of molly, and fifty empty dime bags gift-wrapped in tissue paper. She reached around the seats to hug us. She said, "Happy Wedding," and ran off. It was her present. We dipped a key into one of the vials and tested the stash, riding home with the windows down, hands riding the air, singing along to the ceremony playlist.

At home, we created the goody bags until James knocked on our door. He'd come from the eleven o'clock Megabus near Penn with a fat suitcase and a floral purse. He never traveled light. He was coming early, my best man, to help us put the finishing touches on the party. He was sober for years now and yelped when he saw what we were doing, calling us crooks, mockingly, in the tiring voice gays use to mock things. I was grateful he didn't use a lisp. He knew what annoyed me and utilized this as often as possible. At the last minute, Moans had told James he could stay at our apartment. Moans said he was necessary comic relief for me, although I didn't think I felt that tense. I felt hot and rich and delusionally young. I spent all the money I had, and it felt like we were doing it right. If I had anything of my own, I wanted it gone. With the exception of my name. All my life I'd gone by nicknames. The man who had sold me had used monikers. Sean, Adam, Johnny. And Moans called me Monster, which was a lot, coming from him. After James settled in, we hid the drugs and let James talk away the hours.

James knew more about me than most people, even some of what happened when I was a teenager. We flirted online for a year when

I was seventeen and he was eighteen, and when on my eighteenth birthday I fled from New York to California I thought he could have been the one to save me. He picked me up from the airport in a Honda Civic that scraped the street, wearing half a pair of broken glasses, pinching the left up to his bad eye like a monocle. He pushed out his lips and kissed me once, tasting like menthols and sunscreen. I felt nothing and tossed my single duffel bag, held together by duct tape, into the back seat, and the car sagged even lower. As he swerved, he prayed and changed CDs. Did we tell each other we loved each other as he drove us to my hotel? I don't remember, but whatever hope I had for James died on the white queen mattress, as he nervously undressed and hid beneath the covers. I did not find him attractive. Yes, we had sex; it wasn't anything more than that, but it felt like a lot less. He was sweet, naive, plain—the sort of guy you said was cute and you're sure he would find someone, but that person could never be you.

When James went to school the next day, I hit up another guy I knew online, a photographer from Chula Vista named Izzy. He picked me up in a jade windowless Jeep, the paint burning off from hours at the beach. He was deeply tan, with straight black hair that pressed back in the wind, dark eyes that never left me alone. We had planned to go eat, catch a movie, but as we peeled down the highway Izzy turned onto an exit and drove us back to the hotel. He wore black leather boots and carried a huge Nikon and walked with a hand on me, always. We entered the elevator and slammed each other against the walls. I was leaking precum that he thumbed off my cock to glaze my tongue. I was shirtless before we entered the room. He was fingering me as I sucked his uncut dick on my knees, my shorts caught around my ankles. He spit on his dick, my thighs resting on his biceps—I took the one

34

long slow breath you take as a man you want to love you enters you—and only pulled out to cum on my face so that he could take a picture. I still have it, his thumb guiding my cleft chin up to the light, the very first instance of love. I went to grab a towel but he knocked away my arm and used his tongue to clean it off before we fucked again, dirtying the whole room, removing the layers of longing that make up a gay youth. I thought this was the man to save me, a passion to guide me far from home.

We fucked for hours until a knock at the door became a banging, a crying, a screaming James, telling us he heard what we were doing, asking why and how, questioning me and God and himself. James burned out, but I knew he was waiting in the hallway until Izzy would leave. I envisioned a whole lifetime in those brief minutes. Izzy would take me down to San Diego. We would live together. A brand-new life. Izzy laced up his boots after he dressed, lifted his Nikon for one last shot, and hurried past a devastated James in the hallway, who looked like death and had somehow secured a bottle of Jäger. I ended whatever he thought was between us right there. I told James it wasn't about him.

We didn't speak while I lived with Izzy, but it didn't last long. Only a year. After I met Moans, a loneliness I couldn't name crept into my life, and James appeared to fill the time. We grew a deep friendship. That's what I thought of it. I never wanted more from James than that. He had to have known that, too. As the window took up more of my thoughts, the wedding, and the rest of it—James always found a way to be near me. Seven years of support. He would even save my life. When I told him the plans for my bachelor party, he said, *No no no no no.* And when I told James that we had to keep the secret from Moans, he said, *I'll be there.*

CHAPTER 6

Moans and I decided to have our bachelor parties on the same night. His sister, Laela, would take him out to dinner, followed by a few clubs, and an overnight hotel stay with a spa trip the next day. Laela used to be a dancer, quitting halfway through her ruined pregnancy, and now she worked for a traveling hospice company in the desert, collecting the final stories of retired Los Angeles gay men. Laela was the type of person who wanted to learn from the dying, believing every whisper a piece of wisdom, carrying horrors casually into conversation and claiming her work never weighed her down. This was bullshit, of course, but the useful kind. Whenever she involved herself, Moans became completely preoccupied with her own need to escape.

Moans kissed me goodbye with an overnight bag and took a car to the West Village. I turned around and popped an early sleeping pill to alleviate the terror of the upcoming event. James was already slapping a pack of menthols against his palm. I watched him smoke outside and scroll through his phone as dusk peeled streaks of golden light off the city, revealing the night's blue bruise. The pill held me in a state of grace, and I dropped a single dollar bill into the street. Nature would deliver what somebody needed on the wind.

I handed James the car keys.

"You know this is a mistake, right?" James said.

"I said you could stop at a drive-thru."

"So I can eat fries while you get killed?"

I laughed. "You think they'd last the drive?"

"I still can't believe I'm doing this," James said, as he put the key in the ignition and started the car.

We left Brooklyn as the temples let out, under the purple dusk, heading north. Congregants walked home in groups of two. I was on the way home, too, or at least toward where I grew up. A lot can be said of Mount Vernon, none of it great. I wasn't born there. My parents adopted me from Texas, where I had been abandoned at a hospital moments after I was brought into this world. My adoptive parents flew down and brought me back to New York. You know, the problem with New York is the suburbs are as horrible as everywhere else, if not worse, because there is a better place within thirty minutes. I didn't meet an openly gay person until I was fourteen, and you know how that went. These days, I spend my anger wisely, so I don't waste it on places, but every now and then, when I talk to people in the rehabs or before last call, I sometimes wish I could hate a place as easily as other people instead of hating the people themselves. But that is growing up. The world is a promise that nobody wants to keep. Kill yourself while you cultivate the flowers. Thank God I was high because my mind was turning dead earth. I didn't have the address of the house I wanted to find, but I knew when I got to Mount Vernon that I'd be able to find the right one. I downloaded Grindr and refreshed the screen, waiting to find the face of the man who had raped me. I felt like a god, swiping faces off the screen and in control of my fate. The reflectors on the E-ZPass turned red, and I stashed it in the glove compartment.

I gave James the directions, pressing my finger into Google Maps. The screen rippled like water. I needed to make sure my bravery lasted all the way to the pedophile's house, so I had taken another pill when James wasn't looking. James obeyed the speed limit and occasionally changed the song on his phone. He couldn't understand why I needed to do this, and I should have wondered why he wasn't pressing me. What did we talk about? I can barely remember anything except the feeling of sailing, the way light iced over the dark pavement. The highway looped into Main Street across from a gas station. I told him to turn left, but he pulled into the 7-Eleven.

Red-eyed strangers combed the aisles for food that I thought might never expire with lost, worried looks. If they were high, I was higher, and I spooked them. I looked each in their eyes. I was becoming who I needed to be. A gauzy sheen covered the lights. James bought bags of sour worms. We got back in the car and he followed my pointed finger through the suburbs.

"This way," I said. "Now that."

We came to a narrow one-way road. James slowed down. I leaned against the dash. The homes were built close together on thin lots. I showed James a spot between a dark maple and a black Ford Explorer. He parked and upended the candy into his mouth. I exited the car and stood beneath the single orange beam of a streetlight. What set apart the house I was trying to find was a screened-in porch and a blue-eyed rapist who had shotgunned crystal into my lungs when I was fourteen. I wanted to remind him that I hadn't forgotten. If he read the news, I wanted my face to appear in his head. He wasn't the man who had sold me, but he had bought me. I needed to ruin the rest of his life.

I opened Grindr on my phone and searched the grid for his face. I refreshed the app until each face settled in its box, showing how far each person was from me. In the second column, I saw him. He had short hair, blue eyes, dark purple bags, a gaunt face with silver stubble. He was listed as R, but his name was Russ. I reminded myself he was a person, a human fucking being. What had I been to him? A kid he paid a man to shave completely, a head he pushed into a blue pillow as he put Vaseline on his huge dick to shove inside my ass, the ass you filled with piss to get the body high on meth. I was a boy so afraid I never screamed. My heart skipped a beat as my pulse romped around my junkyard heart.

I walked back to the car and showed James his picture through the open window.

"He looks sick," James said. "A sick old man."

"You're staying here."

"Obviously. One man showing up at the door is a hookup, two is a robbery."

"Nobody would ever be afraid of you."

James ripped gummy worms with his teeth. "I'll keep watch."

I walked across the street to the house. The screen door to the porch was unlocked. Shovels leaned against empty clay pots. Purple stalky flowers bloomed on a shelf. The whole room reeked of mulch. I tried to look through the stained glass window on the front door, but it was too dark. I knocked twice and rang the doorbell. First, a light went on upstairs. Then I heard his steps as he walked down from the bedroom. He cracked open the door and stuck his head into the slate of light. He rubbed his eyes. I was taller than him now. He wasn't fully awake. I wasn't exactly either. I distinctly felt like this was a rehearsal, that I would be back here soon.

"Beautiful flowers," I said.

"They're hyacinths," Russ said, hoarsely. He had a voice destroyed by glass pipes. "What are you doing?"

"That depends."

"It's the middle of the night." He turned on the porch light and squeezed the front door closer to the frame. Less of his face showed. "Do I know you?"

"You'd remember me if I got naked," I said. Russ sucked air through his tiny teeth and shook his head, as if that were not enough. I hardly looked the same, and I didn't know who else he'd paid for, who else might show up in the dark night. I needed to do something so undeniably like myself that he would have to recognize me. But I didn't have a clue what that might be. This choked me up. A cry rose out of nowhere. His eyes were as blue as I remembered. I started shaking and sobbing, totally unprepared to see him. He grabbed my wrist as if he was going to shake me free of the moment, and maybe it was the arresting nature of his flesh against mine, but I looked at him in such a way that the color drained from him completely. I thought he might cover my mouth to keep me from making another sound. He didn't need to. He'd taught me well. I stopped crying, only for a beat. For a second, we both seemed to travel back thirteen years, and this time he let go of my arm and closed the front door without a word. The porch went black. I ripped the hyacinth out of its pot.

I held the flowers by their neck. I got back in the car, dirt falling off my shirt onto the passenger seat. James was speechless. He took the flowers from my hands, stepped out of the car, and dropped them in front of the tires. We ran them over as he drove off.

"I fucking cried," I said.

"It makes sense," James said. "You were a child."

At a red light, James showed me a picture of an absolutely hideous guy. "This guy wants my rotten ass."

I directed James to the last place I wanted to visit. It was a dark house, shrouded by leafy trees, up the street from my high school, where all the trouble started: Vincent's house. The man Russ had paid, the one who sold me.

"Back in high school, the walk took no time at all," I said.

The darkness was broken by a mosquito lamp that zapped glimpses of the blue and yellow house. There was a raised porch, three floors, and a detached garage in the backyard. I wasn't scared, but James put his hand on me. The trembling came from the pills. I swear. That's why I was shaking. Or at least that is what I told myself then.

Vincent no longer lived there. After he had been arrested twice in New York for assault and battery, I knew Vincent moved out to Colorado. His mother was a lawyer, his father a doctor, and this was their home. I cannot say that Vincent never suffered, but he never had to answer for what he had done to me. All Vincent had gotten was a few nights in jail for busting a man's jaw at Pieces, which was both stupid to do and an embarrassing place to have done it. I had an old friend from high school who had told me all of this, that Vincent was now working in a wilderness program, like the kind his parents had forced him to attend a few years before he met me. Vincent had been kidnapped in the dead of night and taken to a program that taught him the proper methods for cruelty and obedience, fear and reward. Apparently, Vincent was now taking teenage boys into the wild to teach them how to survive. The thought made me so sick I pushed it from my mind. I told James to cut the lights from the car so that we could see Vincent's room.

"I never thought it would look like this," James said, leaning over the wheel.

"I need to see his room."

James pressed his eyelids and unbuckled his seat belt. He turned off the car, and we got out quietly. If Vincent's family was home, they had to be asleep. I walked carefully up the gravel driveway. The rocks felt like crushed eggs under my feet. I lifted my foot and expected to see dead hatchlings under my shoe. Two cars were parked in the driveway. I went to lean on the window, but James slapped my hand.

"The alarm, idiot."

I motioned to the detached garage. Moonlight braided the grass. I pointed to the second-floor window, which had a direct sightline to where we were standing. James understood. I cupped my palms around his ear. I felt his skin on my lips. I knew he could hear the wetness of my mouth. "This was the spot I used to stare at when I was on his bed. It used to be a barn, but he set it on fire. I knew what he would do if I did anything wrong." We both looked at the garage. "*Boom.* Up in smoke."

James cupped my ear. "This is the worst bachelor party of all time."

"He set his house on fire twice."

"That's not the worst he ever did."

"No," I said, looking at my hands. "It's not."

We snuck back to the car. I imagined I'd be seeing Vincent soon. The window was open. If he was served papers, he'd have to return to New York. Our names would appear beside each other in the lawsuit. Everything he had done would be listed in a document that would follow him for the rest of his life. I thought returning to his house would help me choose to prosecute, to chase my civil case to its rightful end. But I didn't want his money. I couldn't find out what my body was worth again, after the years of knowing such a slim price. I needed to find another way. James started the car. I rolled down the window and leaned out to get a clear view. I wished I could have seen the motherfucker burn.

CHAPTER 7

We stood outside my cousin Vita's apartment in the East Village, a neighborhood, like Williamsburg, that you remembered for what it wasn't any longer. You got the sense walking around the barefoot people selling single shoes on the corner, vintage clothing stores, and old New York bars that this was where people who once considered themselves eccentric came after they happened into a wealthy marriage or developed a debilitating anxiety disorder or decided they could ignore about the city what they simply could not stomach. Vita was all three, hosting the rehearsal dinner because the place was beautiful and she didn't like to leave. We each took a hit of a joint and Moans stowed it in a box of mints. I looked up to the fourth floor and felt the tiny exasperation that comes from living in New York, full of proximity, little access, and the lucky condescension that comes from never really wanting to live in the neighborhood where the nice people always seemed to reside. It was a sexless block, far from the train, surrounded by businesses that I had not once seen open. I felt a touch of drool on my lips and wiped it. James pointed out the fact that the three of us looked very high, but nobody had eye drops, and I didn't really have a way to look more alert. I slapped myself lazily.

Nobody expected much anyway. The brutal walk up to Vita's

penthouse tired us out, and we panted as we entered her apartment. We had noted on the invitation that there was no elevator, to keep as many people as possible from coming. As we stood near the front door my sister, Devin, walked over to us, staring blankly for a second before saying, "You look like shit."

"They're very high," James said. "Not me. It's my special day."

"Okay," Devin said, enduring a hug from him.

"Look at Mom," she said to me.

Devin grabbed my sleeve and brought me through the bedroom door, where my mom, who was known for being an accidentally vicious bitch, was sitting with her eyes closed in an armchair as Vita held a glass bowl over her head, circling the rim with her fingers, which made a sort of low hum. I mouthed *Is she okay?* to my sister, who rolled her huge blue eyes. I realized she was wearing makeup. I could barely see my sister's freckles. She was actually wearing a dress, her nails were painted, and, for once, she didn't look like the girl I grew up around. The sign of her natural self was the shoes, which were slightly dirty sneakers.

"Mom picked it out?"

"Everything but the sneakers," Devin said.

"I'm working on your mother," Vita said, the hum slowing as she reprimanded us lovingly. She was wearing a loose floral dress, speaking in the tone unencumbered by annoyance that only healers who worked in the East Village could master.

"I'll be right over there," Mom said, without opening her eyes.

Moans went to greet them, but we turned him around and paraded ourselves in front of the guests. My father said, "My son! My son!" to Moans and squeezed my shoulders. I saw Moans' mother stop what she was doing to watch the affection. She was holding balled-up tinfoil in her hand, dumbstruck, staring way past the moment, her lips parted. I was looking at her, but she didn't see me; I was really seeing her, in a way she wouldn't understand for a while, knowing what she and her ex-husband had done to Laela and Moans when they were kids. She carried herself like a guilty person—with remarkable cheeriness and a ghostly quivering voice—and had never atoned for the abuse in their early lives. Her own family had come from cow country in California, and she still had a bit of that rural quiet. Even her eyes seemed to tremble, as if they were switching violently from the present to the past, unable to focus on the very moment in front of her. Truthfully, I did not like her. She had helped her ex-husband conceal his striking violence throughout their youth, even as he pulped the kids in his drunkenness, sparing no bruise for her, yet still whispering to the kids before school to keep their home a secret. Had she hit them? No. Had she whipped them with her Sunday best? Had her own arms been pulled from their sockets? Had the Lord intended, according to her and her ex, to light that path for them? Was she now, as the candles flickered beside glasses of wine, viewing the history of their family collapse onto Moans and my father in this open room? Was this world a mirror to the past? Was she the type of mother who could never give an answer to a lifetime of questions Moans had asked her? Such as *Why, Mom, why?* I could see her side—Caroline, as Laela referred to her—and I knew I would never love her, and she knew this, and still she dropped the foil to give us a giggling hug.

Just as I was about to lose myself in a wave of rising anger, my mother called out, "Where are my fans? Where is my biggest fan? There he is."

"The fact that it's not us," I said to Devin.

"Obviously," Devin said.

"Should it be?"

"What?"

"Us."

"Should we turn on Mom Radio and request a Mom hit track?"

"'You're Getting Fat' featuring 'Don't Give Me That Look.'"

"'Your Tattoos Are a Betrayal' (the one month later 'I'm Sorry' remix)."

"'Finish Your Meal' (1943 Jewish Immigrant Edition)."

"You're not too high," Devin said, patting my shoulder. "That's good. We love the bitch anyway."

I felt somebody looking at me as my mom hugged Moans, and this time it *was* Caroline who was staring at us. She waved with a spatula. I wondered how much she knew about our family. Caroline knew my sister and I were adopted when we were infants from different families. While I came from a decrepit Catholic hospital in the oil-rig fields of borderland Texas, my sister was plucked from the cornfields of Iowa. My parents were East Coast Jews, and I never asked if it was broken pussy or rotted nut, but they couldn't conceive. Our family was slapped together, as if made for television. They snagged us in their midforties, and now neared seventy. They didn't seem that way to me, but as Caroline watched us, I saw them in their twilight. Very clearly. We had passed the halfway point as their children.

"They're getting old," I said to no one in particular.

Maybe it was the weed, or my wish to simply rise above my anger for the sake of my own family in the presence of a woman who had failed her own. It could have even been seeing Laela ignore her stepfather, who was a blond dick with a terminal disease nobody ever named. Life was slowly depriving him of everything he enjoyed—red meat, dark beer—and he was not becoming nicer, just less of a threat. It could have been how the stepfather told me how proud he was of me to have overcome some bad history or James standing on a chair to begin his speech, but I was subdued by a feeling that I was leaving my life behind—the life I had lived for so very long, going out the fucking window—and craved a hit of crystal meth.

"I thought you said no speeches," Devin said.

"Nobody listens to me," I said, making my way toward the door. "Cover for me, bitch."

While people surrounded James, I walked out of the apartment and returned to the street, where I could breathe again. Waiting outside the building was the party photographer, who lifted his camera to take my picture and thought better. My phone kept vibrating, but I was only getting some fresh air. I would get a soda and return to the party. I circled a bodega and opened a fridge door for some fluorescent cool. I didn't have my wallet, so I returned to the party, where the group had cleared a path for me to stand next to Moans.

"I'm not mad," Moans said, holding my hand. "I expected it. We waited."

James decided to tell the story of the night he had met Moans. At the time, James was in the worst of his alcoholism, each outing a nocturnal prayer to the Deer God: Jägermeister. We had gone out to a bar in Hillcrest, San Diego, and James—in what remained of his drag persona—started accosting strangers on the street. Like a street preacher, James screamed homophobic shit like *Hey, shit dick!*, *did you botch your honor killing?*, and *God said a dash of AIDS, a pinch of Kaposi for you.* I was laughing, of course, until something inside him truly died and he began to quietly tell people: *You will never be loved. A faggot will never be loved.* It was shocking, even for me. Somebody pelted us with water bottles. Another slapped James, but he was too gone to register it. We ran away, and by the time we got back to my apartment, James had lost most of his clothes and passed out uglily on the mustard couch. Moans couldn't believe we got reverse gay-bashed, but we had been through worse, mostly by our own hand.

Nobody laughed.

The Moans family found it shocking, and my parents couldn't fathom why James had told a story about *himself* to a group of strangers at his best friend's wedding rehearsal dinner. As my mother put it: "What the fuck was that?" At the time, I was happy that James shielded me from more unwanted attention, and I thought he had done it for me. Although, after what would happen at the end of the year, I'd realize he never wanted me married at all. But, back then, I hugged him.

"Why did nobody clap?" James asked.

The next day, we had a very brief ceremony at a club in Bushwick with just our immediate family before the party. The family stepped down from the street into a circular concrete bunker with a single chandelier. They looked at us like we were a sacrifice. Laela read from a short story about love that I had chosen, but this time my family had found it shocking. There were a couple amputations, a suicide, straight-up raw butt fucking, and true love. So what? My parents knew what I'd been through, and I hated when they acted like the world existed without its major characteristic: violence. They moved away from the makeshift altar, and then, after the story ended, returned to kiss our cheeks. We waited for whatever was supposed to happen. The photographer lifted his camera. We didn't move. James pushed us to kiss each other. We turned to each other and kissed in a silent club. *Boom.*

Our parents left. We had a good time. The coke lifted our spirits, and the molly lifted our bodies. James found a coked-out date with a useless cock. Moans and I danced in our bright short-sleeve shirts like honeymooners who walked into the wrong party. The bunker created a small respite. The after-party at Metropolitan ended early when the bouncer kicked us out for being too obvious with our dusted keys. The after-afters at The Rosemont was simply oblivion. When we woke up later that day, two women hooked IVs into our arms. I felt fine, but I'd had more practice than the rest of my friends.

At the end of the month, we received the photographs. Some were marked in a separate file labeled PRIVATE. Moans reviewed the photos. He was puzzled, staring at the computer, and I wanted to know what he found. He turned the computer toward me. The photographer caught a terrible moment. We looked like boys who had been warned that if our lips touched our whole lives would explode. I didn't click on the next picture. I knew what would happen. I didn't transform into a different person. Moans eyed me as if I would always be a stranger. What could I have said? I had been dreaming of this day for thirteen years, ever since Vincent had carved a wedding date for us into the wooden window frame by his bed—the date when I would finally be free. For all that time, I confused escape with healing, and not for a moment in the bunker, not even for the camera flash at the altar, could I sustain my own lies.

CHAPTER 8

We planned on flying to Europe for our honeymoon. We had never left the country before and wanted an adventure. I was afraid of flying, and the flight was going to be seven inescapable hours long, buckled into a rickety seat with the doors locked. I insisted on the best flight insurance, just in case. We had a stash of sedatives, sleeping pills, and natural remedies. As long as I didn't think about it, I thought I could make the trip.

Moans packed our bags the day before while I went for a long run. In Prospect Park, there was a moment as I was running against the flow of joggers, dodging the current of people, where I lost complete confidence, a moment that happened on most runs, thinking to myself, *You can only fight the tide for so long before it takes you*, but I doubled down, running faster and harder until I exited the park and found myself in a trance all the way to the Brooklyn Bridge. I stopped the run to email my psychiatrist, begging her for pills to anesthetize me for the transatlantic journey. *Please, put me out of my misery*, and she called in a script to a pharmacy so I could pick them up on the way home.

I came home soaking wet, avoiding the suitcases in the living room, and snuck into the bathroom to run the shower. I played music on my computer loudly and played white noise on my headphones as I sat on the floor. I needed layers of protection, layers and layers, to email the Center. Now that the law was in effect, the Center had hired a lawyer, and I wanted to set up time with her before we left. I also didn't want Moans to know.

Moans didn't really know what happened to me—a single rape, a beating or two. It was all he had ever needed to know, and that was the extent for years of what I had been able to reveal, even to myself. If he knew what I was doing in that bathroom, Moans would have been afraid of the ripples, that I might hit some terrible jackpot of fear and ruin the trip, which I didn't want to do. I didn't want to let him down. I never had the money to take him on his dream vacation—to a hut over the water in Fiji, legs hanging over the deck above clear turquoise water. I would make sure he, at least, got this.

When I left the bathroom, Moans put his hand tenderly on my ribs, almost checking to see if I were alive.

"It's still me," I said.

"That's the problem," Moans said.

The next morning, a few hours before takeoff, I took the pills my doctor prescribed me (plus a few more; I doubled down) while Moans made coffee. (Really, I took the dose tenfold.) Our bags were stacked by the front door, and we would call the car in an hour. Sip by sip of water, my fear drained from my throat and dissipated. I lifted a bag to see if I could carry it. Moans looked lovely, too. His hair was recently cut. He was wearing new sweats for the flight, a deep madder blue, gracefully arranging the last necessities for the car, attempting to avoid anything that might trigger me. The word *flight* was missing, even time itself seemed to have left the earth. Our bond felt divine, and while I admired him I lay on the couch.

Two days later I woke up, in the same spot, with a deep ache in my lower back. Nothing felt right. All light meant pain. From the kitchen table, Moans stared at me while he smoked a joint, wearing a tank top and jeans. I tried to stand and fell. My arm, covered in bandages, stung.

"What happened?" I asked, in a voice destroyed.

"You overdosed, blacked out, and tried to tattoo your arm with a blue pen."

"So we didn't go."

"You don't remember?" He rubbed his puffy eyes. "You weren't asleep the whole time. You weren't getting on that plane."

"I'm sorry," I said, and stifled a growing embarrassment on my face, burying my head in the cushions. I should have known to have pretended I could have handled such a long flight. My psychiatrist had contacted the airline, and we got our money back. I felt guilty and told Moans we could have sex, but this only saddened him. I didn't have anything else to offer.

"I found a room on Fire Island," Moans said. He wanted to shatter the damned vibe. "We wouldn't have to pack."

I took too long to respond, and he saw me creating an excuse for why I couldn't leave the house. He was shaking his head, and I really couldn't argue. I didn't blame him for wanting to celebrate. Moans deserved joy. I couldn't have it. I didn't want it. I never considered it a possibility. How could I explain that I had been living for years, from moment to moment, with no real purpose other than to live? I was trying to get from one moment to the next. I was running! I was moving! I was just trying to get away. I didn't explain. He knew. It was terrible to see how little loss of hope changed his face.

Moans walked outside. The dogs were already boarded, and

the room was quiet. I poured myself a glass of trembling water. I followed Moans, out to where he sat on the curb, hugging his knees to see the planes descend from JFK. He smoked his joint and picked pebbles off his palms. Moans resembled his younger self then, the man I once filled with hope, and I got distracted by ideas of love. He stood when he heard me, and we started walking toward the park.

I'd been so distracted by the news that I hadn't noticed the leaves had begun to turn, yellowing the green light of summer. The wind blew the first weak leaves down the block. I chose to pick a leaf and trace its path, block by block, as Moans said things to me I could not hear, tiring himself with accusations and frustrations, practicing a speech I would hear for the next few months that only now was in its rawest form, until eventually we were far from home and the tension between us broke. Only exhaustion remained. We had traveled too far. Moans looked up the avenue as if he could see our home, but of course he couldn't.

I began to regret the wedding. When we first planned it, I hadn't known the Child Victims Act would come into effect, and I didn't know the two would crash into each other. I hadn't believed the past ran under the present. I didn't know it was a reservoir, that I was sinking with every step. It seemed unwise to add a postscript to the invitation: *May postpone, if justice permits. Please send cash, either way.* A fire engine coasted silently down the street.

"Let's go," I said to Moans. I didn't think he heard me. He was staring at the truck. "Let's go. I want to go. Let's fuck up the island."

"Really?"

"I want to get away."

"Let's go," Moans said. "I have been thinking the same thing."

CHAPTER 9

Moans and I met in San Diego. About a year after Izzy and I broke up, when I was nineteen, living in the place we had moved into together after I left James in shambles in that hallway. I had enrolled in massage school and rarely spoke to my parents. They didn't understand why I had fled to California, and I didn't understand how they could have cared so little for my where-abouts as a teenager, how I could spend weekends away and they barely noticed.

This era in San Diego—where, if you've heard me talk about it, I might say I feel like who I am now was born then. I worked in a bakery during the day and as a go-go dancer at night. The massage school line worked to pick up men who would pay me to gently rub their backs before I sat on their dicks in their bedrooms for a hundred dollars.

I think of moving to San Diego as the first great decision Young Dylan ever made. If you're lucky, even when you're younger and life is incomprehensible you act in ways to avoid pain, no matter how drastic, and years later might be able to live better because your younger self knew more than you gave him credit for. I threw away the life I hated for the one I hoped to have now.

It was good that I met Moans at the bakery. He arrived with two friends, but I only saw him, his strong jaw and small dark eyes: two black eclipses I stared at. I stole desserts for them, serving plate after plate, just to keep him there longer. We stared at each other. Moans handed me his number on a napkin. They left for Balboa Park, and I texted him the second he was out of sight, and we made plans to meet in a couple hours.

That night we smoked a joint on Coronado Beach, beneath the pulsing military choppers running drills over the base. He asked to see my tattoos, and I lost my shirt. He traced the black circles down my back. I told him they represented the endless cycles of life. Moans didn't run away. I reached into his shorts beneath the lifeguard tower. He drove us across the high arched bridge to his place, where I lay on my back as he planted his arms above my shoulders. He parted my thighs with his knees and asked if I wanted to get fucked; I had never been asked that question before. He was smiling, laughing a little; he didn't know this was my line of work. I said yes, and later he told me I was very quiet. The men would always talk after. The men would tell stories. But I couldn't yet, so I didn't know how to be any other way.

What bonded us? The San Diego summer, an ideal set of days that could make a man feel like he was meant to live on Earth. We would smoke weed and steal passion fruit as we walked around my neighborhood. They were plump and easy victims on the vine. We fucked everywhere in my Texas Street apartment, even in the shower, where I'd cut my knees on the tiles, and after he'd cum in my ass he'd pull the bedsheets from my wounds as I scream-laughed into a bare pillow. Once, in the trunk of my car on the bluffs overlooking Black's Beach, when we couldn't wait to fuck. A car fuck could feel triumphant like nothing else in this world. Occasionally, a face passed by the window like a cloud. After, I climbed down the precarious mountainside to wash off at the nude beach. It became very clear Moans hadn't had a lot of sex before me, even though he was seven years older. I showed him how far you could take a body, but he never tried to break it.

Nobody wanted a person like me for more than a night, so I gave up the work for Moans. We moved in together. He paid for almost everything. I picked up jobs where I could outside the bakery. A weekend barista, an errand boy, and, every now and then, when Moans left for a business trip or to vacation with his family up in Mount Shasta, I'd hit up the old gigs. I knew my secrets would catch up with me. And it didn't take too long.

We were at Golden Donut, right after dawn, holding cups of coffee whose steam rose into the blue morning gloom. Moans pulled out his wallet, but the man behind us said, "I got it."

The stranger was like any other retired surfer reading the morning news.

"Thank you," Moans said, boyishly.

"Thank him," the man said. "What that kid can do to a guy. Consider it a second tip."

That morning at home, we fought over grand ideas of love: loyalty, betrayal, honor, cheating. I didn't understand any of it. I believed you did whatever you needed to escape the past. To survive. Even now, as I talk about this era, I'm not sure my beliefs have really changed, only that I am less ready to hurt the men I love, especially as the past recedes even further back. I'd been homeless. I'd been owned. I would never go back to those. Nobody would lock me in a room from the outside and tell me not to make a fucking sound. Moans didn't understand what I was doing because I hadn't told him any of that yet. I didn't want him to get it. The more a person knew what happened to you the more they knew what they could get away with doing to you, and I wanted to preserve what I had with Moans. But I needed money, and the same pattern continued. When we were together, I stayed inside, and when he left I ventured out.

I searched farther and farther away from home. I took the bus east to Lemon Grove, or the trolley up to the mansions in La Jolla, where I had a client. The lawyer liked to open his grand oceanfront windows, and after I finished with him he would point out seals and dolphins and whales in the coves. The ocean made him giddy, like a child at an aquarium, and he'd tell me fun facts about the currents or bark like a seal. The lawyer handed me binoculars, and I'd scan the beach, waiting to find Moans on that strip of white sand, skipping work for the day or looking for me, combing the beach for a boy who was meant to be home. I never found him out there. The binoculars revealed the true nature of my life. I would never be free, but I could get close and keep my past secret. I would always be a dancer with a fake name, but, unlike when I was a teenager, I could leave and go home to a man who wouldn't even choke me unconscious if I placed his hand on my throat. That's all I wanted.

Moans forgave me. I never told him that I did it for money. I became paranoid that the men would find me. We stayed home. If I wasn't high, I was asleep, and if I was sleeping, I was screaming. Privately I blamed being afraid of the clients finding me, but it was the men from my youth who populated my nightmares. The night terrors worsened, and what Moans had once found strange—inexplicable eruptions in my sleep—came to seem like a symptom. One night, I screamed and threw myself off the bed.

"Come back," Moans said.

He wanted to know what I was dreaming about, but I didn't tell him. I had heard a key in the door, and I had tasted menthol, and I knew what was coming: a hand over my mouth, a pressurized explosion forcing its way inside me, but I spared Moans the truth.

When my night terrors began to rouse him from sleep four times a week, he demanded to know what was happening, but I told him I didn't fully understand them, which wasn't exactly untrue. One night, my feet got twisted in the sheets and I gave myself a black eye. Moans asked again, as he held ice to my face. He told me that when he was a child in Big Sur, when his parents were out ministering, he would ice Laela's face after his father had smacked her. Another night I shattered a bottle of cologne on the floor. As he daubed up the mess, he told me that when they had stayed at a parishioner's house their father had spilled red wine on the shaggy white carpet, and they knew that unless they cleaned it perfectly they would be homeless again. I never responded to the stories. I only listened. I got to know a man who had been on the run as a boy, who now wanted a permanent home as an adult, enough money to not live in parched fear of having nothing, and some sex. He could take care of me, clean up some minor messes, but the truth was that I didn't have a nightmare every night. It was only after we had sex. Since we had sex almost every night, since I screamed every night, since we spent the quiet hours together telling stories, I learned more about him than I think he had ever planned to reveal. They were run out of towns after his father was caught stealing from churches. Moans only escaped because of a random day. After Laela went to school and his father was preaching, Moans had a strange feeling that his mother was doing something, so he pretended to be too sick to go to school. Little Moans begged for an answer. She decided to escape, had packed a bag and was going to leave without them, by telling him she was going to get groceries. Despite what she wanted, Moans followed her, and he grew up in a house with his mom in Mount Shasta while Laela spent a few years with her father in Santa Cruz. They divorced and Laela moved in with Caroline and Moans. Laela never forgave her. When Moans came out—well, you already know—she kicked him out. I fell asleep to these stories in his arms. We never really spoke about them during the day. Eventually, he started to run out of stories and would just beg for me to tell him what made me tremble. I said I had nightmares like this for a long time, but he didn't believe me. Moans said, *I know what fear looks like*. He told me I had a problem. I needed to get help or he would leave me.

Moans convinced me to return to New York to seek help. I knew the San Diego era was over; what I mean is that I had found a place in the world that I loved but my past was ruining it; I had taken myself as far as I could go, and now Moans would take me home. A psychiatrist prescribed me pills to sedate me for the journey. Every couple of hours the day of the flight, Moans handed me a pill. How did it play out? Like you would expect. I wilded out and never made it on the plane. The Feds kicked me out of the airport. I felt sorry. We tried again the next day. This time they threatened to arrest me.

We made the decision to drive.

I knew I wouldn't remember the ride, so I bought disposable cameras at the gas station and collected free maps at rest stops. In Arizona, we abandoned fields of blue stars. I neglected the medication through Texas, a state I hadn't been to since my adoption, to set what I could of my origins to memory: a strip club, dead railways, a trucker I probably would have blown had I been given a second alone. We smoked a blunt in St. Louis, overnighted in a town so wrecked by heroin that the Holiday Inn worker told us to only eat at drive-thrus. We found Voyager somewhere along the way. She slept near our car in a motel parking lot, and after we watched her all night, when we opened the door, she jumped in with me. She slept on my lap. The rest? All gone.

Five days later we pulled up to my parents' home. They lived in a small white house in a city north of the Bronx. My father had lost his job and taken a chain saw to the swing set, which lay in pieces in the yard. He set me to work with remedial tasks. I carried the broken swing set to the curb, the wood splintering my fingers. I raked my fingers through the dirt to bury compost in the garden. I passed rooms where Moans sat with my parents before they closed the door on me. I didn't think they were talking about me. I didn't understand anything.

A few nights later, Moans told me that if I didn't go to the hospital he would leave, so they drove me to a building that resembled a castle. That's how you know a psych ward will be good—if it looks like you'll be tortured there you will be treated better. I spent two terrifying weeks in the psych ward. Blue halls, locked rooms, the green outside that we only got to touch once a day, for an hour, if we lined up early and were lucky. I was so lonely I held flowers in my hand to trick the bees into landing on me. The doctors medicated me, told Moans that I had been smoking too much weed, and released me after I detoxed from weed and proved my sanity, by which I mean I spent some time acting completely subservient to people I did not believe or trust. They reminded me of Vincent and the other men. Vincent's solution to pain had been to rub cocaine on his dick before he fucked me. As he tore through me, I went numb. Russ smoked me up with crystal meth. I never hit the pipe myself. Russ would shotgun the smoke or he would grab my hair or slap my face until he could piss inside my ass. I didn't know back then that's why he did that. It was just one more task to withstand, another rush of extraordinary pleasure when I was at my most afraid. I still don't know how men can do that to a child. I probably won't ever get an answer. They were so plain and lived normal lives. What I mean to say is that now I know it is hard to accept that some people are capable of more than you, for better or worse. Even Moans was capable of more than I thought. When I got out, Moans and I lived on a blow-up mattress in my parents' basement. We watched a TV that still had a VHS slot. We did not have sex and fought. Within a week, he moved into an apartment in Harlem and got a job managing a now-departed hair-care store in Midtown. In his absence, a crystalline loneliness, even sharper than what struck me in the ward, plunged my world into near-total quiet. I would smoke joints with Devin on the grass at night to talk about our parents. During the day I'd powerwash the moss from the white siding and occasionally sneak off to suck off lonely fathers. I began to feel like a teenager again, in touch with a world I had thought was long gone.

CHAPTER 10

The ferry departed Long Island for Fire Island, and the shore diminished from our blue pews. Hideous gray waves slapped the lower deck. I felt deprived of nature. The ocean had no scent. The boat hit a wave: a spray of salt water stung my arm. Working teens checked our tickets and ran into the enclosed sections of the boat. I'd officially reached the age where I began to see the mistakes of people younger than me. It started with their tans and continued to their vapes. I knew the trivial moments would add up. The people they now kissed in the dark corridors of a late-summer ferry would become future fantasies. I could see their marriages ruined, right there on the ferry, before they realized that every pleasure had a consequence.

I knew then I was falling out of love.

"You look handsome," Moans said, as he took a picture of me. I flipped my hat backward. He took another, and then I did the same for him, trying to capture his best angle, while directing him to soften his smile and raise his chin. I showed him the pictures, and he seemed pleased. We posted them. I laid my head on his shoulder, and I tried to believe I could find our love again.

The ferry approached the island, a skinny green-gray strip on the horizon. The afternoon breeze warmed, and it began to feel like summer again. Like the window hadn't yet started. We got off in Cherry Grove and walked between two bayfront restaurants, each with competing performances from screaming drag queens. Few people attended, but everyone around was forced to listen. Disco lived in a hellish rotation. A drag bar was purgatory for many of those artists, where each high note, the more time went on, sounded more and more like a screaming protest.

At the market, we turned down on Bayview Walk, the wooden path lifted above the ground and surrounded on both sides by reeds and vacation homes. Men walked by us winking, double-taking, drunk and horny. I wished this didn't work on me, but I felt better, among people who would never know who I was, even if they were inside me, which was where they wanted to be. I felt like we were supposed to be here, like this was the vacation intended for us. I grabbed Moans' hand and told him I was happy.

We could see the hotel above all these homes, the white spires towering. It was called the Belvedere, and it was a Venetian palace, or that was what it was meant to look like, huge and campy, painted a flat white with light blue accents. In pictures, the hotel seemed like something meant for Las Vegas. I was ready to burst out laughing. As we stood outside the wooden door, unable to see over the high walls protecting the guests of the hotels, as I grabbed the gaudy metal door knocker, I wanted to hate how out of place it seemed, how tacky, how silly to build a cathedral-like palace for a bunch of wealthy-enough dick suckers to vacation, but, in truth, I was kind of stunned. I thought it was beautiful.

Behind that gate, the lustrous plants grew thick and wild, glazed gently with drops of water from a hose. The naked gardener tipped his hat as we stepped up to check-in, pressing a button at the locked glass door. A man opened the door and hugged me, welcoming us to the Belvedere. A very cute guy about my age kissed our cheeks (and despite what I wanted I did not follow him) and took our bags as the attendant asked for our name. The cute one took our bags to our room as the attendant gave us wristbands that would allow us to enter and exit any party we wished.

Beside the front desk, there was a pool, a hot tub, and an outdoor gym.

"As you know, we are a clothing-optional facility."

"That explains the gardener," I said. "Did you know?"

"No," Moans said. "But it's fine."

"Better for me."

"If you like you can get undressed now," the man said, inspecting my arm. "Did you break it?"

"In a sense."

The man gave us a tour, showing us an upper deck above the bay with navy lounge chairs where a hung man slept, his hand still holding a beer. We descended a spiral staircase to peer down on a roped-off sitting room. There were candelabras, crystal chandeliers, light green curtains that he said were *chartreuse*. The room was off-limits, more of an installation than an accessible place to relax, although we could take pictures in the mirror if we liked. He said, "It's a famous online pic to show your friends," which made me laugh. Through the doors, there was another outdoor patio full of fountains with naked statues shooting white water out of their mouths. "Yes, it does look like cum."

"Was that intentional?" I asked.

"Your boyfriend's a funny one," he said, without laughing, and I hadn't been joking. The nude statues shot ropy, opaque water out of their pouty lips into a basin.

"My husband," Moans said.

"We got married last week," I said.

"A honeymoon?" the man said. "How delightful."

The man continued to show us through various hallways to our room, telling us that we would definitely get lost, but that eventually we would find the way back to our room. We could always ask for help. The lock used a retro key, and inside the room he showed us the three amenities. There was a small fridge, complimentary beach towels, and a wide glass door that opened to a courtyard where two men were fully jerking each other off. They stopped to wave at the man, who they called Dave, and he said, "I realized I hadn't introduced myself to you. My name is Dave. Would you like a glass of champagne? Had I known it was your very special honeymoon, I would have had some ready."

"We had a last-minute change," Moans said. "We were supposed to be in Europe."

"This is actually a very European facility," Dave said.

"Is it?" Moans asked, sounding like me, and I kissed his cheek as Dave left to find champagne.

The room wasn't too small. We had a queen bed, two dressers, a small TV, and a hit-it-from-the-back-sized shower. The thin walls allowed us to hear into the next rooms, as people talked about the Spartan Party, and I felt like that thinness would protect Moans from ever fully going off on me. He lay on the bed, and I unpacked the bags.

"*It's very European,*" Moans repeated.

"He could be right," I said.

"Don't."

"I'm saying we don't know."

"How are you the one in the good mood?"

"I think we are in the right place," I said, taking off my shirt to lay next to him on the bed. I raised my hand and let the wedding ring hover above our faces. "You ever get that feeling? Like you're exactly where you're supposed to be?"

Moans raised his hand, too. The ceiling fan cooled us. I was too nervous to straddle him, to suck him, to even let more than the sides of our arms touch, but I stayed there while he gathered himself, watching naked men pass in front of our glass door, who every so often stopped to wave or grab themselves or turn around completely, their attention glitched by some other better thing. When he was ready, we rented bikes and got ice cream and rode around the island as men in togas started to leave their rentals or water taxis.

"Let's give in," I said.

"To what?"

"The Spartan Party."

We ate dinner in Drag Hell, or Island Breeze, as it's commonly known. They didn't have vegan food, but I had french fries and a BLT without bacon and mayo. Moans kept eying the dish and giggling, as if he were happy for this little punishment. We hated the food and felt very married. We drank Long Islands, vodka sodas, whatever extra drink the bartenders would give us as we barhopped and told them about our wedding. Sometimes the drunks next to us would scream congratulations and give us shots. One old man, alone with a cane, even handed me fifteen dollars, whispering that I didn't have to do anything for it. This time.

We left the bar, walking with the toga-clad men toward the hotel, their golden laurels catching the dusky light, as the wind lifted the cloth and exposed them. Nobody cared. I was ready to be butt-fucking naked too. I was ready to be undressed by the wind, like the pink hydrangeas next to the walk that were left only with their green stalks. I tried not to crush them as we walked. Moans unlatched the gate. I got undressed in the courtyard and dropped my clothes by our room. We kissed in the courtyard until we couldn't see our reflection in the glass door. My oiled, sunburned skin looked purple, dark at night, and even though my arm still hurt I ran my body all over Moans on the patio furniture. A few people gawked, jerking off beneath the canopy of trees and umbrellas.

I reached into his briefs and felt his dick. I stroked him until a drop ran out and licked my finger. He sat up and I kneeled in front of him, the sandy wood rubbing against my knees. I took him fully in my mouth, making him harder and slicker. He tasted like sweat. I asked for his hand to stand up, and he was going to lead me back to our room, but I turned around, my ass facing him right there. I touched his wedding ring, I kissed it, I let him know I knew we were married, I made him feel like I wanted my husband to fuck me, to claim me there. I had my hands on the bamboo edge for balance as he took a random bottle of lube off the table and pushed his dick into my ass. My bandage fell into the plants, but I didn't care. I liked the way my arm bled lightly on the wood. I preferred a bit of pain to guide me through the pleasure. Moans hooked his fingers over my hips and slammed into me. He didn't have a big dick, so he could easily use the whole force of his body. He pulled me into him, over and over, and came inside my ass. I felt him slowly pulsing, each contraction slower and weaker than the last, as if his heart were failing. I was seized by the dullest terror of long-term love. Each fuck had once felt like puzzling ourselves together. Before this, our sex mostly felt like we knew what worked, but how he was treating me there, in this honeymoon theater of love, felt like he might want to break me. He might just break himself into a person I could love again. If we stopped, I knew we would return to the people we had been before, not who we were starting to act like on this trip. The future collapsed until all our possibilities felt contained in that courtyard—oxygen, cum, a little bit of blood—and I felt the need for resuscitation. I gripped his dick and milked the last drop of cum onto my tongue. He wiped the sweat from my brow. As I was about to cum, he was still slightly hard, and I placed my dick on top of his. I eclipsed him completely. The weight stiffened him, and I jerked off with both hands until I came all over his dick, and when I turned around he started to fuck me again.

Our sounds filled the courtyard. Each slam sent a pain down my leg. He turned me around, my back on the chaise lounge, lifting my ankles to press the tip of his dick against my hole. Apollos in the courtyard treated us like porn. One held my ankle in the air. They lingered. My legs were bent over my head, my lungs compressed, and soon we heard another couple fucking, and the Apollos moved on to other rooms, other courtyards. How briefly we held the costumed gods' attention ruined the vibe. We were just another stop on the journey through the pines. Our love felt deeply mortal. Two fools who fucked in the open. We finished and walked back to the room to wrap ourselves in sheets for togas. We were going to join the Spartan Party.

Before we left, as I was weaving wreaths from brittle weeds, Moans said, "I got you a wedding present. The only present you would like. The only thing that will make you feel better."

"Why do you think gay people love costumes so much? I know the answer, but as a culture, I wish it were something less ridiculous.

God is watching us and having a good laugh. Do you think God says 'fag' or 'faggot'? 'Faggot' is just funnier."

"In this moment, he'd call you a dumb fag. Listening to this conversation, that's what I think."

"God says 'fag,' but the devil says 'faggot.'"

"You're out of your mind." Moans kissed my head after I handed him his wreath. He examined the drying leaves and shrugged. They weren't perfect, but they were acceptable, and the Spartans would be drunk enough to excuse our little failures. We checked our costumes in the mirror, and Moans pulled out a plastic bag from the suitcase and dumped a mound of shrooms onto a novel I hadn't started reading. True love! I kissed him. He split it in two and we made off for the party.

CHAPTER 11

At the gates of the Ice Palace, a chorus of drunks slapped name tags on guests. They were singing showtunes in harmony; a few mistakenly believed they were sopranos. It was easy to tell who was the most deluded by the level of detail in a costume. The chorus had human hair units, heavy gold brooches, silk togas, and extraordinary wreaths. On my chest they pressed *Paris*. On Moans: *Helen*. Moans reached to switch the name tags, but a fairy named Eris slapped his hand, saying, "You don't want to mess with fate."

"That's exactly what you want to mess with," I said, but the fairy's toga grew into angel wings, and the fire in the torch behind him leapt brilliantly, and I didn't want to fight with an angel, even if he was an idiot. Moans pulled me into the tented party. Even under the influence, I saw people I knew from home. The slutty Pulitzer winner I'd once fucked in Manhattan kneeled in front of an ice sculpture, but nobody poured a shot into the sculpture for him to slurp out of the statue's icy cock. What fame he had in the city deserted him here. Soon he quit and approached the bar, but the bartender completely ignored him.

"Maybe this is kind of like Europe," I said.

"No," Moans said coldly.

"Dylan's not making the joke. I'm Paris. You can't be mad at an ancient hero."

"I can be mad at anyone."

"I'm sorry," I said, placing my hand on his lower back. His stretch marks shined blue. I grabbed his hand and brought him to the metal railing at the edge of the bar that overlooked a pool. People on the balconies around the golden pool cheered for the shivering Spartans in the water who were fighting and fucking. We made fun of how they folded their togas on the lounge chairs and used their phones to check their headpieces. Athena pushed Hera into the pool, and her breastplate sunk to the bottom. Hera lifted herself on the lip, and the two wrestled, losing their costumes, piece by piece.

The night continued like this: an end-of-summer revelry, a drunken orgy interspersed by vital acts of violence. We couldn't betray the atmosphere. Costumes fell easily. Soon, we were all in our jocks, carrying bedsheets in our hands. We danced, moving as much as the shrooms allowed, stepping tentatively, rating the attractiveness of others. Random men ran their hands over my ass, and I felt blissfully attentive to my body, the island, the potential of my life here. I asked if Moans was okay. He wasn't like me. He couldn't lose his clothes at a moment's notice. He nodded, distracted by the blue ice sculpture, glowing with moonlight, flushed every now and then with liquor, which cascaded terribly through the angel, resembling both blood and light, sucked out by whatever man waited with an open mouth. I told Moans I would take the sheets back to the hotel so we wouldn't lose them. When we tripped, I was always the guide. I never lost the ability to see the falseness of the experience, what others occasionally referred to as the truth of hallucinogens. I knew to lean into fear, to feel and let go. Later, I'd understand I wasn't some spirit guide; I'd learn that shrooms were a treatment for C-PTSD, and whatever effect they had on me—the surface knowledge of the temporary nature of all experience (the trick of all this light)—was in fact a medicine that worked on my wrecked mind. It said nothing about innate vision, nothing of supernatural skill, only the fact that I was sick and treating it. I helped Moans undo his toga, and then I wrapped both around my arm and walked home alone. Along the path I passed a hundred passionate strangers kissing people in the moonlight. I dropped off the sheets, did what people do on drugs, and returned to the party.

I couldn't find Moans.

He wasn't by the bar, or the sculpture, or the pool.

I asked Hermes, the bartender, if he'd seen a man in black briefs.

"A thousand," Hermes said.

I scanned the room again before returning to the entrance to ask Eris, who told me he'd seen Moans walking toward the beach. I should have known better, but I ran to the shore, which was littered with crowns, as sharp as broken seashells. I ran over the packed sand until I reached the Pines, where a condemned house collapsed in the water. The porch was painted with strokes of moonlight. The magnificence of shrooms wasn't some secret access to what lived below the surface of experience. It was attention, that's all. I saw the dark water greet the house in shadow. I couldn't tell the broken beams of wood from the breaking waves. I could not tell you exactly when my relationship had ended. For so long, I had been nobody, and with Moans I had been such a part of him that I didn't know a future for myself outside of him; maybe it was the window; or maybe it was what the window had done to us; or maybe I finally had a space that was my own where I could tell Matan that I did not want to live forever afraid, and I knew with the window being a single year, during which time I would have a grad school stipend and not have to rely on a man for money, that I could not live if I didn't take this chance.

I returned to the path through the forest, through the Meat Rack, lit by torches that marked the way back to the Belvedere. Dunes rose along the shore, where a silhouette of a man would lift out of the darkness of the horizon, and trees cloaked men who kept running into the darkness when they heard another seeker. Men approached me, and they disappeared. I couldn't do anything right now. I needed to find Moans. Aries pissed on Aphrodite's face. Odysseus stumbled nakedly into the path to bellow, "Who has lube!"

"Use spit," Artemis said, as I watched Telemachus bend Polyphemus over a rock. Artemis lifted both their togas to finger them as Odysseus asked lovingly if he could fuck the shit out of my mouth. The gods were what I wanted to be: free island sluts. Moans wouldn't be among them. I wished I could stay with them. It felt like avoiding my future to not lay with them, but I wasn't there yet. I had to find Moans and tell him the truth. I covered my face and cried, feeling completely alone, like I had failed him. I felt a hand on my back and found Apollo, trying to comfort me.

"Shoot," Apollo said.

"I'm trying to find someone."

We both looked at the people around us, all dressed the same, all wanting the same.

"My husband," I cried, really feeling the wetness on my face. I felt the mask of myself washing off. I was devastated. Even if he found me then, I was afraid Moans wouldn't recognize me. The pain in my hip returned. Apollo handled me softly. "I can't find him. And I'm not the person I want to be."

"Go home," he said, and he ripped the name tags off our chests and switched them. I was Apollo; he was now Paris. For a few quiet paces, he joined me, a hand on my lower back, until a deer leapt into the path, staunchly blocking us with a twitchy tail. After a moment, the deer returned to the woods, and I wanted to look at the new Paris, to share a wild moment, but he was already gone.

I exited the woods, closing in on the homes, and I saw the Belvedere, where I decided to check for Moans. When I got to our room, I saw him on the bed, the sheet wrapped around his shoulders, as he changed the TV channel. Beside him, there were seashells spilling out of his underwear.

"I lost you," I said.

"I didn't want to be Helen," Moans said, showing the name tag *Achilles* on his chest. "I was distracted by the ocean."

"You got naked."

"Look at this," Moans said gloriously, holding up a bland shell. I couldn't see what he saw. He spread sand over the mattress and giggled. He lifted another and screamed, "Oh!" as he laughed even louder, dispersing the sand even farther. We didn't mind. It's not like we'd have slept at all that night. I examined what he'd collected. Some were shells; others were pieces of broken vodka bottles, not yet sanded down by time. Moans was lucky he hadn't cut his hand open, although his feet were nicked. I washed off his finds and stored them in our suitcase. I was reminded of when we first started dating, taking long high walks on Black's Beach. I wanted to ask him, *Do you remember? Do you remember, Moans? Do you remember how much I have loved you? I don't remember much, but I remember how we walked through mist so thick I lost sight of you.*

CHAPTER 12

One month into the window, I sat in Matan's office, telling him that the future seemed very dark. The marriage had done something to my mind. I had trouble getting out of bed in the morning, and I would lie there thinking, *If only I could uncross my ankles I could go get iced coffee*, but my legs felt bound, as if I were trapped in my parents' house, Vincent's room, the psych ward. Even Moans acted strange. He kept asking if I was going to be destroyed by therapy after every session, telling me he thought it was making me worse.

"He thinks you're becoming worse?" Matan asked, looking extra pale. I never saw the man with any color. Only the slight growth and graying of the stubble on his crown. He seemed like an early dinner, Lincoln Center type of gay. I could not imagine him in the sun.

"He's not totally wrong," I said. "Sometimes I am completely empty after a session. Sometimes I want some crystal. Sometimes I get so angry I start little fights with Moans, over little things, like him going to bed early."

"There's a curve. When people come to therapy like this, they are engaged with memories they have repressed for quite some time. Awful, violent memories. Usually, when a victim engages with this, they are also losing the defining narrative that held their lives together."

"I'm shedding some old shit."

"Yes."

"I want to shed it faster."

"You're moving at a fast pace. Faster than most."

"I don't have the time."

"We can slow down the pace," Matan suggested. He wasn't bullshitting me.

"For what? To lose time? To spare Moans a few fights?" Sometimes I got the sense that he was afraid of me. Not that I would hurt him, that I would damage myself in the pursuit of whatever it was I truly wanted. "To fucking like do a little dance break?"

"What you—"

"I fully get that thinking about rape nonstop isn't great for the soul, but I can't waste the time. This is only a temporary thing."

"Are you afraid I will drop you as a client?"

"You literally said the CVTC treatment is a short-term thing."

"*Short-term* can mean a few months, a year, a couple of years."

"Exactly. Short-term. I'll get my first check from grad school next week. Then I can go see a lawyer, who, by the way, I don't trust, and then I can see what the fuck my options are, and then when nothing works I can break down in this little office and we can repeat this sick sick sick sick pattern until the year is over and I'm magically healed or just over it."

"What don't you trust about the lawyer?"

"I've never met a lawyer I trusted."

Matan opened his mouth to speak and then he smiled. "The lawyer we hired is a different sort of person. She works on cases for people like you."

"There are words for that."

"Not how I would put it."

"Fine. *Traumatized people.*" I suddenly became inexplicably sleepy. I knew he would notice, so I stated the obvious: "I can barely keep my eyes open."

"What is it? The lawyer?"

"No," I said, fighting to stay awake. "You know, I don't mean this in an offensive way, but I am convinced that I am retarded. I believe the state couldn't even kill me if they wanted to, because the doctors would analyze my brain and literally tell the judge: *Oh, not him.* And I obviously don't mean mentally ill, or PTSD, or disabled, or whatever. I mean, there is no word I have for myself that properly addresses what it feels like to be in my head."

I could tell he didn't want to say the word, but Matan said, "What would it mean if you were?"

"I don't know."

"I believe you do."

"I'm so tired," I said.

"Do you need a moment to reset?"

"No." My eyes were heavy, my body a sinking fact. Looking at Matan felt like watching an old video. The scene wasn't clear. I couldn't hear correctly either. He sounded far away. "I'm so scared, sometimes, that none of this is fixable. Meaning, it's done. This is all a waste of ruined brain matter."

"What if I told you that this was normal? I was saying there's a curve. You will feel so much worse before you feel better. You might feel worse than you have ever felt as an adult. Dylan, you are an adult. I am an expert. What happened in the years between when you were trafficked and now should prove that you aren't gone. You are traumatized. That's all."

"I'm awake now."

"Should we ground ourselves even more?"

"Are you falling asleep too?"

"You do seem awake."

"I am," I said, and the time ended. I took a deep breath in the chair and laughed.

"What?"

"There's nothing better than the end of a session. You run trains on my heart these days."

"What does that mean?"

"Nothing." I checked my phone. There were fifteen texts from Moans. I showed Matan. "See."

"What does he want?"

"Attention," I said, and told him I'd see him next week. I stood to leave, and I looked back at Matan, who said I could sit for a few more minutes. "I want to take care of myself. I just wish Moans could accept that. He takes me rejecting his help as a rejection of him, which I was going to say wasn't true, but is kind of true. But maybe I have to reject him now. I wish he could give up his role of caretaker and let me have some control."

"Do you think if you asked him he would do it?"

I laughed.

"Probably not," Matan said.

"He thinks I'm ignoring him, cruel, indifferent, but I think the exact same of him. He's afraid of losing me, and I'm afraid that if I don't lose him I might never get to be myself."

"Wow."

"But maybe I don't know what I want yet."

I left the session, and I was wide awake outside. There were police officers with machine guns who I didn't want to shoot me. Tourists on Wall Street who I gently pushed out of the way. There was a whole world, and I lived in it, and it felt pretty cool. I had a brief vision of running into Vincent on the street. I thought, *I will beat the fuck out of you. I will be so fucking free.* I knew that's what I wanted most. Moans was only one more person starting to get in my way—into my path of what I sometimes thought was justice, but what I really hoped was revenge.

CHAPTER 13

Matan tried to help me see what I wanted. Every few sessions he would ask a leading question—*What would your younger self say to Moans? (Fuck me!); Did the men leave after they finished? (If I was lucky.); Do you know you can leave the session if you want? You aren't trapped here. (What?); Do you know where you are in time? (Sometimes.)*—and I could easily imagine the end of my relationship. He wanted me to establish a narrative, ordering the events of my life in such a manner that they would be stored properly in my brain. As they were currently stored, the memories permitted my reactive mind to take over, like a hitchhiker picked up on the side of the road, and a simple trigger would take me from lying beside Moans to being with Vincent. Some days I was wary of Matan. Other sessions, he said a word like *green* that sent me traveling back thirteen years and only through the sound of his voice could I return. Anybody who wanted to be a time traveler needed mental help.

I had once asked my sister if she ever remembered seeing Vincent, which she did, of course. Vincent sometimes came around my house, introducing himself under a fake name, pretending to be in my grade, and I went along with it. He always smelled like cigarettes, Devin said, as I smoked joints and blew smoke at the stars. My thoughts returned to Vincent endlessly. I would cook breakfast and remember how he would cook Hamburger Helper. I would shave my face and think of how he would run cold blades over my skin to remove the hair. Sometimes when I got too high I would experience the same blur—a high that makes the present feel immediately inaccessible, a memory before it ever felt like an experience. My mom would light candles and I could see the flames of his Zippo. At night, I would go on Craigslist and see Vincent creating ads for me, using pictures with my face cropped out, just the body of a boy, and the responses Vincent received went straight to his email, where he would set up a time for them to come over. They always asked if I was eighteen, and he always said no. That's what sold them.

Matan needed me to know when certain events happened. He needed me to know they weren't happening now, even if they sometimes felt like they were. I knew Moans wasn't Vincent. I understood that. Some nights I could see a connection between them, a through line of men who liked me under their control, even if the effects of both were different. In theory, I knew all of this. I lived in the now. In the now-now, full of nowness: sweat and hunger and desire, the lump of my wallet, random insignificant objects that populated the city, like the dumbass statue of the bull outside the Center. If I tried, I could see this with Moans. He was not my captor. Our apartment was no prison. Nor was our relationship. I could leave if I wanted to, as Matan annoyingly repeated. It would be different once the check was deposited in my account, and I wouldn't have to wonder how I would eat. My family would think I was losing my mind. But I would have room for error, and I needed that. I was failing. Failing toward my goal of freedom or justice or revenge, whatever it would end up being, and that was the only way forward. I was beginning to understand that there was a difference between being a person and becoming who you were. I was learning what some people called *worth*. It was very simple. I had paralyzed myself, confused myself, stunted myself inexplicably, like when you question the automation of your own lungs.

In the next session, I told Matan about the first police investigation—when I had gone to the police, not long after Moans and I returned from San Diego.

One night, when my parents were asleep and Moans was in New York at our first apartment in Harlem, I snuck out to get fucked by this couple who tied up my arms and legs—one took my ass, the other rode me—and the whole time, even though I wanted to be there, even though they were kind to me, I could only feel Vincent tying up my arms with the black rope he kept in his closet. Vincent was still with me.

The next day I knew what I had to do.

I went into my father's office, which once had been my childhood bedroom. The bed was still there. The rest had changed. He was sitting at a desk, wearing a headset. I waited to make sure he wasn't on the phone, and I told him, as if I were hungry: I need to call the police. He turned off his monitor and slowly swiveled around. My sister was sleeping in the adjacent room, and I closed the door behind me to sit on my old twin bed. My father told me to do what I needed, and he asked why, although I think he suspected it was related to Vincent. I had told him that Vincent had raped me. I had blamed them. Why had they let me spend so many weekends away as a teenager? Had the bruises not worried them?

My father asked if I wanted to use the landline. I shook my

head. I held my phone like a mirror and stared until I was ready to dial. I found the number for the non-emergency line, and I pressed the blue link. I was not worried; I wasn't really there; I was somewhere in the future, granting myself resolve I did not yet believe myself to have; I was hoping someday this day might be useful to a person I wasn't yet. When the responder answered, they asked why I was calling.

"I need to report an assault that happened when I was a teenager."

"Did this assault happen to you?"

"Yes," I said, as my dad stared out the window.

"Did the assault happen here?"

"Yes."

"What's your address?"

I gave it to them.

"We will dispatch an officer to take your report," she said. "Will somebody be there to receive them?"

I nodded.

"Hello?"

"I'll be here."

"They will be there soon."

The call ended. We waited a few minutes. My father obviously wanted to speak, but he didn't know what to say. I wanted to relieve him of that duty. I wasn't doing any of this for him. I could tell he had questions that he didn't want answered. So I told him, "I need to do this or I will kill myself."

"Do you want me in the room with you?"

I didn't answer.

"Of course not," my father said. "When he gets here, do you want the kitchen or the living room?" His phone rang. "Or some privacy." The phone kept ringing. "You can have this room."

"Thanks," I said, and we continued to wait. It didn't take very long. The cruiser parked. An officer walked up to the front door. He seemed like he was in costume. White hair, mustache. Like a guy who would pay me to fuck him. As I led him through the front door to my former bedroom, I knew what he looked like naked. I knew the pink belly, the short, fat cock, the sweat that lingers on the sheets after a man like that leaves. Very much like men who had bought me. The officer sat in my father's chair, and he pulled out a slim notebook and a pen, and he asked for some basic information. After I was fully registered as a person who could be found, the officer asked me for the reason he was called:

When I was fourteen, Vincent hit me up online. He liked my pictures, he liked the music I was posting, he left a message asking if I lived near him. He was the first gay guy I ever met, and I was attracted to him. He was nineteen, thin but worked out, with short brown hair and a deep tan. He had high cheekbones and hazel eyes that lived in shadow under his brows. He said he had spent time modeling and was a photographer. Vincent claimed he knew beauty. Vincent lived near my high school in his parents' home, which had been built hundreds of years ago. They were never home. His bedroom locked from the outside. He got me very high. We lay down. He fucked me while I thought I was having a stroke. I couldn't move. I could only seem to track my heart, which wanted out of my chest, beating powerfully against my ribs. After Vincent finished, we got higher, and he told me that he could love me, that he was already feeling like that was the path. I cleaned up the blood in the bathroom and showered away what I believed was the literal proof of love. I didn't mean that in any romantic sense. I had never spoken with other gay people. I heard it could be messy. I was high enough to let the pain drain in the shower, and I told my friends in the morning, after the bus dropped us off at high school, that I had sex, and we all marveled at how grown-up we were, even with the braces cutting our lips. I returned to the house almost every day after school.

I heard my sister wake and speak to my father in the hallway outside the room. My father told her that the police were speaking with me, that I had done nothing wrong. Devin wanted to know more, and when my father wouldn't tell her, she said she hated that she was always the last to know, if she ever found the information out, and she slammed her door. I didn't hear my father walk away. His shadow marked the light under the door. He was listening, and I raised my voice a little, to let him hear if he wanted.

Vincent and I spent so much time together. He would get me high on the porch with blunts, in the bedroom with pills or powders. Sometimes he would sprinkle dust on bowls we smoked. I was down for love and whatever that entailed. I had been a very lonely child, and I had spent my childhood afraid of being found out. Vincent told me that I didn't need to be afraid anymore. He would show me the way, telling me smoky stories of the old men he had fucked, the ways he had gotten drugs, the routes a young gay guy takes to become an adult. I would spend the weekends there, and if my parents wanted to know where I was, I told them with a friend from school. He always had that Zippo and he liked to have me light his cigarettes, seeing his baby fumble with flames. On the weekends, if his family was home, he would lock the door from the outside, and I would silently await his return. I read books on his bed. I slept. I listened to the sounds of his parents in their bedroom downstairs, cooking or cleaning or listening to loud music, which, at least, meant that I could move a little.

After he set his house on fire the first time (once he said it was a candle, a cigarette's ember, a friend who had been partying carelessly with him), his parents had paid men in black to abduct him at midnight and ship him out to a wilderness program, where he learned the ways of the world. The only way to survive was to keep what you loved secret. Otherwise, you might soon be handcuffed in the dark. Pain is temporary. It is the harness that straps you to your future. Sometimes, I thought he was the dumbest guy in New York State, but sometimes what Vincent said seemed truer than anything I had ever heard. Everything gets taken from you, Vincent used to say, and I believed that to be true. That's why he loved photography. You could keep whatever you wanted. I was telling the officer about the concealer Vincent used to buy from the store to cover up bruises when I reached the end of my ability to speak. I leaned over my knees and held my head in my hands. My mind stopped me from continuing. The closest I could get to the truth was that Vincent liked to get me high and rape me, and then the now-familiar exhaustion overtook my whole body. I wasn't ready to speak about the rest. I could barely think about it without my mind turning off.

The officer told me that he knew about the fires. There was a news story about them online, the officer told me. They had questioned Vincent back then, too. Especially when the fire happened again. They knew, but this was back when the officer was fully on the force, before Vincent had ever met me. The kid even went to jail, he said, which I already knew. For beating up a fag, my words, not his. He told me he would set up a time for me to speak with a detective, and then, with an absolute lack of awareness, with a precisely chewed-up unoriginality, he said, "Let's get the bastard," before leaving. My father told me I had done the right thing, that I did a good job, and for the rest of the day he swung a golf club outside. He hit nothing. A wind carried grass right into the air.

A week later, I received a call from Detective Threader, who invited me to the police station for an interview. The building resembled a bank. Inside there was a bulletproof glass window with an officer behind it and a few chairs. I told the woman who I was there to meet and then sweat through my clothes until the detective walked through the automatic doors. Detective Threader looked like a man who would save you. He was muscular in a blue suit, with his sleeves rolled up, showing a tattoo that I would laugh at if a friend got, but on him it made sense. He did not feel like anybody who had harmed me, so at least I was only afraid of the situation, not the man himself.

"This is important," Matan interrupted.

"Which part?"

"All of it."

"Okay."

"Do you feel afraid right now?"

"No," I said, but when Matan shifted in his seat I recoiled. I knew he saw it. "I would rather be literally naked than feel like you see everything."

"You will never be naked here."

"I know."

"I think what you want is to be seen."

"It's hard not to roll my eyes."

"Because you agree?"

"I don't know if I agree."

"Let's try something," Matan said. "I'm going to stand up and move my chair and face a different direction. I'm telling you this so you're not alarmed when I get up."

"Okay."

"I'm moving the chair back now, and I'm facing the window." Matan rearranged the chair slightly, so that his chest was angled a little away from my chest. We were no longer parallel. "How does this feel?"

"Like you're talking to an idiot."

"I'm not playing a game," Matan said. "How do you feel? Do you want to find the birds?"

"No." I did what he said. My shoulders had lifted and now they were sinking down. An alertness I had not realized faded away. Matan was moving in the chair, changing his posture slightly, but I did not brace myself at all. "I feel calmer. What happened?"

"You think I'm a threat," Matan said, which I wanted to fight but I sometimes did feel that way. A man this close to you in a room was bad news. He didn't look like anybody who had harmed me. I knew the door was closed, though. I knew what happened. To me. To others. I knew what I had been through, and if I was being honest—if I had to be honest with myself, something I needed with the short amount of time we had—I lived most of my life in fear. "Do you think I am a threat?"

"No, but I feel it."

"What does it feel like?"

"I'm waiting for you to attack me."

"Do you think I'm going to attack you?"

"No."

"Why don't you tell yourself that."

"I hate stuff like this."

"You might think it's silly . . ."

"It works," I said. "I can feel it work."

"Do you want to continue?"

"And stop now? When I've come this far?"

I continued: At the police station, Detective Threader brought me into a room where he hung his suit jacket over a rolling chair. I told him everything I told the officer, except this time I started crying. I wasn't gone. I told Detective Threader that I had done so much in the name of escape. I had overdosed on all types of drugs and slashed my arms open when blacked out. I had cheated on boyfriends and hated myself. I had kept the secret so tight that I felt locked inside myself. My body was a locked room I could never escape. I was so angry and shocked and felt so alone some days that I . . .

Detective Threader asked if I wanted a glass of water. He left the room and came back with a plastic cup that I knew I couldn't hold without spilling. I tried for a second before the water spilled and set it on the table. He closed the door again and said my name before he paused to take a deep breath and lean over the table. I had no idea what he was going to say.

"Dylan," Detective Threader said again, "we are going to find him. We are going to put him in jail. This is a very sick person. What happened to you should not have happened to you, but it happens more than you think. I see stuff some days that no longer bothers me. I have days where my eyes feel open. Days when they are closed. When stuff happens to kids, it is harder for them to feel shut. Do you know what I am saying?"

"I don't think so."

"We are going to sit at my desk, and I am going to type up this report, and I want you to figure out what evidence you have."

"I have some emails from him."

"What is in them?"

"Him telling me how he wants to fuck me, how he's gonna

marry me." I felt my spine go cold, my arms go numb, a rush of paralysis to my lips. "He sent me some pictures. I'm not naked. Just shirtless. But they put me in his room."

"That's good," the detective said, and he walked me to his desk, where he typed up a report using only two fingers. Each word took forever, as he pressed index finger and index finger into the keyboard. What should have taken just the time of the interview and a quick report took almost four hours. We chatted about his vacations and my future and Palm Springs. We had enough in common to actually talk. The whole event was painful. Every detective in that building saw me crying as they made phone calls or poured coffee or grabbed terrifying forms from boxes behind my head. This was a hellish place, and I was small-talking my way through a man who was going to help me as he typed like an absolute fucking dumbass. When I'd signed the report and forwarded him the emails, Detective Threader told me they would investigate what they could and forward the evidence to the DA, who would start the case. Except a few weeks later, I got a call from a restricted number: the voice announced himself as Detective Threader in the world's most terrifyingly fuckable voice. I answered and he told me that he had bad news. There was a case. They had proof. Vincent no longer lived in New York, but that didn't matter. But like I said, the statute of limitations expired five years after a child victim turns eighteen. I was twenty-three, and I had turned it only a few months prior. He said he was sorry, and I believed him. Life continued, like everything had happened but had not mattered. The years I had escaped were the years that mattered, even though I never would have been able to say a word of it.

"It sounds like you were very alone," Matan said.

"That's when I adopted Empedocles, who became known as

the rape dog. Another phrase that sounds bad but makes sense if you know. If you know, you know," I said, through a growing smile, and laughed in a way that stunned Matan, who let out a single laugh.

"Did Moans know?"

"I called him crying from my backyard smoke spot and told him, but only what Detective Threader knew, too. Nothing more. I wasn't ready." I closed my eyes and leaned back against the arm-chair. "Moans said he always suspected something because I had once referred to an older ex-boyfriend I had when I was fourteen who used to do fucked-up shit to me, and he was like . . . 'That's not a boyfriend.'"

"No, it is certainly not. And your parents?"

"The detective asked that, too. I don't know. I wasn't home. When my father told my mother, she was kind of upset, and they said they had no idea. Which I don't totally believe. I had all these bruises. Hickeys! Like, I came home hiiiiiigh some days."

"Did you ever think of telling them back then?"

"Not really." I glared at Matan like he was stupid. "We had no real relationship. My dad and I used to fight. My mom was . . . not maternal. I was a guest at that house growing up. I was never home. They said that when I was gone, they were just happy I had friends, which I don't totally understand. But they stick by it. That they had no idea."

"You had no supervision."

"None." I shrugged. "And what people don't understand is that when you're adopted, whatever freaky connection biological families have . . . adopted families don't. Like I love them, but there's no weird psychic shit. That sixth sense people talk about? Like, oh, I know what's going on with my daughter because that's my blood? None of that. I was a mystery in the small bedroom that they hoped would one day reveal himself to be their son."

"We are almost out of time. I have one last question."

"Sometimes it feels like I'm not talking about myself. Like I'm talking about someone else. So go for it. Ask Old Dylan a question and I'll relay the message."

"What does it feel like to work through this with me? That you're not alone? Can we sit with that for a minute?"

"Yes," I said, and we literally sat there for a literal minute that felt much longer. I almost felt like Matan wanted to help me stand. Matan didn't offer to help. He knew if he touched me that I would never return. What I mean is I believed he wanted me to heal, and he thought he knew the way. I wished Moans felt the same way. We had so many years of ease between the horrors, like the years after the first investigation. We had moved to Harlem, and I went to college in Union Square. Moans started making money that nobody in his family had ever touched. Even the betrayals I forgave as they came (at least, that's what I thought), like when I had this amazing month of happiness that turned out to be him microdosing me with shrooms. This was back before I ever realized I had C-PTSD, and he had learned online that it was a treatment. It was how I grew to later love shrooms, and even though we yelled, I was able to forgive him. I felt like a normal person. I believed the end of the investigation meant the end of that period of my life. I worked at a pizza place near The Strand. I would go to Nowhere Bar after class with friends and meet Moans on his lunch breaks. We told people we were happy!

Now, I know that period was an outlier. I hadn't gotten justice, but at least telling people a version of what happened calmed me. Moans and I vacationed in Woodstock, where we fucked under curled fly tape, and Myrtle Beach, where we fucked only in the hotel room because every other person seemed like they hated us, and Fort Lauderdale, where we fucked all over the naked resort. I graduated from college and Moans dreamed of the day when I would finally earn enough money to help support our future. We even visited San Diego, where we dined at the restaurant where we'd met with some of my old friends still working there. During the holidays, Moans would grill with my father like a family. We became regulars at restaurants and hated everywhere that wasn't New York. Even San Diego we talked about as if we would only move back when we were old and decrepit. Moans got a promotion. He had enough money that we had stuff to waste.

His mom called once to say, *You really got a life over there, don't you?*

Those three years were unexceptional, which made them feel great. We had both come from worlds most people never touched, and to be normal through a few years was a nice relief. We even felt like we belonged there, in that wonderful place that was never meant for us, which was what made the Child Victims Act feel so shocking. To him, at least. Looking back, I can't say it was hard to ruin my life at the chance to tell my whole story. We had so many great years. And yet here we were. I focused on the cobblestone streets outside the Center. I wanted strangers to know a person like me. I wished I could say to Moans: *Please, forgive me. You have to know I was hoping to be saved.*

I LOVE
NEW YORK

CHAPTER 14

I woke early to meet with the lawyer at the Center. A month and a half had passed since the start of the window. It doesn't sound bad until you realize that you don't get it back. I needed to be the type of person you wanted to help, and I didn't know what that type of person looked like. I certainly didn't think that person looked like me. I tried on all I had and left a mess. Pants covered the couch. In my hands, there was a newspaper-gray and a teal sweatshirt, which I was holding up to the morning light. The teal was more fuckable, but the equations for fuckability to access in terms of the law wasn't available. In general, if you were fuckable you got what you wanted.

Moans walked up the stairs with the dogs at his feet.

"Teal or gray?"

"That's turquoise."

"For the lawyer," I said, raising the teal.

"The gray." Moans pressed the coffee machine and waited with his hand around the mug. "The teal is too much."

"I don't think I'm a gray person, though."

"It's not a bar."

"It kind of is, though," I said, as Empedocles stretched by the door.

"That has nothing to do with how you're dressed. Dress professionally, that's all."

"You know that's not true."

"Could you bring the laundry before you go?"

"I can't be late."

"Or take the dogs out quickly."

"I'm not doing this right now," I said, as he sipped his coffee on the couch. The dogs were ready to go outside, but Moans wasn't working for hours. He never got up this early. If I hadn't had somewhere to go, he would have stayed in bed. "I'll clean this up when I'm back."

I didn't see him take the dogs out as I walked to the train, and I knew he wouldn't for hours.

The subway dulled my mind. As it rattled from stop to stop, strangers played musical chairs. It was possible to love the city for this reason: the million distractions that made me forget, if only for a few seconds, what I was trying to do. The faster people moved, the less they had to think. It's impossible to carry a single thought across subway stops. I held the silver pole and rode the aisle, staring at the end of the car, waiting to be sized up by the lawyer who was allegedly my ally. If everything collapsed, at least I could throw myself on the train tracks. This wasn't suicidal. At some point in New York, everyone imagines jumping on the tracks—or, worse, imagines lifting a fallen stranger from the pit as a honking, potential dismemberment squeals into the station. Dreaming of heroism must be the least honorable fantasy.

At Union Square, everyone stood and struggled to exit the train. Any second wasted could have a fucked-up impact on our day. But the transfer wasn't there anyway, so we stared into an empty tunnel until two bright lights came at us like the eyes of God. I don't believe in heaven, but that's what people say appears in front of you when you arrive at the great unlivable afters: a church, a cross, white lights. What I tell people I believe is that every person you know you have known before in a different incarnation. In your last life your father was the love of your life. Your sister was the town doctor who amputated your rotting leg. Your mother was your prison guard or a stranger on the train. You didn't pay close enough attention to notice her, to catch her staring at her phone as she tried to do her makeup. That one frame is all that would hold you together for a lifetime. And now it's gone. Each incarnation barely resembled the last, but all the spirits of the people remained the same. I was pretty sure then that I was hot in all my past lives. But nobody cares for that part of the theory. People are mostly horrified by this cycle of time, but I want to know if people can change, if my adopted father could ever become an artist, what my mother would be like if she ever had a biological child, what Vincent would do in any other version of life.

At the Center, the office manager was haphazardly balanced on a ladder, adjusting a huge painting of a plant being watered. The waiting room had a horseshoe couch with a coffee table and a bench across from the door, which was always where I sat with my back against the wall. This way I could see the whole office. Nobody could sneak up on me, and if I wanted I could walk right out. Another man rang the buzzer, entered, and sat on the couch, allowing me to view his spiraling baldness instead of greeting the terror of recognition in his eyes. I wondered if he needed to invoke God to get here. He possibly walked here on his lunch break. He knew I was staring at him, because I knew when I walked down the hallway he would stare at me, making sure I wasn't a threat.

The receptionist lifted her phone.

A minute later a woman in a dusky violet hijab and black pantsuit leaned her head out of her office and waved me over. The legal counselor, Natalia, told me to sit in a rolling chair in her unfinished office. I wanted to snoop through the yellow pads in the boxes, familiarize myself with the local atrocities of the waiting room population. While I was dreaming of going through her email, she introduced herself as an immigration lawyer who had been recently hired to oversee the Center's legal program. She would not be my lawyer but would help guide me through the process.

"Like a doula," I said.

"No," she stated.

Natalia didn't know much about the Child Victims Act, except that she knew firms were hungry for clients. A gold rush, she called it. I shouldn't have trouble finding a firm. All these cases were a test for the country at-large. Activists were following, hoping to enact similar laws in their own states. In only six weeks, thousands of cases had been filed. New York wanted as many wins as possible, to show the country what was possible. No pressure.

Her hands distracted me. She moved them as if conducting an orchestra. Gentle movements rehearsed into her unconsciousness. Natalia hadn't given this speech before, but it was clear she spoke to idiots like me, people who were swayed by hand movements along with words, kind of like a living picture book. Easily I could imagine her before a jury. Some people could hypnotize you. This was different from how actors (the least fuckable genre of artist) tried to convince you of anything because it was actually effective. An actor thinks leaning into you all big-eyed with emphasis con- jured belief. Of course, that's lunacy. That's how people in the ward spoke to doctors. I was barely listening. Truthfully, I was afraid. She must have noticed because she said: "The legal system is hard."

"Oh. Okay."

"Do you have any questions?"

"All I have are questions."

"Let's check them off."

"How do I get a lawyer?"

"You want a personal injury lawyer who specializes in sexual assault."

"How do I find one?"

"They're everywhere. The ones on benches and billboards. Search 'personal injury lawyer child victims act.' When did the assault take place?"

"What?"

"What year?"

"Years."

"How old were you?"

"Fourteen."

"And how did you meet?"

"Online." I was swiveling in the chair. "He sent me a message, and I responded, and then I went over to his place and he got me high, and that's how it started."

"You reported this to the police?"

"After the statute of limitation expired."

"What did you report?"

"Some of what happened."

"You have to guide them." Natalia shook her head. "They can barely interpret the law."

"I feel like me and you aren't speaking the same language."

"The lawyers will help you."

I didn't believe that, but Natalia referred me to the National Crime Victim Bar Association. They would refer me to three lawyers at a reduced fee.

"You need to be ready," Natalia said. "They will ask for the facts over and over again. It might help to write down the details."

I lifted my hand from her desk, leaving a sweaty imprint. I tried not to draw attention to evidence of my fear. Not too much embarrassed me anymore. Once you are kicked out of the airport by the Feds, or locked in the psych ward for weeks, or even just having gay sex for a decade, you become less afraid of public embarrassment, but I would rather have shit myself on the steps of my new grad school than let these people see that what happened back then still had an effect on me. I needed to go.

Natalia stood up and reached for a handshake, which I did, and then she peered down at her own hand, mortified that she had broken a rule. I could see the signs they had taped in the back rooms: *No touching the rape victims! Victims may bug out!* Natalia glanced down at her hand again before meeting my eyes, and then I was the one who went rigid. She evaluated me as if she knew every secret I contained. That's why I didn't tell people.

"Don't worry," I said, walking out the door.

"Wait," Natalia said, her hands behind her back. "When I had a case. Not about this, but still a personal case. I had to search for many lawyers before I found one. I didn't stop, even when firms said no. You will have an easier time than I did, but you might need a touch of perseverance. You still have ten more months."

"Four," I corrected. "I'm doing this without my husband knowing everything, which means I can only touch my grad school stipend."

"When do you get it?"

"This week," I said. "And I don't get paid over break, and I don't know what will happen if I take a break. I'm forcing myself to do it now. If I take a break, I will stop. I can't rubberneck twice."

"Then you need a lawyer by mid-December. Call the place I sent to you as soon as you leave."

"Thank you," I said, walking through the lobby. The receptionist told me to have a good day, which she must have said every time I left Matan, but I hadn't been able to put in my headphones. I grabbed a Jolly Rancher from her desk and cracked the candy between my teeth on the elevator ride down. I promised myself I would make the call as soon as I got outside. I would tell the next lawyer everything. The truth would run out of me, even if I had to dash through Wall Street, screaming phrases so perverted—*child porn, sex trafficking, forced drugging*—that people would have to notice. *That's what happened to me*, I wished to say, as I stared a security guard in the eyes on the way out.

CHAPTER 15

On Exchange Place, a flower delivery truck approached the rising metal barricades as I spent a moment gathering myself. The whole city blocked me. A tourist took a picture of his son in front of Federal Hall, posing beside a bronze statue of a hideous man. Almost nothing in America disfigured a person more than a monument. Every time I stopped moving I grabbed my phone and vividly recalled Russ' face when I visited him with James only a couple months ago. I wanted to bleed him out over his flowers. I didn't want his money. I really didn't want to have him sign over any amount of money in my name and call what he did *in the past*. His face was a monument to my own torture, and I wanted to rip it down. I didn't want peace. Nobody cared when boys were raped. My heart beat fast. I was angry at this world, pissed at my love for it. Why should I love something that did not love me back?

I walked south and turned onto a strange narrow street jammed with rustic pubs to sit at a table at Ulysses. I called the number for the National Crime Victim Bar Association, the one Natalia had given me, as the waiters set up for the day. After a few rings, a soft-voiced woman picked up the phone. She wanted to know who referred me, and I told her the Crime

Victims Treatment Center. The words made it seem like I lived in New Victim City, in New Victim, in the United Victims of America. I knew I was lucky that New York had these programs, but you could only say *victim* so many times before you soured on the word. I preferred the word to *survivor*, though, which I always thought was for losers. I didn't need the designer word for a simple act. I wasn't trying to stunt.

Some people mistakenly believe language has lost its power. That the Word has been bastardized, but they're wrong. Language has reached its peak. We now live in an age where people claim words designed by people who want them to suffer. People have been stripped naked and tortured by this life and given the badge *survivor* by the very people who raped them. This is not the age of degradation, but the age of language surpassing sound and becoming a product. I see people joyously sing their oppressor's songs. They plant the words across their chests while they get burned alive.

The woman asked for the same information as Natalia. I told her everything I told Natalia and more. I said, "My name is Dylan and between the ages of fourteen and seventeen I was drugged, raped, and pimped out by a man named Vincent, who was a pedophile that made child pornography of me." The woman said, "Okay," and proceeded to email me the names of three lawyers I could reach out to for a meeting. The lawyers, who normally charged more than I could ever afford, would only charge thirty-six dollars. As we were wrapping up, a waiter told me that I needed to leave. People would be coming to eat soon. I didn't know if he heard the conversation, if he had waited until I was almost done to ask me to leave, if he was one of the men who had been unlucky too.

CHAPTER 16

I didn't want to go home, so I wandered up Broadway until I found a courtyard bench at the Church of the Ascension. In college, when I worked in Union Square, I used to get red-eyed under the cherry blossoms, stupid and high. You could even meet a man here if you waited long enough. Over time, the church's courtyard became my way station. I'd been hanging around its black iron gates since I was a teenager sneaking into Webster Hall, and now that grad school was starting a block away, I'd be around it for another couple of years at least. I believed, without evidence, that the priest who had baptized me in the Catholic hospital where I was abandoned as an infant in Texas had moved through this very church. I liked to think we crossed paths again. Two strangers moving through eternity.

I texted James a picture of the black door, which was engraved with a saying I never understood: THE WATCHMAN STAYS AWAKE IN VAIN. James called me immediately to explain the quote, but I wasn't listening, and James didn't care. James believed he could understand anything and everything; I knew I could barely understand my own life. He liked to talk, and I liked to hear his voice when I felt alone.

"Why are you at the church?" James asked.

"Honestly . . ."

"You're cruising."

"No."

"Cruising for some midafternoon cock in a holy location."

"I spoke to a lawyer today," I told him. "About the act. I'm waiting to get referred."

"Did you tell your husband?"

"He's blowing up my phone with texts, but I seriously don't want to think about whatever bullshit he's saying."

"Look now because he's blowing me up too."

"Beautiful," I said, and read the texts to James:

I did the laundry

What time do you think you're going to be done?

I could meet you for a late lunch

Or an early dinner

Why do the dryers take so long to dry things if they are so huge

Vita might want to come over later

Or I could meet her in the Village

How did the meeting go

?

Do you think I don't know what it's like to be like this?

What did you do with James that night?

Why won't you tell me?

Dylan?

You can't ignore me. What were you doing?

Your behavior recently has been unacceptable. You won't respond to my texts and that's really not asking much. We got married not that long ago and suddenly you are acting like we are not together. It is not too much to ask of you to loop me into your activities.

If I got the chance to get back at my father, I wouldn't act like this.

"True love," James said.

"True something. I haven't talked to a fucking lawyer yet. You need to talk to twenty people before a lawyer will read your name on a piece of paper. Too much foreplay and it's killing me."

"You know you don't have to do this all in a day."

"The lawyer said shit like that, too. But if I don't do it now, I won't ever do it."

"Make a list. Complete a task every few days. Call me and tell me about it. I can help you through it."

"I've never made a list in my life."

"You're going to burn out."

"That's my only option. You remember what happened the last time I let time run out? Absolutely nothing. I was shuffled around by my unconscious, like some demented old person in a nursing home. You know how dirty that thing did me?"

"You will always be moved by your unconscious."

"The number of times I have to threaten you about Freud."

"It's sad that that's the only psychoanalyst you can name."

"Sorry that not all of us are getting a PhD so we can apply some literal pervert's theories to *Charlie's Angels* to prove that people want to fuck their fathers."

"Everyone wants to fuck their father."

"Some of us want to fuck other people's fathers."

"What a blessed life," James said. "I'm coming down and staying with you in a few days to give a lecture. Your husband informed me that I could stay, and I in turn informed your husband that he should come, but maybe I should take it back."

"Cool," I said, refreshing my in-box.

"Cool?"

"I got to go. They emailed."

I hung up and saw the subject line, drawing circles in the leaves while the email loaded. The groundskeeper approached with a broom, sweeping the leaves into pink snowy mounds. I made sure he wasn't staring. He kept his eyes to the ground. I returned to the phone.

Dear Caller,

My name is Ian; I am an attorney referral specialist with the National Crime Victim Bar Association. I am very sorry to hear about what happened to you; and thank you for providing information about your case. Below is a list of attorney referrals. Please call or email them at your earliest convenience.

- *Gaildon & Pritchard - The Gaildon & Pritchard Law Firm PLLC - New York, NY*
- *August F. Quigley Law PLLC - New York, NY*
- *Nicholas & Baptiste PLLC - New York, NY*

If you would like to complete a survey to help us improve the Attorney Referral Service, you may complete our survey here.

Best,
Ian

I called Gaildon & Pritchard immediately. When the receptionist picked up, I told her how I had been referred, and she transferred me to a junior associate, a woman with a deep voice. She sounded like one of the bartenders at Cubbyhole—the one always in a tank top who bellows at people trying to give her credit cards. I hadn't seen her in a couple years. It was possible she was a lawyer now. This was New York. One day your bartender was another person you fucked at midnight after too much coke, and the next they were speaking to the Supreme Court in skinny pants with a Connecticut accent.

"First off, I'm sorry that this happened to you. Is it okay if I get the details of the case?"

"Yes," I said. "Yes."

"Was it the Boy Scouts or the Catholic Church?"

"What do you mean?"

"The abuse. Was it perpetrated by the Boy Scouts or the Catholic Church?"

"Neither."

"Oh."

"It was by a regular person."

"Can I place you on a brief hold?" She put me on hold, briefly, before returning. "Was their insurance involved in the abuse? Did it happen on public or private school grounds? Anyplace that may have an insurance policy?"

"Private homes," I said, letting her down. "Sometimes at the home of a guy who pimped me out. Sometimes the other men's houses. I bet they had insurance."

"The alleged perpetrator—are they well-known?"

"I'm sorry. He was some random guy."

"Does the family have money?"

"They're rich," I said.

The woman placed me on hold again, and I knew what she was going to say when she came back. I left the little garden and watched the groundskeeper clean the flowers I had occupied with my nervous feet. I gripped the iron bars, staring as he swept. The hold extended. I doubted she would return.

"Sir?" the lawyer said. "I'm sorry to tell you we are mostly taking class action cases."

"Thanks. Can I ask you a question before you go? What do I do? He wasn't a pastor. He worked for nobody. He *was* nobody."

"Smaller firms may take on smaller cases. Which is not to diminish your suffering. Only to acknowledge the fact that larger firms take on larger cases. May I ask you a few more questions?"

"Please."

"How long ago did this occur?"

"Thirteen years. You know, I had this conversation already today. It happened a long time ago. I am young, and this case is old. I get it. Who knows where the evidence is? I only know that I can see the past. I can see where all of this shit happened. That lasts, okay? Do you know what it's like to lie down on a bed while a man waxes all the hair off your body so that you can be raped like an even younger boy? Do you know that what will make you scream will also force you to be silent because you cannot let out a sign of pain? Your lungs will feel like that spinning thing in a tornado. Like the motherfucking rooster on the top of a church? Do you know what's it's like to have porn taken of you after that? That there is a price attached to that? I'm just asking, if you were in those pictures, what would you do?"

"I would gather as much evidence as I had of the child pornography since the court can offer financial restitution for each picture. And I would pursue total financial devastation. Even if the settlement came down to pennies, I would fight for pennies. I would take whatever I could that was not mine from a person who had stolen from me."

"What if I don't want money?"

"Then you should call another firm. I am very sorry for what happened to you."

The call ended while I still grasped the iron with cold hands. The groundskeeper took a break to smoke a cigarette among the flowery dunes. The man had a look about him that I knew from the psych ward—a missingness, the ability to disappear. I asked him why he made the little piles against the grass. Why not sweep directly into the street? The man told me to come over, and I entered the garden, where I crouched beside him as he got on his elbows and knees. The groundskeeper pointed at the insects that had sought refuge in the flowers that now crossed the bricks into the grass.

"Watch this," the groundskeeper said, as he pulled a long drag of the cigarette. He brought his lips to the petals, like a hummingbird to a flower, that close, and he exhaled the smoke into the mound. From the petals moths emerged, as if born from smoke, to fly up into the branches. "They rest here, too."

"How did you learn that?"

"Nobody talks much here. I spend my time with plants. This is my world." He blew out another hit and more took flight. They rose broken and manic, poisoned by smoke, into the haven of leaves that had yet to fall.

CHAPTER 17

Outside the offices for Quigley Law, I texted Moans an update: *Met with a lawyer. No help. But they sent me to another bitch. Be home later.* The offices were on the second floor of a glass building in the Flatiron District across from a tiny triangular park full of people eating lunch alone. Nothing seemed real if I looked too long. These businesspeople, lawyers, and whatevers in their indistinguishable suits seemed like extras. Not film extras—life extras. People who knew they were alive but whose generality made me doubt their liveliness. I waited for the birth of a moment when their humanity would clearly appear. For a fist to swing over a bench. A kiss or two. To see a man answer a call and hear news of a tragedy that would alert the whole park to the crushing of his heart. I saw nothing, of course, except my own wanting. Like I've said before, sometimes I doubted I was alive, and now I was renting a belief in my own humanity, mustering a brief importance I needed to defend, in order to walk across the street right into the offices and demand what I deserved.

When the traffic stilled, I crossed over and entered the building. They had a Rothko above the security desk, cast in a green light from the tinted windows. I took the elevator to an office where I sat across from an empty desk with blurred glass walls separating the rooms. A few minutes of other people's conversations passed before a receptionist exited the elevator with an iced coffee, swinging his blue coat over the chair. He sat and scooted up to his desk, slurped the straw at the corner of his lips, and observed me strangely.

"I got a referral from the NYCVBA," I said, waving my phone. "Quigley is listed as the contact."

"It's his lunch hour, but I can see if we got the referral," the guy said, typing as he sipped. He had a red Botox dot on his forehead as if he had just come from the plastic surgeon's office. I was jealous his face hardly moved. His lips were pumped, but not recently. He looked like the type of guy I would have sucked off in Chelsea when I was an undergraduate in a blue-lit bar that felt like an aquarium where the men spoke behind the glassy partition of drunkenness. When you kissed them, you still felt like you hadn't actually touched them. He was handsome, but not my type, unless I was tipsy. "Would you like my name?"

"Sorry?"

"You were staring."

"I was zoning out."

"Alexander," he said, shaking his head. "You are Dylan."

"I should have said."

"Let me review your file quickly and I'll see who might be able to help here."

"You don't need—"

"It's all private," Alexander said, leaning toward the computer. My history glowed on his immovable face, which I felt grateful for. He stood, smiled, and printed a document that he brought to a closed door. He knocked, handed over the paper, and whispered to a man I couldn't see. Alexander waved me over, winked, and introduced me to Mr. Quigley, who was eating salad at his desk.

"You were supposed to call," Mr. Quigley said, forking leaves into his mouth. His tie was slung over his shoulder. If there was a scale of looks that every man fell on from hero to rapist, Mr. Quigley sided with the heroes. He possessed the opposite effect of the heebie-jeebies.

"Sit," he said.

"Thank you."

"You call and pay the fee and we set up a time to meet."

"I didn't know," I lied.

"Is this your first case?"

"I went to the police a few years ago, but it didn't work out."

"The police," Mr. Quigley said, chuckling. He seemed to be having some difficulty eating a chopped salad, grabbing a pile of napkins stained with balsamic to wipe his hands. "You'd fucking think they wouldn't chop it into such infinitesimal pieces." He eyeballed me and said, "Small," before setting down his fork. "You probably know what that meant. Can I blame the food for my annoyance? This is why lawyers don't take lunch meetings. We are good at a single thing, and eating a salad isn't it. When I asked for this, Alexander told me I wouldn't like it, and I told him that I'd find that out for myself." Mr. Quigley lifted the phone and pressed a single button to say, "You were right." I could hear Alexander let out a single barking laugh, and I smiled, too. He continued: "You're getting a rare view. I wish there was a bone or something to stab my tongue. A beautiful corporate settlement for this piece of chopped shit."

"Thank you," I said again.

"I'm doing this as a favor. We are breaking protocol, but because I am attempting to eat we must pretend this isn't a legitimate meeting. I'm interested in the law. Do you know much about it?"

"No. I had a meeting earlier with a lawyer from my therapy

place who tried explaining it to me, but I don't totally get it. I called a place earlier that only wanted people from the church or the Boy Scouts."

"That's an intelligent strategy." Mr. Quigley took a note. "Not everyone is lucky enough to be an Eagle Scout. I was a Scout, but those were different times."

"I don't think they were," I said, and Mr. Quigley cocked his head. "My therapist told me the figure used to be one in six men get assaulted, but now it's one in four. And the guys who report are sometimes talking about stuff from a long time ago."

"I have three brothers and a father," Mr. Quigley said. "One in four?"

"Sometimes I look around a gay bar and feel the ceiling come down."

"What happened? In your own words?"

"When I was—"

"And I have fifteen minutes, at most. I don't mean to rush you. I certainly abhor what you've been through, so please don't take this as disrespect. In fact, I'm showing you respect by breaking the rules. This salad is trash." He swiped the salad into a bin, cleaned his hands, and fixed his tie. "What are the main problems?"

"One guy used to get me high, take child porn of me, and pimp me out over Craigslist. There were probably a dozen men. Maybe a few more. They did whatever they wanted." I remembered what the other lawyer had told me. "This was thirteen years ago, and it lasted three years."

"Do you know what brought its end?"

"I grew up and didn't look as young."

"Could you qualify the damage?"

"There was a lot of blood."

"Long-term," Mr. Quigley said, drawing out the word.

"It's hard to say."

"I have two clocks, and all I check is my phone."

"I have C-PTSD, and I am in therapy at the Crime Victims Treatment Center. I don't like to include the C because some-*how* it both makes it seem worse *and* like I'm exaggerating. Some people talk about their PTSD as if it's a badge of honor, and I roll my fucking eyes. I'm not trying to be the PTSD-est of them all. I ignored it for a really long time. I overdosed at seventeen. I had no home for a little while. Every night I have nightmares. It's gonna end my marriage, too. I want it to end. He can't stomach my suffering and hates that he can't help me and doesn't want to do what will actually end this era. I think he loves me too much to see me in pain, and the pain he does see reminds him of his own, which is just as fucked as mine. Why can't he just let me fucking cry? When the men came over, they would drug me, and I still crave those drugs to this day. Every man I look at either reminds me of those men or they don't. All men are mirrors. Whether they want to be or not. I think about those old men all the time. I walk in a world where people have seen me naked as a child, cracked out and fucked. Raped. He took hundreds of pictures of me. He bragged about it. This is not the world I want to live in."

"Your quality of life has been impacted. The problem is that all we can get is money through a civil case. Normally, the settlement occurs through some kind of insurance. You might never see a dime."

"I get that now."

"Without that, we are pulling pennies from the penniless."

"The family has money."

"Were they away from the crime?"

"I ate dinner with them once at Yom Kippur. I have a few emails included on a chain with his parents."

"What about the illicit pornography?"

"I have none of those. I think if I ever saw one I would straight up kill myself. They were all his, from his camera to his computer. I have a few pictures he sent me, but none like that. Shirtless in his bedroom."

"That helps," Mr. Quigley said. Alexander knocked on the door, informing him of lunch's end. "Listen, kid, what you need to do is call the office and give the details to an associate. I take an interest in these cases. Not for the money. We wouldn't make much off you, but I know we live in a world where without a strict and violent assertion of one's right to restitution we would soon have chaos. Maybe you will never get what you need, but we will hit them where it hurts. People love money. This is all off the record, of course."

"Thank you, Mr. Quigley," I said as I left his office.

Mr. Quigley screamed for Alexander to give me an associate's number, and at his desk Alexander told me that Jackie was a great associate. He finished writing and quizzically stared. "I feel like I know you from somewhere."

"Me?"

"Yes, you, but I can't figure out from where."

"Honestly you looked familiar too."

"Where would I know you from?"

"Nowhere."

"Do you go there a lot?"

"That's not what I meant, but I used to."

"Meet me there in an hour?" He checked his watch. "A half hour."

"I'm not in the mood to dance."

"It's happy hour."

"I'm not really in the mood for that either."

"You look like you need a drink."

"I'll be there," I said. "Alexander."

"Dylan," he said. "Run along."

"Run along," I repeated, laughing at him as I left the office and sat on a bench in the now-quiet park. I called Jackie the associate from a bench that faced the building. Someone picked up the phone, and I thought I saw her answer in the conference room next to Mr. Quigley's office. She took notes while she swiveled on a chair. I gave her the details as I thought I saw her kick off her heels. I answered as best I could. When she asked where Vincent was now, I told her I heard he was working in a wilderness program out West, and she made a disgusted sound. There was no way he wasn't taking advantage of these boys in the dark and empty wilderness. Every time I thought of stopping this journey, I thought of the campfire illuminating his face of awful beauty. I doubted I would ever stop. For years I had been pathless. I couldn't trace a single desire to its source. I was moved only by a fear and rage that I thought had been unsourceable. People thought I was simply wild. They saw a symptom of craziness, not a tangent of history. I was wild. I was on the run. I was trying to survive.

After the end of the conversation, the woman walked into Mr. Quigley's office. To get a better view, I ran across the street. By chance, he moved to the window, not peeking down at me, but regarding the whole park, as if he could see the world for what it was. I received a call from him personally as I stood under him and he declined to take my case, citing reasons I didn't want to hear. He did seem sorry. I was sorry too. You think some people will take you where you need to go. Then, as he was giving me advice, he looked down as I was looking up, and the sight of me felled his shoulders, and Mr. Quigley said, "The truth is I want to take your case, but we are a busy firm with a major caseload. We have our own class action against the church. I don't think we could divert the right resources to give you justice. If you run into trouble at the next firm, would you give me a call? Would you let me see if I can do anything? If it sounds like I am doubling down, it is only because I am ashamed temporarily at my inability to be who I want to be for you. It is only because I am not who I am meant to be."

"Thank you," I said, for the last time, and I walked away to sit on a fire hydrant, where I wished I had asked him to tally what I could have potentially received, but the question sent bolts of future regrets from my brain to my stomach because I knew the number would chase the rest of my days.

CHAPTER 18

While I waited at Nowhere for Alexander, I drank away the realization that he knew more about me than most of the people in my life. Only Matan had access to the whole history. Alexander knew the secrets. He could sketch a story that resembled the truth. I couldn't decide where I wanted to sit with him, where I would be seen for the first time as I had been made, and I switched between the couches by the window, the nook by the DJ booth with a bench and an armchair and a mirror, the two lounges by the pool table, the barstools by the wall, and the bar itself, and I settled in the back room behind the bathrooms that at night turned into a fuck room. Nobody would sit near us at this hour, and we could see down the long hallway of the bar to the door. I had escape in my line of sight—and yet I wanted the door as far away as possible. I wanted to be locked in the room with him. I hoped I could taste the truth on his tongue. I didn't mind that the happy hour lights cast away the shadows of this place. Alexander would see my face as I had been afraid of being seen for so long, and I hoped he would spend the whole day with me, take me home to let me crash my life into his. I knew I didn't want to fuck up this already fucked-up meeting more, so I fingered the two-for-one drink token in my hand until I could no longer slurp the ice and got another vodka soda.

I texted Moans: *Still meeting with lawyers. This is very hard.*

Two people approached the pool table, racked, and broke the pool balls with a crack.

Alexander entered the bar with a breeze of light rain. His hair was slightly wet, losing the gelled composure. He still appeared like a bitch who could captain a sailboat with his rain-dotted pale blue oxford, skinny black pants, and gold-buckled black loafers. Like somebody who knew what Martha's Vineyard looked like, who had a friend with a home in the Pines, not just a share. Alexander came from a world that I have heard of but would never touch—not in my history nor in my future—and whatever happened between us would be an eclipse. I knew that even then, before the rest happened, as he walked up to me at the bar and ordered us two vodka sodas.

"I am two deep," I said.

"Is that a pun or a confession?"

"Huh?"

"Cheers," Alexander said, handing me another. He shuffled the two drink tokens in his free hands, and we returned to where I was seated. "They don't give tokens like this anywhere anymore. Can you think of another place? Outside of Hell's Kitchen."

"Where you live?"

"Is that what you think of me?"

"I don't know what to think."

"That's not what you give. Are you interested in hearing my take on you?"

"From what?"

"Not your file," Alexander said, widening his eyes as he sipped from a tiny red straw. "How you look."

"How I look." I laughed. "Please."

"You act like a private judge of the world. I see the manner in which you look at everything, from me and my peacoat to Mr. Quigley to the way you keep looking at your drink."

"What way?"

"You tell me now what you think of me. Truthfully."

"Obviously I think you're a Chelsea gay."

"What if I told you I was nothing of the sort?"

"I've got a better bullshit meter than you."

"Why is that?"

"You know," I said.

I knew Alexander understood. He silently stirred his drink and started complaining about work as if I worked there too. I was waiting for him to name the reason for these drinks. Most of what he said was lost on me. He was no different from an office manager at a prison or a bank. The law was sleazy. And he was monologuing about nothing important. He tapped his red straw against the glass, sucked it clean, and leaned back against the wall.

"You were a theater kid."

"Am I going on?"

"A little," I said, feeling drunk. We both leaned our heads against the brick wall and stared at the ceiling as if it were the stars. "Why are we here?"

"One more," Alexander said, turning his face toward me. I thought he might lay his head on my shoulder, but he smiled with his lips closed, and then pushed himself up and got us two more. When he sat down again, Alexander took a deep breath and tapped his heels twice. I didn't know I had missed it: the sheen of sadness across his whole being. Really, I had barely been here today. I was thirteen years in the past, I was in the future waiting for Moans to yell at me, down the line at a courthouse waiting for a verdict. I hadn't been paying close attention. He surveyed me over the edge of his drink as he took it to his face. Alexander reminded me of myself.

"Are you going to say something?"

"You kind of remind me of me."

"I was thinking the same."

"So why are we here?"

"I'm sorry we couldn't help you," Alexander said. "A feeling of helplessness while searching for help is not a feeling that passes easily."

"No. It's not. I didn't know what to expect. You read my file."

"Not many people show up like that." He ran his fingers through his hair. "That was a first for me. I'm not making fun of you. I wish I would do the same. I have been considering it, you know? Walking into Mr. Quigley's office and sitting in his chair and telling him the truth."

"The truth?"

"The firm has taken on this class action case against a church. Long ago, in the church of an upstate hamlet, a quaint little village, a priest took advantage of all these little boys. What did he do to them? You can assume. In time, you might learn. One of those boys might tell you his story." Alexander didn't change his posture, yet a change occurred on a level imperceptible to anyone who wasn't right there beside him, as if a slight drop in temperature, a tiny percent of a degree, suddenly plunged the room into an impossible coldness. "I read their papers, as I read yours, and I help organize their files, as I will shred yours, and I read about events that I went through myself. What happened to me happened to countless others. A couple even came to the office. I knew none of them personally and none of them knew me, and yet I felt a frightening kinship."

"Nobody knows?"

"About what the priest did to me? No. It would be too hard."

"Harder than this?"

"Someone brought in all these photographs from the church, and we were reviewing the pictures, and I kept waiting for someone to find me."

"You wanted them to."

"Would they recognize me? As a child? This Chelsea gay? No, of course not. And the office would treat me well. They would get me something. But I could not imagine my life if I were to be found out."

"It's destroying mine," I said, and Alexander lifted his hand, almost as if he were going to place it on my thigh, and I spread my legs a little so our knees touched. "I'm the destroyer of worlds to everyone I know."

"I can't sleep," Alexander said, spreading his legs too. He rested his hand against his thigh—the back of his hand grazing mine. "I used to be blond. Now, of course, I dye it dark. They should have men who have been sexually assaulted run witness protection. I am not anything like the boy I used to be. You get it. I could tell you the bar was on fire and you wouldn't bat an eye."

"I would fucking bust out of here if I started to smell smoke."

Alexander whispered into my ear: "Pee-Tee-Ess-Dee."

"I want another drink," I said, "but I don't want you to stop touching me."

"This wasn't a sex thing," Alexander promised. "You have a husband."

"For now."

"Come with me," he said, offering me his hand to bring me to the bar, where we got another (plus another free one each). We sat on the stools and linked our drinks around each other's arms. "You said you didn't want me to stop touching you."

Stupidly we drank. Like that. Wrapped around each other. The second glass he lifted to my lips, and I did the same to him. Hand in hand we went to the back room, acting like infatuated teenagers, finding new positions to drink as we tangled ourselves together. We had not even kissed. If he was waiting for me, I was also waiting for him. The other patrons gaped at us as we laughed and spat out our drinks accidentally. What would they do had they known what had made us giddy? Alexander watched me as I thought this, and he burst out laughing over my face, and he hugged me, taking me down on the seat so that he was on top of me.

"If we do this, I don't think there's a way back," he said, his head resting by my neck. "I don't think there's a way out."

"Of what?"

"Can you feel it?"

"Yes," I said.

"Do you want to do this?"

"To kiss the truth on the fucking lips?"

"On the lips."

We kissed, sweetly. And that's how we remained. I didn't really feel him up, and he kept a hand under the back of my shirt. Enough passed between us to make us not want to leave. Alexander sat up first. I didn't know what to say. I thought he didn't either.

"Are you going to do it?" Alexander asked.

"The case?"

"I don't want the money. It's the truth."

"I think there's something you should know."

"Okay," I said, as I stood. "Let's get some air."

We walked under the awning as the light rain continued to

fall. I stuck my arm into the mist and waited for Alexander to tell me whatever I needed to know. A green taxi made a U-turn in front of the bar.

"Your file," Alexander said, reaching into his pocket. Whatever he was trying to find wasn't there. "Can I ask you about something?"

"What is it?"

"You didn't inform the police about the pornography," Alexander said. "Why not?"

"I couldn't talk about it."

"Did you omit anything else?"

I nodded. Another man hurried into the bar, shutting his umbrella near my face. Rain sprayed over me. I wiped my face with my hand.

"Have you been to the West Side Club?" I asked.

"The bathhouse?"

"I need to do something destructive."

"We could go get another drink."

"I need to get this out of my system."

"What are we going to do there?"

"Don't act brand-new," I said, grabbing his hand. "Come on."

We ran down Fourteenth, passing Union Square, and walked up to Chelsea. The cars pushed globes of light through the mist. My stomach tightened, and I thought I needed to find a bathroom. Alexander kept up the pace. Every so often, at a street corner, we would kiss each other. He would run his hand over my buzzed head and wipe off the rain. If I turned to him, I could see a light wind blowing open his coat. He would put his arm in front of my chest to prevent me from crossing the street when a car I hadn't seen would cruise in front of me.

On the corner of Twentieth, we stood in front of the old cathedral, The Limelight.

"It's a cycling gym now," Alexander said, as if everyone didn't know.

"Don't tell me you're one of those."

"I don't live far from here."

"Gay people love to pretend they care that some sacred space was lost. Spare me. Would you go if it was still open? Do you know anyone who lives in New York who would go?"

"Of my people?"

"Gays watch the movie *Party Monster* on a couch with a hag in high school and suddenly want to vogue in a nurse costume. It's like riding a buggy in Central Park. Only a tourist would do it, and both smell like shit."

"Maybe you should give a tour of New York."

"And Stonewall? That's like the 9/11 Museum for out-of-town gays."

"I would not advertise that opinion."

"Would you pay thirty dollars for a vodka soda made by a Jersey City gay in rainbow socks?"

"I have done my time there."

"Never again," I said, and Alexander pulled me in for another kiss. The bull's-eye on his forehead from the Botox had gone down in size. He failed to raise his brows and smiled. I was surprised by him. It's the truth. I didn't venture far from the type of person I liked. Especially who I let fuck me, and I could have stripped down right there for Alexander. I would take the hit and get railed by a guy wearing a peacoat and loafers. Would he have followed a guy like me around the city? Of course not. No future awaited us, and it was easier to chase each other knowing that the end would come sooner than we could imagine.

We passed Boxers, a bar I'd rather be shot dead than enter, and edged closer to the center of the block, where the West Side Club was hidden on the second floor of an apartment building. Alexander looked confused, but he followed me into the lobby where a security guard asked, "The gym?"

"Yes."

"Use the stairs."

We walked down the black-tiled hallway, past the elevators, to a plaque that said WEST SIDE CLUB, 2ND FLOOR. We took the stairs up one flight, hearing the music before I pushed the door into the waiting room. A teller waited behind the bulletproof glass window. In an office, a man in dreads counted money and peeked at the security cameras. Nobody seemed out of place. Everything outside no longer existed. The million desires narrowed into one single want, and the nervousness that accompanied a place like this transformed a heartbeat into a great muting device. I heard my heart, only my heart. Alexander went to the window first.

"Locker or room?"

"A room," Alexander said. "For two."

"Under thirty?"

"Yes," Alexander said. "We are both."

"Would you like the big room?"

"Is that for two?"

"I can give you a locker for one of you, but you can both use the room. We only rent one room to a person. It's the law. How many you bring into your room? As many as you desire," the teller said, as he collected both our IDs, wrote down our names in a ledger, and asked for our signatures. He pulled out a metal lockbox from a wall behind him and we put our valuables in the safe. The teller asked us each to sign a membership card, and he placed them in the box too. Our box was returned to the wall and he pressed a button that buzzed us through the door on the right, where an attendant grabbed two rolled-up towels and two hanging keys and led us through the hallways to a red door. Men in white towels wrapped around their waist slowly walked around us. They met our eyes, or they walked as if they saw nothing. Nothing in between.

The attendant unlocked the door, turned on the light, and threw both towels on the bed with the keys. Our room had a full bed, a single chair, and a mirrored wall. We stared into the mirror.

"How strange is this day?" Alexander said.

"The only weird thing is you coming along." I took off my clothes as I stood beside him. First my shirt and shoes, then my jeans and briefs until Alexander was looking at me completely naked in the mirror. "I would have ended up somewhere like this no matter what after today."

"Nobody tells you about this part," Alexander said.

"Which one?"

"There's nowhere for the feelings to go."

"No." I faced him. "And I'll go home later and wonder what to do with all of this. I have no idea. I really thought I could live a different life."

"It's impossible."

"It's not possible yet," I said.

"Perhaps."

I wrapped a towel around my waist. Two packets of condoms and lube fell onto the bed. Alexander hung his coat on the wall and I told him I would be back. I rattled the doorknob and took a breath and my focus put my mind on automatic. I didn't think about what I wanted. I simply wanted. My body moved for me through the figure-eight halls of the West Side Club. I first made my way around our side of the club, peeking into the dim rooms where men were ass-up on the cots or stroking their cocks as they made eye contact with whoever passed. I had to adjust my towel every other hallway. They were too small, never long enough to fully wrap. All the hallways were dark red. Except the black corners where a man might wait for someone to walk up for a kiss. I never went too fast or too hard. Only the floor creaked occasionally beneath my feet. I didn't make a sound.

In each room there was an offering: a man with a pipe and lighter, two delicate tongues, overtures of ecstasy, a slap, a man with his head in a pillow.

The attendants would lead a new man through the halls, illuminating the hallways briefly with the new room light, and I could catch a glimpse of these people, like the one across the hall. This bald man slumped in the corner, completely naked, rubbed red boxing gloves over his jockstrap. He had a long bruised face covered in petroleum jelly. Lips that hung open. Another pair of boxing gloves waited near his feet. The boxer barely moved as I stood on the threshold of his desires. The setup begged a question I couldn't dare ask. I came here to be pummeled, but now I wanted to do the pummeling. I left behind the gloves and continued to cycle around, passing him again and again, each time wanting the gloves to consume my fists. I left him and returned to our room.

Alexander lay on the bed facing the mirrored wall, the towel around his waist. I joined him. A fan's breeze gently pushed the fabric at our waists. Blades swung above our heads. I turned on my side to face him.

"I don't want the money," I said.

Alexander's chest hardly expanded as he breathed, and he reached behind his back to show me his phone. The screen was too bright, but it was already turned down. I could feel his breath on me as he showed me the law. The statute of limitations had expired for much of what happened, but not everything. Alexander swiped through a few pages, showing me what was possible. I didn't have proof of everything. I placed his phone facedown and kept my hand on his wrist.

"I'm going to ruin their fucking lives," I said, as the exhaustion overcame me, and I rolled closer to Alexander, who draped his arm over me, as I started to fall asleep. Into his fluttering neck, I whispered, "I'm going to end their lives as they know it. I will find them, Alexander. I'm going to send the men away."

"I'll help you," Alexander said.

"Ruins," I said. "Ruins."

CHAPTER 19

By the time I returned home, Moans was cleaning the dishes in the sink in his particular way: soaping each item individually and stacking them on the counter. Only when the sink was cleared did he dip the soaped utensils beneath the water and load them onto the drying rack. He had a TV show playing from his laptop on the table. He looked at me once and waited for a response, although he hadn't asked a question. A single candle burned on the coffee table. Two plates of food cooled in bowls. The scene presented like a celebration. I felt like I was late to a party at somebody else's house because this did not seem like mine. This life, too, no longer seemed like I was the one who had recently been living it. I wanted to step into the room and say, *We can stop pretending. I have moved far beyond this place. I loved it for a time, yet I am in the future, and this is in my past.* But Moans probably would have had me committed.

"So?" Moans asked.

"I don't think—I can't do the lawyer thing. I'm sorry."

"What are you sorry for?"

"The bad timing."

"Are you okay?"

"Yes," I said, as the pressure intensified. I wondered if Moans saw the feeling pass across my face. If he did, he ignored it. "I am feeling pretty good."

"That's all that matters," Moans said, as he placed the final dish in a slot. He carried the computer to the coffee table. He turned the volume up. We ate dinner, a meal I had loved when we first met, pasta with zucchini and potato and bell peppers. Women argued on the screen. They yelled over drinks and their men occasionally intervened to argue with each other. We laughed. I hated the shows he liked, but I loved the lullaby of strangers yelling. The screaming had the same effect on him. We finished the episode.

"I'm not going to press you, but will you tell me what the bill is for?"

"The one from the mail?"

"This one," Moans said, and he showed me a black-and-white picture of James and me in the car from E-ZPass. I had forgotten they would ever send a bill. He curled his legs into the couch, his toes against my thigh. The dogs stood on their hind legs to try to get the rest from the bowls.

"Is that pineapple?" I said, the scent in the air.

"I made an upside-down cake."

"Cooking all the old favorites."

"Will you just tell me what you were doing?"

"James was driving me back to where I grew up." I sat cross-legged on the couch and leaned against the wall. "To one of the houses where a man raped me."

"Why?" Moans rested his head against the armrest. "For what?"

"Do you ever think about reminding your father what he did to you?"

"I don't ever want to talk to that person again."

"What would you say to him if he called?"

"But I didn't go to him. That's if he came to me. Which he does. Every year. For one holiday. And we have one awkward conversation. He says, Hi son. I say, Hi. He tells me about his scams. I listen and tell him I'm happy." Moans pulled a bowl and lighter out of his sweatshirt's pouch. He ran the flame over the bowl and sucked in a few hits. "This way I can say I did my part."

"What if you told him you weren't happy?"

"And give him the satisfaction?"

"I had a long day," I said, and I rubbed the soles of his feet. "But I went to find him to remind him I was still alive."

"Why didn't you tell me?"

"Would you have left the keys?"

"No," Moans said. "I wouldn't have let you go."

"James told me it was a bad idea, but he drove me there."

"You let him drive our car?"

"Do you want to know what happened at his door?"

"And James lied to me too? James told me he wanted McDonald's and you were too high on pills to drive."

"That part was true."

"I should un-invite him. Forget his dang lecture."

"What he did for me was good," I said. "James loves me, and he wanted me to do what I needed to do to move on."

"Why are you looking at me like that?"

"Like what?"

"I haven't been given that look since I was a kid."

"Like what?" I said again, but felt like Moans wouldn't understand, and I was looking at him like I hoped he would snap out of whatever was holding him hostage to beliefs I didn't think he actually held. "How could you want anything other than to be absolutely free?"

"I want comfort," Moans said. "I want a home."

"You can have both," I said. "I don't know if that's true."

"What do you want? Just tell me?"

"I am going to find the men who did the stuff to me that has ruined so many years of my life, and I am going to get the truth out of them. And then I will find a way to get justice for myself."

"The men?"

"What do you know?"

"What you've told me."

"I want to hear you say it."

"I don't think I can."

"You don't like to think of me as myself."

"I don't like to think about what happened to you."

"Why?"

"Do you like thinking about it?"

"Sometimes." I smiled horribly. "Sometimes I love nothing more than to think about it. Sometimes one thought puts me out of mind."

"You're my Dylan. You're not that boy."

"What happened then put me in your arms."

"I don't think that's true."

"I think about what happened to you all the time." I took in the shut windows, the motes caught in the weed smoke. If I moved, this conversation would end, and I didn't know if I would have this chance. "I wish you would think about what happened. You think I'm making a mistake."

"I don't know," Moans said, picking up the dogs. They curled on his lap. "Your therapy is making you worse."

"Matan said that it gets harder before it gets better. I think he called it a curve."

"I think he's negligent."

"Do you want me to tell you everything?"

"Don't change the subject," Moans begged. "I want to know how it feels to leave that place so much worse every week. You can't see what I see? I could make you better if you let me."

"I wish that were true," I said, and I ended the conversation by playing the next episode of the show. I laid my head on his chest. He smoked over my face. We watched the arguments on that small computer screen until we fell asleep. When I woke up, Moans was still down and I went downstairs to text Alexander that I wanted to see him soon, and then told James that Moans knew the truth. I placed the West Side Club membership card in a Vietnam War novel on my nightstand.

CHAPTER 20

Two months after the window started, in the weeks after meeting with the lawyers, I lived in small doses. My heart thumped begrudgingly along, and I blamed it for my problems. Too much thinking would make me explode. Wouldn't it please just stop? I wasn't present. I felt like a bomb being flown over my own life. I could see the end coming from above. I went to school and the movies and restaurants. Alexander met up with me for drinks. We talked about our childhoods and teenage years and young adulthoods without mentioning the future. I lived my life—as if I had already done what I needed, as if I were long divorced, as if I had accosted the men and Vincent and was at the afters. Even Moans and I got along fine enough. We didn't have sex. Occasionally, I would jerk him off in the mornings before he left for work. Other than that, Moans was my roommate and nothing more. James kept changing the dates for his trip, but he was coming down around Halloween. I told him that I had plans too, and that I wouldn't be able to be with him every moment, and he kept asking what I was doing that would prevent him from being around all the time. The truth was Alexander, but I didn't know how to break that to James, who didn't love competition.

Moans and I went to movies at the Angelika, where old couples like to talk over the movies, and you were allowed to yell at them. We tensely admired a movie about a woman trapped by a rapist without once mentioning what moved us about the film, other than the performances. We saw a triptych film about growing up Black in Miami at the IFC Center, the city's second most uncomfortable movie theater. I paid for the third film we saw, from my grad school stipend, at the Metrograph, the city's best and most uncomfortable movie theater with seats that made you feel grotesque and unloved. The price of entry was mild suffering, like almost everything else about New York. That was also how you were able to tell who would survive the city and who would not—who would take the myriad inconveniences of life here and pretend it was real suffering.

Twice a week I went to grad school for writing in the Village, where I disliked almost every single student. I had two three-hour classes where people talked about things I did not care about while working on things that I did not care about and then went to straight bars to talk about how they were having the time of their lives. Normal people seemed to hate writing programs for the writing they produced, but I learned it was the people they admitted who were casually despicable. It was boring and depressing and sometimes I would find myself so deeply enraged at how people thought that I would show up to class high or drunk and wait for Alexander to meet me outside so that we could go drink at Julius'. I would always tell Moans that I was with the grad school people, and he would occasionally ask to come. But I would tell him that it would be inappropriate. Nobody brought their partners to the writing circle. This would violate the sacred terms of artistic practice. Moans seemed to accept this.

Late October rains started to come down on us, and Moans drove us everywhere. We had parked after grabbing a to-go order from an

Indian restaurant. While we were waiting outside our apartment, a call rang over the speakers from a number we didn't recognize. Moans answered.

"Hello?"

"Hello, son."

"Hi," Moans said, cheerily empty. He grabbed my thigh, bug-eyed.

"How's the weather in New York?"

"It's not too bad."

"Yeah?" They sounded nothing alike. His father had a neutral voice. I imagined something greater, a voice that accompanied a violent man, somebody who could break a woman's back, a daughter's arm, a son's lips. But he had a nasal, forgettable tone. I listened for a break in his voice, a little thunder.

"Yup."

"We're freezin' over here."

"It's warm here," Moans said, as I mouthed *Where?*, but he mouthed back *I don't care.* "The weather's great here."

"Sounds like it's raining, son."

"That's a fire hydrant. You know how kids like to play in the streets."

"Wow." The father whispered to someone else around him. "You doin' okay?"

"Only amazing."

"I been thinking a lot about you, and I wanted to give you a call." I waited to hear anything in the background. A plane landing, a siren, but all I heard was his father's voice, for the very first time, and no other signs of life. The voice was detached. Hardly a scratch in the connection. Where were the birds of California? Where were the cars? Where was the TV? All the detritus of life was missing.

I had never heard his voice before. If Moans had recognized the number, I didn't think he would have picked up. Or maybe he had wanted me to hear. To know the father was real. "We went to the swap meet and got some food. Turkey and ravioli and sweet potato. You couldn't believe the pennies I paid."

"Good."

"Pennies."

"Good," Moans repeated, sounding very tired.

"How are you doing with the sweets?"

"Good."

"Good."

"Yeah."

"Well, I just wanted to call you and see how you were doing and wish you a Merry Christmas in advance."

"It's October," Moans said.

"You can never be too early to call your own son."

"But you can be late."

"What's that?"

"I'll talk to you later."

"This is my landline."

Moans hung up, quietly sighed, and gripped the wheel as if he were going to start driving. We stayed parked. My hands rustled the plastic take-out bags. Rainwater rippled down the window. Moans said, "I can't wait for him to die. You would think a three-hundred-pound diabetic with a shredded liver and no insurance wouldn't live that long. Nothing horrible. I just wish he would die."

"Is there anything I can do?"

"Let's watch a movie," Moans said, opening the door to the roaring rain. When we stepped outside, we were drenched, and then the rain halted, all of it gone, halfway to our door. In bed, we ate as a WWII movie played. He played a game on his phone. Then he went to sleep for almost fourteen hours.

When he woke the next day, Moans asked if I wanted to go get coffee. The shop I liked was off the Bedford–Nostrand G. Three people could fit inside the store. No tables meant nobody sat and stared at screens there. I hated seeing people hunch over their computers next to half a muffin. A sight without beauty. It destroyed my appetite, so we always came to this one place, where you could wake slowly without your day being ruined. Moans was pretty quiet. We sipped our coffees and took the long way back, ambling down a street between an elementary school and a produce garden.

"I wonder what goes on in your mind. You laugh and joke and hold me, all that, and then I see a look in your eye that is so unnatural, so at odds with what you're doing that I know your whole world is a secret. What do you think about that you're not telling me?"

"Do you really want to know?" The garden had a chicken coop. Both sides of the street were ringed by chain-link fences. I decided to be honest. "Right now? Vincent used to finger me with coke, or fuck me with coke on his dick. A few times with Percocet. It would numb me so the rest wouldn't hurt that bad. I was thinking about the feeling of getting fucked dusted. Because, if he used lube, he would have ruined the coke, which I knew was something he wouldn't do. He had told me this story once about how some old guy he was with had supplied him coke, and he shot cum into the coke dish, and the guy beat the fuck out of him, even though they were having sex." I sipped my iced coffee. "So, what's better? Ruining the coke and getting beat, which I only made the mistake of doing once with spit, or taking it dry, which does get you numb? Of course, if you're dry, you bleed, but the coke does numb you so that the blood does kind of work like lube. What hurt was after, when the drugs wore off, and I showered, and I was burning so unbelievably badly." I looked at the elementary school. "Can I have my muffin?"

Moans handed over the brown bag, and I ate while we walked home in silence. I thought he regretted knowing. Moans had been taught it was better not to know, to bury yourself in tasks that make a life—homemaking, as it's called. He had accomplished more than I had. He'd never gone to college nor had a stable home. Moans had a life that was testament to his willpower; he was the sort of person people rooted for because he succeeded where others couldn't imagine the possibility. All with that beatific smile. One of the best I'd ever seen in my life. Without it, the relationship was drained. At the time, we didn't understand that we made different attempts at recovery. For every truth he pulled from me, an accidental question was posed that he didn't want to answer: What was due to him? Did Moans see the end as he entered our living room, as I sat cross-legged on the couch?

"I always knew something worse happened to you," Moans said. "Looking back, it's obvious."

"I'm sorry," I said.

"I'm so angry for you. Why aren't you angry?"

"It's a lot of pressure."

"Is there anything I can do?"

"Don't add pressure."

"Sometimes I wish we met when you were older," Moans said, sitting beside me to stroke my arm. "Like if we met when you were this age."

"You want to skip the bad years."

"I wish you had time to process."

"I don't wish we met now," I said. "I don't think I would have gotten here without you. I needed the trouble. Otherwise, I'd be back in San Diego."

"What about the beach?"

"I can give you that. I miss the beach."

"We could go back."

"I fantasize about returning."

"When?"

"When I'm not dreaming of revenge."

CHAPTER 21

Nearly a decade ago on Halloween, James had dressed me and two other young men in wings and white jockstraps. We were angels in the outfield. James charged the night with the idea that we would become other people, even though we barely knew ourselves. We did know that the famous superhero movie director (you know the one) would be at Heaven's Gate, the 18+ club, and he always took the most beautiful boys back to his mansion. James wanted to be one of them, taken away in a limousine for nothing more than his face. The night went as it always did. James was ignored, although he almost made the cut, taken into the bathroom by the club owner, who gave him a VIP wristband. James was never going to become an object of desire. He would always be the watcher—the critic—and I couldn't figure out if that quality predated those nights or was an extension of them. I never asked James this, either. Everyone finds a way to steal a bit of power.

The director let us put drinks on his tab and he left with the shortest angel. I didn't drink at all. When just us three were left, James slammed a couple shots and tripped as he left the club. He crawled to the Sunset gutter and purged his guts.

"Why not me?" James asked. His palms were flat on the boulevard and his legs straightened out behind him. People stepped over him. Where had his shoes gone? It didn't matter. Time to go home.

I had his car keys. Our remaining friend, the big angel, lifted James up, and they hobbled into the back seat of the car. I drove to James' house, as James stared in a terribly quiet manner out the window, where it was so dark I knew he was transfixed by nothing—the sheer vivid renderings of his twisted mind. I couldn't see past their wings, which blocked the rear window, but I didn't want to disturb James.

At the DUI checkpoint, an officer beamed his flashlight into the car. I requested the breathalyzer and blew into the machine. The officer let us go. We rode in silence. Every few miles, emergency beams erupted from police hiding on the roadside. Headlights illuminated a smoking pirate driving with a hook. My phone lit up as the short angel sent pictures of the director's house. The fat angel in the back seat, too drunk to know James was in one of his moods, whispered about golden cabanas, trunks full of extra-small designer T-shirts. I wanted to know everything, but I didn't want James to feel like he was missing out. We were almost home, halfway across the bridge to Mira Loma, when James said, "Goodbye, girls."

James opened his door, flushing the interior with wind, as the car started beeping and the red open-door signal flashed on the dashboard. The angel screamed uselessly while James held the door ajar, peeking into the slit, staring at the rushing asphalt as if he were seeing a face he remembered but couldn't name. Death, you know, is strangely familiar. I reached back to try to grab him, but I made the car swerve, so I slowed down.

"If you stop," James said, "I'll jump."

"Not on Halloween," the angel said, "Not on Halloween."

"If you jump, you won't die," I said. "You'll break a leg."

"Is that a dare?"

A van full of boy pilgrims pulled up beside us.

"Grab his wings," I screamed, "and slam the door!"

The big angel ripped out fistfuls of feathers and managed to shut the door.

I enforced the child lock.

James unlatched his seat belt.

"Kiss him!" I said.

The angel kissed James on the lips, which stunned them both, only for a second. Long enough for James to roll down his window and try to launch himself through it. The angel punched James three times, knocking him out to save his life. I finally pulled the car over. The friend stormed out, threw his wings on the ground, and called the police. Whatever had seemed funny to us about James in the past now seemed as if it were a cry for help. The cops arrived and declared James temporarily unable to care for himself—a classic 5150. Our friend called somebody to take him home, and I got in our friend's face, so close my wings beat against his arms in the wind. The friend seemed terrified. It was clear we'd never see him again. He walked down the freeway, into the dark, and found his ride home.

James curled up on the grass next to the curb as if he were taking a nap, using the feathers as a pillow, as the two officers stood over him. Every so often a car drove too fast past us. The officers would turn their heads and watch the cars until they vanished. I waited for the paramedics, who arrived in costume too. The clown paramedic secured James to the gurney.

I broke the news to his mother. She greeted me at the front door, her wavy dark hair and white gown catching the slightest bit of yellow porch light. She told me I could sleep in James' bed and lit a tall candle beneath his Catholic school portrait, the little flame reaching to his closed-lip smile. James called me from the hospital. He was in love with one of the psychiatrists already, and he was fine. They gave him a banana bag, which made him piss so often it reminded him of bloodletting. He told me to imagine all problems being carried in blood. All they needed was to get out, a little at a time. Not enough to kill you, just enough for the euphoria to arrive. I loved James, even when he was like this. The nurse forced him off the phone. In the morning, the other angels asked me if James turned out fine, and we never spoke to them again. They knew James had a problem, and they didn't want to see it through to the end. I picked him up alone.

Now, James would arrive at our apartment with a suitcase to pre-pare for his lecture on horror films. He had always been obsessed with the way people suffered, whether it was St. Sebastian or the people jumping from the towers or a boy getting killed in his dreams. For his two-year sobriety anniversary, for example, James had wanted to go to the crucifixion at The Eagle, the leather bar in Chelsea that had become so run-down it was easier to piss in a man's mouth than a urinal. Photographs weren't allowed, and they had a coat check behind a chain-link fence. There hadn't been a good crucifixion in years. The days of leather had passed like a trend. I hadn't truly been alive for the heyday, and I never wore it in my life. I was not a person who dressed up as anything other than myself. We took a cab to the bar. That night, there was barely anyone on the second floor for the event. A dispirited bartender wiped dust off the black crucifix for an idiot to be strung up. The young man leaned back against the dark wood, extending his arms for the bartender to tighten straps around his limbs. When he was secured, the bartender abandoned him and returned to the line that had formed in his absence. The young man made awkward eye contact with people who considered him an embarrassment. It was one thing to attend the crucifixion, but another to actually partake. James had too many Diet Cokes. I wasn't high enough to believe in anything. Nobody punished the man on the cross. They barely acknowledged his existence. He seemed bored, like now he really wanted to die, and his desire for punishment turned increasingly into shame. I felt bad for him.

"The great shame of your life is that you weren't raised Catholic," James said to me. "You've got suffering, but you don't have the aesthetic."

"I don't know what that means."

"What do you think this guy is?" James approached the young man, whose posture became rigid and alert. Maybe he thought we'd be the ones to dole out punishment. Instead, James pushed the hair out of his eyes. "We were wondering if you were raised Catholic."

I made a face to excuse me from whatever was going to happen.

"I don't mind," the guy said. "I wasn't. My parents were atheists."

"So this is just a sex thing?" James said, grimacing. "Nothing religious?"

"I like the feeling, is all."

James grabbed the leather strap around the guy's wrist and began to loosen it. I called his name, but he handed me his empty soda. The guy writhed against James, attempting to stop him from undoing the binds that suspended him. He told James to stop, but I knew James wouldn't. The priests at his Catholic school had molested his friends, like the film director at Heaven's Gate, and they never chose James. The men James dated often had boyfriends, and the attention they gave him ended when their boyfriends returned. The court chose to punish James, too, for a night he couldn't remember. Some days he hated himself so much he could twist his own good fortune into a curse and consider the lucky way he'd never been abused into a punishment for whatever he believed he had done wrong in his life. He felt undesirable, even for violence, and those who chose to be punished misunderstood a crucial element to James he couldn't forgive.

"You don't deserve to be up there," James said. "You don't get to choose."

"Leave me up," the guy said, calling for the bartender to save him. He jerked on the beams, shaking the floor around us. The crowd that hadn't materialized earlier now formed around James. Half the guys seemed like they were going to ask James for a kiss, but James paid no attention to them. Nobody intervened. When one wrist was undone, instead of fighting James off, the guy kept his arm frozen in position, as if freedom immobilized him. A minute passed as he stared at James, after he finished undoing the binds, before the guy walked straight out of the bar. The crowd wanted to know who was going up next, if anything was going to happen at all. I felt again the strange sensation of being watched, and when I turned to find who was staring at me, everyone else was doing the same, attempting to find out who in their loneliness would volunteer for a little bit of pain. One by one the crowd disappeared until James and I were alone with a bouncer striding toward us.

For the lecture, James wanted me to go alone, but I was bringing Alexander. James would have to be there the whole day, and I didn't like to hear academics talk about almost anything. I didn't even really like to fuck them. They all believed they were good at sex, despite their job, which I had heard so many tell me after they barely lasted two minutes. *So many of my colleagues can barely kiss. My peers . . . The union senate . . . Tenure committee . . .* If anybody uses these words after they bust—run.

CHAPTER 22

The day of James' lecture, he woke us by snoring. No amount of tape on the bridge of his nose prevented his croaking. Moans turned to me in bed and said that it began to seem as if James was moving into the living room. I didn't think Moans minded. Moans had somebody to talk shit on me with, and do things to their faces, like coat their foreheads with blue algae, which had the texture of cum. They ordered food with real meat and James sang in the shower in a pure falsetto, which made Moans laugh.

That morning, Moans said, "You should get keys made."

"I already have a spare."

"Do you really?"

"How do you think I let myself in?" James said, as Moans left for the day. The second we heard the front door close, James asked: "Who is Alexander?"

"A friend."

"I want to meet him."

"I have to go to therapy," I said, and left James behind to rehearse. The whole trip to the Center I wished that James wasn't at home. I didn't really want him to meet Alexander either, while simultaneously wanting him to see me with Alexander. I couldn't explain it, which was what I told Matan, who was dumbly listening to me talk.

"James has done a lot for you," Matan said, adjusting the white collar under his salmon sweater. "So why now?"

"I don't want to hear what he is going to say about Alexander."

"What do you think it will be?"

"He's going to tell me it's a mistake. That whatever is happening between me and Alexander is a placeholder for whatever should be happening between me and Moans. Or that he doesn't like Alexander. Or that Alexander doesn't make sense in my life. That I would normally not like a person like him."

"Alexander."

"I'm saying his name a lot."

"Why do you think that is?"

"We haven't fucked."

"Did you think you would have? Fucked?" Matan went all googly-eyed, trying to imitate me, and he sort of got it right. "Did I sound right?"

"The moment we fuck it'll be over."

"Why?"

"Because neither of us is attracted to each other. We're attracted to the situation," I said, and I saw that Matan was going to ask me to clarify. "*The situation* being that we can say the word *rape* a thousand times and not feel bad. He can say anything to me. I can say anything to him. Even though we haven't done that in a while." I watched a pigeon fly into a glass building across the street and fall. "You know what's wild? I feel fine. I have been completely okay for two weeks. Maybe even three. I have been on vacation from myself."

"Do you like being there?"

"No," I said. "Because you spend one day in San Diego and it turns into three years."

"What does that mean?"

"That I'm going to invite James and Moans to drinks tonight with Alexander."

"And what are you going to tell them?"

"I don't know," I said. "I don't want to talk about it. I just want to do it."

"Nobody is stopping you."

"I'm going to take out my phone and text Alexander."

"Feel free."

"Okay," I said, and texted Alexander while reading the messages aloud to Matan. "Hey. I got a bad idea that is going to sound good. Want to meet my husband and best friend tonight? I am ready."

"Ready for what?" Matan said.

"It's annoying being asked questions all the time," I said. I could feel my eyes go wide but I couldn't close them. I could barely blink. "I'm done with this bullshit. I want to tell Moans that I am starting the hunt." I grimaced. "Hunt. Yes. That sounds right."

We had some time left in the session, and as Alexander responded Matan and I worked out the plan. Alexander would come with me to James' talk at six, and then after his speech we were going to wait for Moans and James at Red Bamboo on West Fourth. We would have to lie a little. Alexander would be someone I read about online who had his own lawsuit with the Child Victims Act, and we had been talking to each other about what it had been like to go through something. Alexander agreed that it was smarter than saying he was from a law firm. He didn't want to get in trouble, and I had told him that Moans would occasionally flip out. The plan felt right.

///////

When I got home, James was smoking at the park, and I sat next to him. A children's playground beside us had a statue of a camel sinking into the concrete. As he lit the cigarette, I told him I was planning on introducing Alexander to both him and Moans that night, and he blew the smoke out over my face. I almost threw up. James looked far away. The atmosphere changed instantly, and I could feel the breeze that had once traveled through the cracks in Vincent's window blow over my face. Over what was happening in front of me, like two negatives superimposed, I could see Vincent holding up a camera. The camera had two quick flashes. Then Vincent would instruct me on how to move as he pulled on his cigarette. The angle needed perfecting. Nothing identifiable from Vincent's bedroom could show in the photographs. Vincent centered me on the black quilt on his bed, spread my legs, and raised my hips. If he found the right angle, he would place his hard dick on my ass to take more pictures. All this, I felt. I couldn't see. My face couldn't be in these pictures most of the time. Sometimes, if he wanted to break the rules, if he wanted to break me, he would take a picture of me sucking him off and then later crop out my eyes, and I would know that what was coming was to be feared (until he brought out the drugs). In some pictures, Vincent obscured my face by pressing my head into his pillows, which reeked of the cigarettes. He would spread my ass and enter me. He didn't use lube because it was too reflective, he used to say, and would ruin the pictures. He would tell me that it wasn't just my pain, that entering dry sometimes hurt him too. We both had to sacrifice for a good shot and use a tiny bit of spit. If I moved too much, he would tie my hands to his bed with cuffs he kept in his underwear drawer. When he was inside me, he'd sometimes hit the spot and make me feel an evaporating pleasure through the dead-armed, blacked-out pose. Almost everything Vincent did always missed the mark a little. I used to dream of challenging him to an old-fashioned noontime duel. When I shoot I don't miss.

"Hello?" James asked.

"You're smoking his cigarettes."

"Whose?"

"Vincent's."

"Camel Crush?"

"Yes," I said. "Do you know what the worst thing about having child porn out there is?"

"That it is out there. That it happened."

"Also, that you don't know who has seen it. I look in people's eyes sometimes and wonder."

"That's your favorite word."

"I don't think so."

"Sometimes," James said, blowing more smoke over me, and I asked James if he wanted to hear what I was remembering. Of course he did.

Russ, who we visited two months ago, had a little black case where he stashed the drugs. He had a pipe, a lighter, a needle. I begged to avoid the needle. Now I know he never would have done it. The track marks would have been evidence he couldn't hide. The bit of blood Russ pulled from me satisfied him enough. After the men paid Vincent, it was his turn, and blood was nothing compared to shit. If after he fucked me it was unclean, he would scream at me for being dirty. Vincent would knock my head into the window or push me off the bed and yell. I couldn't let him see me wince. He could choke me and my face wouldn't change. I could take it and return a smooth face, the way a rock dulls beneath a waterfall. To this day, people tell me they can't read my face. I thought they were stupid. Who could be more transparent than me? But I remembered. To see Vincent's face when he pulled out meant learning what would happen before it happened, and my own face worsened this. A second of silence, a soured look, a broken lip. Hadn't he known I wanted to be a good boy? I rarely made that mistake again, and I never complained. If I bled, the briefs would stick to my flesh, and I could get high enough to forget.

"I've said enough," I said, and we got ready for the lecture. James tried on a few identical outfits. He wanted to know which I liked best, and the answer was I liked every single one the same. They were all bad. I didn't understand why he did this. James would bring a black turtleneck, black pants, a black sweater, dark gray pants, all too tight. I personally didn't like it, and I found it hard to imagine that how his appearance would get him anywhere, and to dress like *that* on top? And ask for my interest? I kept telling him he looked good as he cycled through the outfits, and James' face continued to fall until he sat on the couch with a shirt in his hands.

"You don't support me," James said.

"I am coming to your event," I said.

"You can't even tell me that I look good."

"What did I say?"

"You didn't believe it."

"It's not my world," I said. I thought about telling him that I would never fuck him. "You're the expert in the field."

"You make it sound like I'm not human."

"You're snapping before an event. It's normal. Put on your shit and let's bounce."

"My shit," James said. "You know what Freud would have to say about that?"

"Of course. All hail the god of my life. The great and powerful king of shit."

"Finally some respect."

James dressed. I hugged him, and he grabbed me tighter. The great lie of best friendship made itself known. We had nothing connecting us beyond a span of time already gone and a body of knowledge that others did not. He knew what Moans did not. I knew what the people in his program did not. I really had thought he only wanted to fuck me. Okay? I did not understand he was in love with me. Of course it's clear now. He didn't want my approval, or my thoughts, or my ear. James wanted to love me better than he saw other people love me, and he wanted my rotten love in return. James always wanted men that never loved him back the same, and I think with me James believed that he could bring something dead back to life. I don't know how I didn't see it. I thought the possibility of a romantic connection was so far-fetched it never occurred as a possibility, or maybe—and this I wonder the most at night when I hope he's doing well, good and far away from me—I used him.

The talk took place at The Frick, a museum that bordered Central Park on East Seventy and imitated a temple. Grecian columns held up a domed ceiling. James and I walked in together, and I immediately felt as if I were trespassing. A golden fountain was surrounded by plants more alive than the people around us. Dark frogs shot water from their mouths into a pool. It was exactly the type of place I avoided in the city, a space with an opulence that seemed to conquer history, as if nothing but art mattered, when what originated all of this, this building, was what happened when two people with faces like jewelry fucked their way into creating empires. This place had been a destitute library. Frick got rich off iron, destroyed a few unions, and survived an assassination attempt. The library became Frick's mansion, death became Frick, and art his legacy. I imagined destroying this place. I would rip out the throaty frog and toss it through a window. I never liked animals turned into stone. The urge to freeze a frog as it throated white water seemed like the work of an absolute pervert.

"Don't say it," James said.

"It's beautiful."

"Is that what you think?"

"There he is," I said, and I pointed at a man clicking through the lobby with one hand in his pocket and the other smoothing back his hair. Alexander broke a smile when he saw me, and we embraced each other and laughed. I showed Alexander how I was looking at the place, all wide-eyed and repressed. Through the translucent ceiling, we could see birds perching in a nest. Alexander cocked a finger gun and aimed it at the birds as he whispered in my ear, "We don't allow trespassers here." He had come from a barbershop. Little brown hairs crosshatched his cheek. I wiped them off with my thumb.

"Gauche," Alexander said, pointing at velvet ropes blocking off paintings that nobody was trying to see. "I heard someone on the Six today refer to life as a series of cringe-inducing embarrassments. They were fourteen. Maybe fifteen. Referring not to their own lives but to a dog in a vest sniffing at an abandoned coffee cup. Hi, I'm Dylan's friend Alexander."

"Nice to meet you," James said. "Thank you for coming."

"I've heard so much about you," Alexander said. "A doctoral student?"

"The correct term is *doctoral faggot*," I said.

"Film theory," James said.

"Same thing," I said. "Have you been here before?"

"Don't make fun of me," Alexander said. "Of course."

"I've heard a little about you," James said, opening his blue folder to play with the pages. "It is nice of you to come."

"I told Mr. Quigley I had an optometry appointment."

"Who is that?"

"The lawyer," I said.

"My boss," Alexander clarified.

"We're not telling Moans that part," I said.

"Do you ever feel strange calling him Moans?" Alexander asked James.

"And you two have known each other?"

"A month and a half."

"How sweet," James said. "Young love."

"We're not in love," Alexander said.

"We haven't fucked," I said, and my voice seemed to carry. Around us, people bored right into my life, and their faces told me that not only did I not belong, that James should be chastised for bringing me, and if they were lucky that they would only ever see me on the street. It was that type of look. Not of exclusion, but of placement. They said, *I know where I will find you, and I will see you there later.*

"Don't," James and Alexander said, surprising each other.

"What?"

"You scream *fuck* in a place like this?" James said. "You're gonna get a look."

"He didn't scream the word. They are simply alert to riffraff."

"I'm riffraff?"

"Scuttlebutt."

"Now you're making up words."

"Now you're fucking attempting to get the stare," Alexander said into my ear. "You know what to scream in case of fire?"

James walked away into the golden auditorium with a wooden stage. We slummed in the back seats while James sat up front with the speakers. There were ten empty rows between us and James. Nothing filled up. A few New York accents complained in the middle rows. I didn't know the scene, but this seemed sad.

An old man took the podium and announced four speakers. James was second. He rehearsed, moving his lips, as the lights went down, and a very hot man talked about depictions of Jesus. He sounded stupid, and he acted like a top who fucked floppily, a cartoonish humper you endured to let him spit on your face as he nutted in seconds. He showed a picture of a wonky Jesus, the type of thing I imagined old emperors had shimmying on their chariots, like a taxi tiki dancer. I clapped when his time ended. Alexander shook his head, crossing his legs above the knee. The hem lifted, showing the light brown hair bending on his calves.

"I know what you're doing," I whispered.

"Show me," Alexander said.

I crossed my legs, and Alexander reached behind me, slipping his hand into the back of my black shorts, running his finger over the hair at the top of my ass. He didn't go lower as James started to speak. He moved his thumb horizontally, the finger rising and falling over the flesh. I didn't pay any attention to James, who was showing images of freaks swinging chain saws, girls on the backs of trucks with wind in their blood-streaked hair. A single touch could freeze me, and Alexander knew this, only I wasn't afraid of being hurt. I was full of such longing for him, and I didn't want to fuck it up. I wanted to stand up, hand in hand, and rip away the faces we showed the world, leaving this gold auditorium for the future we would never give each other (really give, fully surrendering)—the dark riding rooms in bathhouses and checkered-table meals on Bleecker and full-throated screams of ecstasy as our rapists were burned to death in court as we consumed ourselves in the writhing anger we did not allow ourselves during the day.

James' presentation ended. A woman asked him a question, as the lights returned to the room, that I didn't hear. For a silent minute, the whole room stared at James, who turned to the screen behind him at a frame of a boy with firelight on his face. The computerized image trembled slightly, and James said, "Why is there a shadow if there is no fire at all?" He adjusted his glasses. A man stood up and moved closer to the podium. The strangers wore their search for meaning on their faces like masks, as if in a moment they all might rush up to the stage and loot the world for all it was worth. Alexander and I left as the next presentation was announced.

We walked down the park, ignoring each other, and I felt strange around him. And the trees did not help. What had been green last week turned, and whatever color I named the living would be out-of-date in a day. I was pretty sure the trees had been green last week. Certain people you were supposed to see in the specific lighting of certain places. Central Park almost made Alexander seem too alive. I wondered what he was ruining to be here with me. His job? Dates? A chance at actually joining his case. If I were Alexander, I would be spending time with me to hopefully get fired and then, with nothing to lose, join the case that his firm had taken on. We waited for the train to take us down to Washington Square Park. I mouthed *Are we there yet?* as we pulled into the station. The day moved without us, without me, and I collected myself near the basketball courts on West Fourth, The Cage. Somebody was screaming across the street at Papaya Dog that he was going to kill himself over the price increase. I didn't want to ask Alexander what he was destroying. (I wanted to destroy everything with him! I wanted to beat the shit out of him at that very moment. I dreamed of the diamonds imprinted on my cheek from the fence, blood from my lip flying onto the court, the skin peeling away from my flesh as he dragged me across the ground. I wanted him to make me scream. I wanted him to love me.) If I broke his spell, maybe he would leave me, and if he left me I would be even more alone.

"What?" Alexander asked, his hand on the chain-link fence. "Don't give me that look."

"If I told you what I was thinking you would hate me."

"If I told *you* what I was thinking . . ."

We decided to grab a drink at the closest bar before ending up at Julius'. I imagined myself already there, sitting with James and Moans, talking to them across the divide of my life. You could either join me or watch me go. I knew James would come, and I had given up hope that Moans would too. At the bar, staring at two beers in a basement room, Alexander told me that his firm's case was ready for trial, even though it wasn't going to get that far. One of the boys—men—had killed himself, leaving behind a trove of letters that were exchanged between the priest and the dead guy when he was a child.

"It is always love," Alexander said. "That's how they get you."

"Fear too."

"That's what traps you, but I mean what entices you."

"What enticed you?"

"As if I can remember that far back. If what this boy said is true, then it was probably love. I think I was loved dearly as a child, but if I return to the imaginary scene of the crime, why do I feel so unloved? Why do I want to feel love?"

"You were younger than me."

"Much younger," Alexander said slowly. "The experts say a part of you is trapped at that age. I don't feel that age. If I told you I feel like I'm eight years old on occasion, would you put me away?"

"How would you feel that age?"

"I used to urinate on myself. Not as a child. When I was dating my ex, who knew nothing of this, I would take an extra pair of briefs to the bathroom, stand in the shower, and soil the briefs."

"Soil," I said. "That word."

"I would dispose of them, wrapped in a plastic bag, in someone else's trash. I believe that's how one might feel that age. Can I say something offensive?"

"This is a safe space," I said, and he laughed.

"I can't actually say what I want to because I fear that I am both correct and incorrect simultaneously," Alexander said, pointing at the bartender. She was leaning over the bar, texting, occasionally scratching her scalp with a single nail.

"Oh, I know what you're gonna say."

"You're about to roll your eyes, but spare me the moment, please."

I waited.

"I would like to institute a test, like the Bechdel—I asked you to refrain from the eye rolling. Let's say it's true that one out of every four men are actually assaulted. I want people to count the men in their lives, in their families, and I want them to calculate how many men they know to have been assaulted. I think more men know this than women. I wish I could tell you why. This is anecdotal, and it's based on my own experiences."

"You don't need to shit on yourself here."

"We can call it the Dylan Test, then."

"Yikes."

"If you are really part of the world that we want to build, and I am reluctant to admit that is what I desire, aside from revenge and all the sweet stuff, then your rape roll call should come close to a quarter of the men you know."

"Let's test it," I said, and I called the bartender over. "Should we test out our theory?"

"On the bartender?"

"Let's have her guess how many men she knows and figure out how many men have told her about what happened. It should be somewhere from a quarter to a sixth. Probably a little less than that since most people don't talk about that shit, but according to the Dylan Test . . ."

"I don't want to know the answer. I'm terrified that I already do," Alexander said, looking at her again. He wanted to be proved both right and wrong, right in the moment and wrong as times changed. I didn't want to be there any longer, so I pushed back my stool and made for the outdoors. A breeze was promising fall, even though fall had already come. It was going to be a warm year, one without any storms I hoped. I hated to see the world like this—as a fateful place of signs and symbols—but that is how I saw it most days. I stopped to feel the wind, and Alexander rubbed his hand over my head.

"It feels nice," I said, distracted by the store we were passing. Jewelry hung over a black backdrop. I saw a diamond-encrusted necklace that said I Love New York, silver chains, a palm tree made from pink stones. A sticker on the door read We Buy Gold.

"See something you like?"

"Yeah," I said, and we entered the store, where a woman sat behind bulletproof glass. She zoned out on the flat-screen TV above our heads. A boy played in the back. Inside the case, there were watches, pens, bracelets. Gaming consoles too. Discounted luxury, framed in glass.

"How much is the New York necklace?"

"Evan," the woman called.

"What?"

"The man wants to see the New York chain."

"Man," I said to Alexander. "Am I there yet?"

"Fine," the boy said, walking to where we stood and unlocking the front window display. He passed the chain to me, and I held it on my chest in front of a mirror on the wall. I knew it was ridiculous. I didn't want it. I handed it to the boy, who placed it in the window display again. The boy was waiting to see if I wanted to look at anything else. I wasn't a jewelry person. I ran my finger over my wedding ring and took it off.

"I just need something to pass through my hands," I said. "How much for this?"

The woman pointed to a slot for me to drop the ring. I wasn't going to sell it.

"Never mind," I said. "I won't tempt fate today."

"You are tempting it enough," Alexander said.

"How?" I said, laughing, as we left the store and walked by a pet store with horrendously cute dogs. "The second you are attractive you are sold. It transcends species."

"You're triggered," Alexander said. He stopped on the street. "It's okay."

"I'm not triggered."

"What does your therapist tell you to do?"

"Pick the color."

"White."

"Those pants," I said, pointing as we walked to Julius'. "The pigeon. It's not *not* white. The line on the ground. Clouds. White chalk on the Jeffrey's sign. The cleaner's name. The hanger. The frame of that window on the brick wall. Post no bills. The name of the ice cream place. Bestsellers in the window. And we're here."

"I thought you were only supposed to name a few."

"Why don't you try it?" I asked, as I pushed open the door to Julius', where nothing good happens. The cash-only bar had a reputation for being an elderly gays' type of place, where someone who wanted something from you sat alone in a high chair as you pulled cash from the ATM. For young people who believed leather jackets made them edgy. For me? It was a dive on the West Side, close to the trains, where nobody I knew would go. Because of the tiny kitchen the bar smelled like grease and was always dead unless it was horribly packed. On occasion, a DJ played music close to the bar, and if you danced it was proof you were blacked out. I had only ever heard disco played here, which at a normal bar has a terrible stranglehold on culture, but here it seemed as though there were no other option. I couldn't blame an out-of-date place for out-of-touch music. The back had cushioned leather seats along the wall and bathrooms without fuckability. Everyone was a regular but I never knew their names. This was not a home bar, despite the fact that I frequented it weekly.

"I think I'm addicted to chaos," I said.

I sat near the front to avoid the feeling that I was hiding. There was a skinny green bench and circular wooden tables and terribly uncomfortable stools. Alexander sat across from me after getting our drinks. The condensation nearly had the drink slip through my hands.

"There is a man looking at me through the window who I believe might be your husband," Alexander said.

Moans walked into the bar and took off his jacket, holding it with a finger from the hook as if it had been raining. He stared down the end of the bar, and he seemed surprised to see me here. I kissed him on the lips as he checked out the two drinks. I had the sense of kissing a stranger. He was wearing new cologne and clothes and ordered a whiskey at the bar. A couple more people showed up. Nothing close to a crowd, but now there was enough noise to feel like our conversation had some privacy.

"How was the talk?" Moans asked, sitting next to me.

"I'm Alexander. You must be Moans."

"Yes," Moans said, wincing. "How do you know Dylan?"

"I told you. Grad school," I said. "The talk was boring. We left after he did his thing."

"I had to work," Moans said. "You don't look like an artist."

"I don't?"

"No." Moans laughed, covering his mouth. "Is that bad to say?"

"What about me?" I asked.

"Of course. You fit the bill. He—Alexander doesn't. You don't go by Alex?"

"I do."

"You do?" I said.

"I think you called yourself a nickname bitch and kept my full name as a joke."

"I don't remember that."

"That sounds like Dylan," Moans said. "Both of those things."

"I'm having a crazy sense of déjà vu," I said, as a man at the bar nodded at me. He patted the seat next to him. The déjà vu disappeared before I could recognize what was happening. I thought, for a moment, that I was going to die. I had a dream where this exact scene happened but my heart failed right after, and I wondered if this was a message from the universe to take an aspirin, to let Moans know that I feared something terrible. I placed my hand on his arm.

"What's wrong?"

"All my déjà vu is preparing me for the moment of my death."

"That's not how that works," Moans said.

"I have a confession," Alexander said, wriggling his drink. He always finished first. He might have actually been a drunk. "I have never experienced déjà vu."

"What?" I said, glancing at Moans. "How is that possible?"

"Not once in my life, and before you describe the sensation to me I have already researched the phenomenon, and, yes, it's true. Not all people experience déjà vu. It's French for *already seen*." Alexander turned to the bartender and motioned for another round. "Once, in a fit of despair, I posted to an online forum that I hadn't experienced it, and people informed me that it means I would only be living as a human once, that my eternity I am damned to forget, that I am an idiot, the latter of which I believed."

"Me too," I said. "The last part."

"At this point, I know I will most likely never experience it. I am nearing forty. I am post-thirty-five. I can't imagine the sensation either. Like, a color-blind person is unable to render green in their minds, and I am unable to render this majestic experience that you can't even see on someone's face. Just now, you looked totally normal. Nothing gave away your interior. Sometimes people look around after, but that isn't substantial. I can look around." He did. "Is it magic? Truly? I am afraid to ask."

"Yes," I said. "Honestly."

"And you?" Alexander asked Moans.

"There's nothing like it."

"I'm sorry," Alexander said, and he started to cry. He gazed at his hands as if they had just grown, and rested his sorrowful face in his palms. I didn't know what to do. Moans was surprised, and he waited for me to comfort my friend. "I'm not in my body."

"Alexander," I said.

"I can't do this."

"Are you okay?" Moans asked.

The old man on the stool gathered the drinks Alexander ordered and walked over to place them on the table. The man lingered, and Alexander glared into his face. He smiled slowly at the three of us and said, "What's wrong, baby?"

"Don't call him baby," I said.

"Dylan," Moans said.

"What are you boys doing here on a night like this?"

"Why are you alone at a bar on a night like this?"

"I know you," the man said to me. "Tell him I know him."

"You don't know me."

"Dylan, is it?" He handed me a drink and put his hand on Alexander's shoulder, saying to him, "You're the sweet one."

"You left your wallet at the bar," I said.

"You're not gonna ask my name? What I was doing earlier? Why I am in a suit?"

"What were you doing?"

"This and that," he said. "This and that."

"Mr. This and That," I said. "Your wallet is on the bar."

"Oh," he said, taking his hand off Alexander.

I stood and lifted the drink to my lips.

"There's no poison in it," Mr. This and That said. "Drink more.

I watched him prepare it for you. I kept it safe. I wouldn't do anything to a friend."

"What about someone who isn't a friend?"

"Dylan," Moans said, again.

"Watch," Mr. This and That said, taking the drink from my hand and downing it. He leaned over the table, his suit jacket half covering Alexander's face. I stared the dumb fucker in his empty blue eyes. All he needed was to put a finger on me. He was shorter than me, and he was wasted. The alcohol had turned his limbs into a masterless puppet's arms and legs. The man turned to walk back to the bar, and I stepped forward, past Moans, who was begging me to stop.

"I'm going to leave," Moans said.

"What? Why?"

"Look at yourself. You're deranged. You're unrecognizable. Just stop."

"He's right," Alexander said.

"Stop, stop, stop, stop, stop, stop, stop," Mr. This and That said. "Listen to your loved ones."

"Shut the fuck up," I said.

The bartender stopped shining a highball glass.

"I'm leaving," Moans said quietly. "You're letting a random man consume you."

"Say goodbye to your man," Mr. This and That said.

Moans grabbed his jacket and walked out of the bar. He never once turned around. Mr. This and That kept talking to me, and when I didn't respond he tried to talk to Alexander, all while Moans disappeared, and I didn't want to chase him, but I didn't think it was right of him to go home alone. Even though I wanted to be done with Moans, I was so unsure of what my life would look like without him that I couldn't pull the trigger. Moans was right. I was consumed by a stranger, and I would have broken his jaw over the bar if I could have, simply because he put his hand on Alexander's shoulder when he was crying instead of keeping to himself.

"Let's go," Alexander said.

"You don't want your drinks?" Mr. This and That said.

"Let's depart," Alexander said firmly. "Now."

Mr. This and That waved as we walked out of the bar. I kept turning around, wanting to go back and break his arm. I didn't understand why anybody would act like that, how you could see a bitch suffer and still try to fuck them. That's what he wanted—a broke-down man who might do anything to not feel so bad. I was enraged, barely listening to Alexander over the sound of my own heart. I hated that I couldn't even ask Alexander about the moment when he started to cry. I stopped walking and tried to place myself. I could see the Hudson. A barge sailed toward where I grew up, and I wished I had killed myself when I was a teenager, and when I let the anger awaken me even more, I wished I had killed the other men.

"I'm so angry," I said, tracking the slow boat. "I lost all my language for a minute there. I was so pissed I didn't have a single word."

"At who?"

"The man. The men. My husband. Even you," I said, rubbing my eyes. "We can't just take shit. You can't just take shit. I wish I could go get fucked at the bathhouse. Do you got some fucking crystal? Do you want to watch me get fucking high?"

"What will make you happy?"

"Let's go back," I said.

"Let's go," Alexander said. "I'll follow you."

I took one last look at the water and jumped a small jump, bouncing on my toes, and started to move fast, jogging into a run, checking to see if Alexander still followed. I saw in his eyes the terrible incandescent joy that comes from enforcing an error. We ran back to Julius', where I slammed open the door and panted as the last daylight retreated from the bar. I went in the back and couldn't find Mr. This and That. We went into the bathroom, and there he was, washing his face in the sink. He met my reflection in the mirror and smiled in the same way everyone who had ever threatened me had: the pleasure of knowing I would let them do anything to me. Mr. This and That started to turn around, and I kicked the back of his knee, forcing him down. He hit his head on the edge of the sink and grabbed the porcelain, near graffiti that read FUCK ME PRETTY GOOSE. Alexander pulled my arm to get me out of the bathroom, but I wouldn't let him. I wanted to see his face. I wanted him to see mine.

"Dylan," Alexander begged.

"Is that it?" Mr. This and That asked.

"Dylan," Alexander repeated. "Let's go."

"Get the fuck out of the bar," I whispered to the kneeling man, his face wet and hands shaking. I tapped his shoulder once. "Stand up, look at me in the face, and leave the bar."

Mr. This and That didn't move. The water in the sink still ran, and Alexander again pulled on my arm to get out of the bathroom. I listened to him, and he sat me on a stool at the bar, where he ordered two shots. As if nothing happened, Mr. This and That limped out of the bar. I turned to watch him leave.

"Of what?"

"Whatever you're pouring," I said. "Fuck it."

"Dylan," Alexander said, with a smile I hadn't seen since that first night.

"You want them?" the bartender asked. "On me."

"Yes," Alexander said.

"To rage," I said, and we hit the shots on the wood before throwing them back and moving to a booth.

"What now?"

"It has to start somewhere," I said. "Wait. Where the fuck is James?"

"Did he say?"

I checked my phone.

"*Bitch. Where are you?*"

"Speaking aloud a text. That's intoxication."

I put my phone away.

"Are you that drunk?"

"Are you?"

"Where do you live?"

"Why?"

"You know why," I said. He was beautiful. I was not that drunk, but I had moved beyond the realm of hotness into a night of beauty. That was the downfall. His skin was covered in a film of sweat. His hair was out of place. He looked like he might make the mistake I wanted. "You don't feel it?"

"I feel it."

"So why not?"

"Why not," Alexander said, and he reached across the table to make out. I lay back on the bench and reached up his pants to grab his ass. We made a mess of each other, and we didn't stop. The energy didn't die when I felt his hard dick through his pants. I could hear people entering the bar and the silence of them watching. I didn't stop. Neither did he. The more we kissed the more we wanted. I didn't know how long we lasted. The orange lights strung above us glowed terribly, casting us in a light of another holiday, another season, another time. I blinked and saw time pass for us. I tasted the ending. It was coming soon. We had waited until the last moment to do this, and so I said what I should not have said to him.

"I love you," I said.

"I love you too," Alexander said.

"Let's go."

"Not my place yet," Alexander said. "The West Side Club?"

We kissed again and stood. The bartender said something about the day. I couldn't hear him. I didn't care. Alexander called a car, and we continued to make out, like teenagers, like boys who had never been raped, like men who had once been—you know what I mean. The driver hated us, and that only made us feel better. At the red light at the intersection, we got out and ran, hand in hand, to the club, where the security guard nodded at us as we hurried to the second floor. It was obvious what we wanted. I started undressing as the attendant walked us to the room, where it only took seconds for me to open the pack of lube and coat his dick. I got on my knees and forearms, but Alexander turned me around. He wanted to look in my eyes as he fucked me in that dim room, which was our whole world for a few minutes. I jerked off as he fucked me, cumming when he came inside my ass, and he laid his head on my chest after he was done. The black fan spun above our heads. The DJ played remix after remix of songs that sounded familiar but that I didn't know. Every time I fucked, a new future opened in front of me. Every single time. I had fantasies of being a new person—to be with Alexander, to stay with my husband, to return to crystal meth in the arms of a wrecked father—and I couldn't find another way to stay alive so easily. Just like that. By getting fucked, I saw myself in somebody else's future. I saw myself in the future. There with Alexander, I could see myself completely healed. I could kick an asshole in the knees. I could watch him bleed.

CHAPTER 23

My heart didn't settle as I took a car home. The apartment was bright. I unlocked the door to James and Moans playing cards in the living room. They stopped when they saw me. Neither said hello. I didn't know what I had interrupted. I felt like a stranger.

"What are you playing?" I asked.

"Now you know what I'm talking about. Dylan comes home whenever he feels like it."

"I texted you," James said. "Why didn't you respond?"

"I didn't mean to ignore you."

Moans placed his cards faceup, ending the game. He looked at James, who adjusted his black nightgown. "Sometimes he's early. Sometimes he's late. Or I'm asleep. Or I think maybe he's dead. You know how he is."

"You left. You could have stayed. We could have come home together."

"If I hadn't left, you would have fought that man. I couldn't see it happen. There are unseeable things. I saw you in the psych ward."

"Unseeable things."

"I'm not refereeing," James said.

"Ask him what's so hard about sending a text," Moans said. "I'd like to know the answer."

"Something happened. I got distracted."

"What happened?" James asked.

"He doesn't care."

"I don't," Moans said.

"You don't care?" James said, slowly to Moans, as if double-checking with a child. "Are you sure?"

"Last week we were supposed to go to Vita's for dinner." The dogs finally woke up downstairs and greeted me sleepily before jumping onto Moans' lap. James wagged a finger at them to keep them away. "I'm sure he didn't tell you this. An hour before we were supposed to leave, he tells me he's not in the mood."

"I had a rough day in therapy."

"It's embarrassing. You're in school. You're in therapy. You've got all these things. We are *married*. You got dictionaries. Do you need to look up the word?" Moans hated me. He barely had to open his mouth. The slight parting of his lips released a pent-up speech, even if I had heard it before. "Unless I'm wrong and it means two people who live together and never conversate."

"I'm sorry, Moans." I sat in the chair and lost my anger. "I couldn't go."

"To a dinner party. Where you could sit in a chair and drink. Really, you would not have to chat. Since that's what you do these days."

"You don't get it."

"I get it."

"James," I begged.

"I see both sides," James said, stacking his cards in a neat pile. He fixed his glasses. A few people walked down the hallway and out of the building. "You want more time. And Dylan's going through something."

176

"Everyone goes through things," Moans said, sitting cross-legged on the couch. I could hear his mother in his voice, and I could picture his mother standing over him, when he was a child, in a motel, telling him that people struggled, and he would need to learn to stop crying. There was no way for me to say what I wanted: You must suffer. It is okay to suffer, and it's better to find ways to relieve it. Moans couldn't even see that he was a child again. That the boys we had once been were tugging us in opposite directions. "Everyone."

"Not to the same degree," James said. "What does it matter if he skips a dinner party? He's messy, but if you love each other, what is a night gone missing?"

"Wow," I said.

"You two idiots treat it like a secret that you're both fucked-up. Nobody believes you. Instead of either of you accepting the truth, you run around like you both haven't been beaten to hell. It's crazy! Honestly, it's annoying. I can see it. Look at Dylan. That's a three-legged dog afraid to get pet if I ever saw one. You want to drag that mangy thing to a dinner party?" Now James faced me. "And you. A text isn't that hard. You could have said, 'Hope your talk goes well.' You could have said, 'We're at the bar.' Instead of getting that carried away with some new friend. You could have written to him. *I need more time.*"

"He wouldn't have given it to me."

"I would have," James said. "I would give you whatever you needed."

I held up my palms searchingly. I reached for the sleeping dogs. They didn't come, twitching in their dreams. None of this surprised me, and yet I felt unprepared. I hadn't paid much attention to Moans or James. Everything revolved around what happened back then. This had always been the case, although it was only clear now. When we had first met, I think we believed we had found a place where our childhoods hadn't mattered. Moans seemed to think that if I looked backward, I would leave him. But it was the fact of our youths that brought us together. It wouldn't be what would end us. We had come too far from that period. If we didn't make it, it was because we didn't change. Or couldn't.

"You're smiling?"

"Me?" I said, checking my face. "It was an accident."

"Do you want to be married? To me?"

"I need to go through all this. You have to understand. It's my only shot."

"That sounds like a no."

"Do *you* want to be married?" James asked, and I mouthed *Thank you.*

"Don't put this on me," Moans said, and he walked downstairs. The dogs followed him. He turned on the television to a movie with gunshots and bombs, and I got the gist he had a private fantasy of blowing me to pieces. I heard Voyager crawl from out of the bed and scratch the sheets to be lifted onto the pillows. James and I stared at each other in silence until he walked outside for a cigarette in his slippers.

At the playground, James lit a cigarette.

"I worshiped him," I said.

"You need to stop worshiping men."

"Give me one," I said, holding out my hand.

"Your husband will kill us both."

"I hate that smell." My lungs flapped haltingly, and I let out a great shameful cry. The midnight hour covered my naked feeling of shame. "I'm done with that shit. I'm gonna kill the trigger."

"Is that smart?"

"How will you hide it? Your clothes are going to reek."

"Good idea," I said, and took off my shirt. My skin prickled in the cold night. "Don't look at me like that. I'm keeping my pants on."

"Do you know how to do it?"

"Suck and blow," I said.

James tapped the package and handed me one. I took his lighter and ignited the end. I didn't hold the smoke long, and James told me to breathe it all the way in.

"I saw you," James said.

"What?"

"At the bar."

"When?"

"I saw the way you were kissing him." James studied my home. The wind blew his nightgown. "I thought about taking a picture to show you what it was like."

"Why didn't you come in?"

"And be another third wheel?"

"Honestly, Moans is the third wheel at this point. I was the third wheel to the two of you tonight. Anybody can be the third wheel."

"That's not how it works," James said.

I didn't know what else to say.

We smoked one more and focused on everything novels say about cigarettes: embers, clouds of blue smoke, the scent it leaves between your fingers, the ashing, ashing, ashing until it was gone.

"Welcome to the club," James said. "I have one thing to say about the fight tonight."

"Spare me," I said, putting my shirt back on. Everything but my clothes smelled like smoke. My skin, the night, the whole city. We started back. "I can't believe what you said to him. He was mad."

"Who gives a shit if you want to skip dinner?"

"You think we'll make it?"

James stopped and tapped the pack against his forehead. Through the window, I could see the light of the TV. Our window was broken. The landlord would never fix it. "You're disappearing. You madly doing whatever with Alexander." James reached for my shoulders and brought me to his chest where he squeezed tight. It wasn't a hug. "The fear isn't that you lose Moans. The great fear is that if you don't deal with this, you will kill yourself."

CHAPTER 24

At the start of the session, Matan seemed strange, and it wasn't that he was dressed fuckably in navy and black. He started the session how he always did, by asking how I was doing, and there seemed to be something missing. His face was in wait, the smile and open eyes rising like a wave. I told him that I was fearing the passing window more each day. I had thought at first I would lose it, that my future would fall out of my hands, but now I knew it was changing me, that I would not come out the same, that I didn't want to be the type of person to take a hit anymore, that if it came to it I would be the one to throw a punch.

"What?" I said, after a minute of silence.

"Did you check your email in the waiting room?"

"That's ominous," I said.

"Your husband sent me an email today, and he included the manager of the Center."

"You look pale," I said. "Fucked-up."

"Would you like me to read it?" Matan asked, and I nodded. He reached to his desk for a piece of paper.

"You printed it out?"

"I figured that would be better than reading off my computer."

"Why?"

"I'm not sure," Matan said. "Would it be okay if I started?"

"I had news," I said with my stomach knotted. "Whatever he said, I had news, and Moans knew I had the news too."

"I want to share this with you first because I don't want you to be operating at a knowledge disadvantage. I had no communication with your husband."

"Fucking read it," I said.

"'I am emailing the boss where my husband, Dylan, goes for therapy. He is being treated for PTSD, but he really should be treated for bipolar disorder, borderline personality disorder, major depression. I'm not sure which one, but I know that the treatment for PTSD has not worked, and I think that must mean malpractice. His therapist, Matan, is negligent in his duties as a therapist. Every session he comes home worse. I must say that in all the years I have known him, his mental health has never been worse, and I think if I have to I will take this into my own hands and do what should be done about his therapist.'"

"Wow," I said. "My whole body is tight."

"I didn't respond, and my boss didn't either. We cannot respond to communications with patients' families, but it has put me in a strange position." Matan was talking slowly, deliberately; he seemed afraid. "When a client's family threatens a therapist . . . I thought about contacting the authorities. I had a meeting with my supervisor about this. What do you think the threat level is? If you had to guess?"

"He's so stupid."

"You don't think there's anything to be afraid of?"

"I threatened somebody at Julius'."

"What?" Matan asked, sitting upright suddenly. He put down the paper. "Oh."

"Yeah, bitch. Like, 'Fuck you, bitch.' 'Fuck you, Moans.' This man had put his hands on Alexander, was getting too close, was doing something he shouldn't have done, and I did something about it. Moans saw me get worked up and left. He saw I was becoming somebody who didn't need help."

"Oh."

"I hate that there's always the same view out this window," I said, looking at the slick glass building. "Don't you ever wish you had a different view?"

"It was important that I not sit on this because you are on this chain as well, and I need you to know that I would never do anything without your knowledge." Matan reached for his water. "How does this feel to hear?"

"After we moved in with each other again, at the start of New York, there was this period where I was so happy. All my anxiety had gone. Moans would make me coffee, and I would drink as I wrote or in bed reading or the couch watching TV. I felt amazing." I sat up, uncrossed my ankles, cracked my lower back. "Then he comes in with this little dropper in his hand, and he tells me he's been microdosing me with shrooms for weeks. I was so mad. He had me so fucked-up. And he didn't get it. He was like, 'I cured you. I made you better.' He had read these articles about trauma and shrooms, and he didn't want to try it first, so I was his trauma guinea pig."

"You never told me about this," Matan said.

"I honestly forget about it, but I know that man read some article about trauma and shrooms, secured the vial, and essentially gave me PTSD therapy."

"So the question is why now?"

"No, there is no more *question*. It's a control thing."

"I would agree with that," Matan said. "And you told him about the man?"

"I told him about the man," I said. "You know how much shit I repeat back to a person?"

"What made you do that?"

I told Matan that I had been drunk, and we had been drinking while I had been triggered, and I didn't totally feel like myself as I was doing it. I had the strength of who I wanted to be and none of the fear of who I had been. Time traveling: what I felt like. I smoked one of James' cigarettes. It was Vincent's brand—Camel Crush. I took Alexander's perfectly average cock until he busted. Out of order? Sure. The most important information relayed? The high from the week had me so far in the future. I was living where I am now, renting who I would become.

Matan wanted to know if I had ever done something like this before. Once, after I'd told Vincent that I was going to the police, we swung at each other. I was trying not to get killed, and he was trying to make me think I would die if I betrayed him. He smashed my phone and wrung my neck. I clawed his skin. After that, if a man choked me, I went limp and he lost interest in choking me. If I could go back, I would fight him again and go to the cops. Matan wanted to know if that was true, and the answer was no. My face was why I survived, and I knew he wouldn't beat me badly. People hate when you talked about yourself like that, but my face was always how I survived. I don't care. I did what I needed to do. I fucked who I had to fuck.

"That's change," Matan said.

"Why Moans sent that shit."

"Do you think you'll talk to him?"

"Now that it's about to be over, I think he might chase me for a few days before he hates me forever. He's gonna think this is all bullshit. He has said so many times that he thinks you're the world's worst therapist. He thinks this is like the toy refurbishing factory, where I come in fucked-up and leave in mint condition. He doesn't get the process. I want to be upset." My voice broke unexpectedly. Hearing the sound hurt my feelings. "I want to be angry. I want the sadness. I want to feel human enough to not be locked in a room. I want to feel. I can't do that without messiness. It's changing the way I think." I closed my eyes. "I'm gonna be sick."

"The door is unlocked," Matan said.

I checked the door.

"You can leave."

"I can leave."

"Do you want to go?"

"Fuck yes," I said, and Matan opened the door, as he said he would if I ever wanted to leave early. Nobody was trapping me in that room. I left of my own free will (with a years-long reminder from Matan). It seems so ridiculous now, after the lookback window has closed, that I had been so terrorized that I couldn't leave a room on my own, but I left the room, and soon after that I left Moans, and soon after that I almost left the world. I needed to test what freedom meant. I was still me, after all.

CHAPTER 25

I picked up bagels and coffee on the way home. The dogs barked as I neared the front door. Our neighbors definitely hated them. The apartment smelled like weed, and the shades were drawn. I heard Moans playing video games, still half-tucked into bed. "Grab your bowl and let's walk."

"Okay," Moans said, barely paying attention, as he paused the game, slipped into his sneakers, and followed me to Herbert Von King Park.

A man ran up and down the concrete outdoor auditorium pews, huffing and commanding himself to keep going. The dog park loudly interrupted us as we sat at an empty chess table. Moans took out his bowl and breathed in a hit. I put the brown paper bag in front of him. We didn't eat, and I didn't yell at him.

"Do you want to stay married?" Moans asked.

"Yes and no."

"That's not a good answer."

"What's yours?"

"You know how much it means to me."

"That's not an answer."

"I want to stay married and go to counseling and I want you to spend time with me." Moans went to take another hit but a police officer walked through the park. He hid the bowl in his pocket. "And I need you to be happy."

"I have made you miserable," I said, folding my arms on the table.

A cyclist blasting a radio passed us, and Moans lay his forehead on my arms. "I don't understand how you changed so quickly."

"I haven't changed that much."

"You did. Who is this person? What happened? Remember when you made me promise to never do drugs? When we were first together? You said you didn't like the taste of liquor?"

"I was nineteen. You know what I was trying to avoid remembering. Encountering." I lifted his chin and kissed his cheek, and he kissed me on the lips. "I have a confession."

"You're not that sneaky. I know about the cigs."

"You want one?"

Moans nodded, and I placed one between his lips. They weren't Vincent's brand. Marlboro Menthol Lights, close, but my own. We split it. He took a pull, I took the next. Moans reminded me of all the stupid promises I had made him when we first got together. No cigs. No drugs. Total honesty. We had even made a contract and signed it: THE RULES OF LOVE. I had even saved a dried rose from our first month together, all blue and old and nostalgic. He had bought me flowers, and I told him that I didn't like getting that gift. In secret, he dried them and made them indestructible. I was young and unable to care for fragile things. The dried-up flower was one of the great gifts of my life.

"Did I ever get you something that good?"

"A family," Moans said. "I always wanted that. Ever since I was a fat little boy on the islands."

"I have something I want from you," I said. "One last thing."

"Anything."

"I want you to come with me to the bathhouse. See the world I'm leaving behind."

"I have seen other bad things," Moans said.

"I wish I remembered all your birthdays and I really wish I could tell you everything that happened to me, Moans, but I have done what I can do with the love we have."

"Are you ready?"

"I'm ready," I said, and we returned home.

All night we lay in bed together, and Moans held me. I fell asleep on his chest. The dogs curled around our ankles. I was sorry that we were reaching the end. I woke with my arms around him, but I hadn't dreamt that we could start anew. We were a dream I had when I was younger. We were a dissolved future. What luck I had for Moans to pull me away from such a wrecked place. He guided me here to this chance at life. I hoped he felt the same.

CHAPTER 26

Worst-case scenarios: You're born into poverty or given up, you're never adopted or your parents beat you, your mother gives you up to live with your abusive father or you find a pedophile who rapes you, nobody cares either way what happens to you (this never changed for us), and your marriage fails. You love a man because of what happened to him, but he was too young to know who he would become. You're so traumatized from what happened to you that you can't handle more pain. Your husband gives you more pain, and you do the same in turn. You will have to start over, again and again, your entire life, no matter what happens. You will have been through worse, you will remember worse, and worst of all, you will never be able to erase the pain of what happened although you will be able to move beyond it, if you are smart enough to realize the difference between what will hurt you and what you are afraid of. That's what I told Moans when I persuaded him to come with me to a bathhouse. I needed him to know the person he was leaving behind. He listened silently, and then he agreed to the West Side Club.

He picked me up and drove us to Chelsea. We waited in a brief line to get two rooms. You can't share a room, so we had to get both. I paid, and Moans nervously followed me through the dark and busy halls. I dropped him off at his room, told him to get undressed if he wanted, and to wrap a towel around his waist. He didn't have to leave the room. Moans texted me to ask if I was okay, and he said he was going to walk around, and when I returned to my room I could see the changing lights of his phone in his room. I undressed and left my phone under the bed, locked the door, and showered off. A Hasidic man with a small dick let water flow over him, and another with a piercing leaned into the showers to see who was there. When I didn't make eye contact he left me alone, and I went into the sauna.

The tiered white-tiled seating was foggy, and the steam obscured a small TV playing vintage porn. Alone I sat in that very hot room.

What rules and regulations existed on the walls seemed silly: *Maximum Occupancy*. I only ever saw that phrase in a bathhouse. The sign warned to avoid the sauna if you were ill with a stomach virus. In the video game I was playing at home, fellow bandits fell ill with dysentery. I had looked up the etymology of the word. It was made famous by Hippocrates of ancient Greece—you know, the Hippocratic oath, the great lie of doctors. He lived around the time of Alexander the Great, who ate shit at thirty and died after binge drinking poisoned wine. The great father of modern medicine couldn't keep a down-low conqueror from a faggot's death. There were more brutal ways to die, but few were as embarrassing.

My father used to tell two death stories before I went to sleep as a child, all from his Jersey beach rat youth. One of them occured on a summer evening, his mother had heard scratching in the air ducts connected to the stove hood. The family put down their hot dogs to listen to the intruder. His mother stood up from the table and leaned over the stove, peering through the aluminum slits to investigate the racket. A squirrel had found its way into the ducts and seemed unable to escape. It was trying to climb into the kitchen, its little paws reaching uselessly through the slats. His mother didn't know what to do. She tapped the hood with a wooden spoon. My father and his sister screamed at the squirrel to go home. His own father wasn't home. She realized she could turn on the fan to gently blow air against the squirrel, urging it outside. My father expected to see the creature transported in the wind, like the house in *The Wizard of Oz*. She pressed the switch for the fan, which whirred peacefully into a terrible thumping ruckus. Caught first in the blades, the tail discarded tufts of fur, followed by a little arm, bones, skin, and guts.

In the sauna, I laughed at the memory of that story, and I didn't know if it was true. My father told the story as if the three of them danced beneath a shower of blood, screaming like lunatics. This didn't seem like my father, a warm and guilty man who was angry at his own father. More likely, it was probably a story he himself had told to his own absent, angry father once his father had returned from work. Like: *Dad, you won't believe what happened today!* My father never recovered from how his father had treated him, and this rejection carried over to my youth, when my father and I used to argue. This happened right before the Vincent era. The last night my father threw my skateboard against a condemned tree in the yard, and I picked up the broken halves in the purple dusk of summer with fireflies rising from the grass. My parents didn't come outside. They quietly asked me to return. After that final fight, my father enrolled in therapy, started medication, and changed. Now, as an adult, I could see it was an extraordinary rehabilitation, but it had also placed a burden on him not to intervene. I had to stop remembering. I was in a bathhouse, and nothing made you feel more like a pervert than seeing an old man's ugly cock and thinking *Daddy!*

Moans entered the sauna in a fog with a goofy smile. Moans had beautiful wide lips that lifted into his cheekbones and displayed all those straight white teeth. He stood like a victor. I was going to miss him.

"I might leave soon," Moans said.

"I understand."

"I'm going back to the room, and I'll find you if I decide to go. This feels too bad."

"I know," I said, and Moans walked away.

The porn ended, and a new video began in a farmhouse. A boy lay back on bales of hay. I heard footsteps, the shower turned on, and my hair stood on end. The steam thickened and felt drugged, like how it sometimes happened in therapy. A man entered the sauna, and he sat beside me. He parted his legs, ran his hand up to his neck, and I saw the chain. A taste of tequila coated the back of my throat. I rubbed my own arms and swallowed. Thirteen years had passed since I last saw that cross swinging above my neck. He'd grown fatter. Time had ruined him kindly, allowing his hideousness to remain unchanged. I could feel the cold cross on my back, and I could smell him still. He undid the white towel and let his dick hang out. My heart slammed, pulling tides of blood, expanding and receding within my limbs.

I felt too human.

He didn't recognize me. After seeing Russ at his house, I thought I was ready now to see the others, even if I had long been afraid of this moment.

"Hey," I said.

"Hello," he said. He narrowed his small pinched dark brown eyes and scratched his twice-broken nose. His lips I could hardly bring myself to look at, not when the taste of tequila was building in my throat. His hairline had receded further. He contained a sense of rot and illness. I wanted to rip his hair out by the roots.

"I think I know you. From some time ago," I said. I could not frighten him. This was a gift, fate doing its best work, why I threw dollar bills into the wind on the street. "You used to live in Yonkers?"

"Yes," he said, smiling, which mirrored the three wrinkles in his neck. "Still a Yonkers boy."

"I thought it was you. A barber?"

"Did I cut your hair?"

"Yes, but I looked very different back then."

"I cut a lot of hair." He pointed at my head. "I take it you don't get haircuts no more."

"I get the buzz at Astor now," I said. "You know how it goes."

"Still kept all my own." He messed with his hair and knocked twice on the tiles. "Lucky genes."

"I can tell. I think I remember your old screen name, too."

"Oh," he said, turning toward me. "Yeah?"

"Hung Fleetwood?"

"Goddamn," he said, squeezing my shoulder.

"You came over to this guy's house with a bottle of Jose Cuervo."

"The quickest liquor, tried and true. Did we?"

"Did we what?" I smiled. "You tell me."

"Oh boy, you're gonna get this thing hard again."

"Do you remember the house?"

"I'm getting overheated, man," he said, looking at the exit. He placed his hand on the tiles as if he were going to lift himself up. I placed my foot on top of his and pressed down. I felt the bones in his foot, and I started to get hard. He looked down. I ripped the towel off his thigh and covered myself. He grimaced, but he stayed seated. I grabbed his wrist and took a deep breath then let go of him. His hands dropped to his sides.

"Dylan?" Moans asked, walking into the steam. I heard his voice, and I saw him, but I couldn't do anything other than look at Moans as if I had never seen him in this life. Moans watched me press my foot on this man, and for all he knew I was trying to fuck him. Moans glowered at the guy, and then he left. After his footsteps faded, I slammed my foot again on top of the man's. If Moans was leaving, let him hear the rapist yell.

"You don't recognize me, but you will remember me."

"I don't know who you are."

"No, you don't, but you will."

"I'm with a friend."

"I don't care," I said. "We're alone right now."

"You got me mixed up with somebody else."

"I remember your face. And your screen name. And your chain. And your little dick. And your tiny little teeth. And you know I remember, otherwise you'd have thrown me off right now, but you don't want me to tell anybody. You don't want me to tell the attendants that there is a pedophile here. You don't want the other men to know what you did." I pressed down on his foot even harder and felt his nails cut into my flesh. "You came to Vincent's house. You paid him money to shave my entire body and have me fucked-up for when you came." The rapist met my eyes, and he seemed empty. "What did you do then?"

"I don't remember," he said.

"Do you remember what you called me?"

"You're wrong."

"Your 'boy,'" I said. "I was your 'boy.'"

"It's just a word."

"And what did you like to do?"

"I don't party no more."

"But you partied back then. Then you spit the tequila into my mouth."

"It brings you back down."

"And knocks you out."

"I really don't know."

"Tell the truth and I'll let you go."

"What do you want to know?"

"How much I cost."

"It was ages ago."

"Not for me. I think about it all the time. The world thinks about it for me. The year is asking me how much I am worth. The window wants to put another price on me, and I can't fucking do it. So I want to hear it from your mouth. I want you to tell me why I can't get what I need. Tell me what I cost."

The rapist looked down at his foot, massaging his calves, and greeted me dead in the eye. "An all-nighter was two hundo and a bottle. The crystal was mine."

"Thank you," I said, crushing my heel as hard as I could into his toes. He grunted. I didn't care. "I'm going to find you again. But it won't be me. It'll be the police. They'll arrest you and you'll see me for the first time with my clothes on in court. I'll make sure you go to prison."

"You're hurting me," he said, and I slammed my heel down again.

I leaned into his ear and told him my name.

"Say it," I said, and I felt his nails cutting into my heel. I only pressed harder. What was a little blood for the truth? "Say my fucking name. Dylan. I want you to know who you should be afraid of."

"Dylan," the rapist said. "I'm sorry."

I let go of him, took the pressure off, and he cradled his foot. I threw the towel at him and walked back to his room. I knocked on Moans' door, naked, and when I opened it he was lacing his shoes. Moans could barely look at me, and when he did he expressed such a solemn acceptance of loss that I knew he didn't understand. This faded quickly. Moans only ever allowed himself the smallest lot of sadness because I don't think he wanted to get over what happened to him. If he ever actually let himself get sad, we never would have fallen so far from each other.

"That was one of the men," I said.

"I don't give a shit."

"Moans, I wasn't fucking him."

"Cool."

"Moans, listen to me. That was one of the men who raped me as a kid."

Moans pressed his fists into his cheeks and started shaking his head. He turned to the wall as if he could see through to the steam room then looked down at my feet. He pointed at the blood and grabbed the little garbage, as if he were going to puke, and then tossed it at the wall.

"I want to kill him but I can't move."

"I know," I said, "but I think I scared him."

"Did you scream? Was that him who screamed?"

"I hurt him."

"Why can't I move? I want to break his jaw. I can hardly feel my legs. Dylan."

"I understand."

"I don't know what else to do."

"Welcome to my world," I said, and he went to hug me, but I recoiled. I had a moment of unexpected fear, but I wanted to be comforted, so I reached for him. I dressed and we walked out into the street, where the light no longer warmed us. As Moans walked, he kept turning around to look behind us, but the guy wasn't there. He wasn't paranoid, only checking to see what was real. The closer we got to home, Moans kept saying he couldn't believe it. Moans asked if I wanted to enjoy a movie. I needed to be alone. Moans asked about dinner, if I really didn't want a little company. We fought in the car, taking turns screaming. I couldn't give Moans my time tonight, and he couldn't comfort me. I stared out the window at the West Side Highway, which eventually turned into another highway named after another forgotten figure, and we passed an island with a building that looked, for all my references, like an incinerator. I expected Moans to drop me there, and I thought I'd affix my lips to the gas pipe. When we got home, Moans started to pack his belongings. I wasn't surprised. I knew what it felt like to be so alone that you had to run away. He packed for eight hours. He took only his valuables, clothes, and the dogs to a hotel, leaving the boxes in his car.

That night, I took a sleeping pill and walked to the bodega in the rain to get a drink that I chugged on the wet street. People walked by me. By the time I started crying, I had nothing left to drink. I decided to live many years ago.

I soaked my heel in the bathtub. The cuts of my cruelty refused to last long enough to remind me of the real mission. One day soon, I would find a way to get Russ to admit everything he had ever done to me. I would do what I couldn't do on his porch. I would risk his rough hands on my neck and my own reaching for the lighter to ignite against his eyes. Because Russ knew what Vincent did, and if I could get Russ to admit to getting me through Vincent then I would have a chance at finally getting what I wanted. Not justice. Vengeance.

I wouldn't have the blood to guide me. I wanted to have a reason, a reminder, proof—I searched through my old Hotmail and found an email I'd sent to Vincent. It was so pathetic I wanted to drown, but it would work:

> *im not insane, im just confused. you did things that are too much for me, and i used to be a brave person but you ruined me which is a chance with any boyfriend. you always said that you werent good enough for me and i still think thats not true. i think that you are a cheater, and a liar, and you get mad when you mean to be sorry. you say i havent had to give anything up but i have. i had to give up my life. and im sorry but vincent, you never should have done to me what you did. i am not going to tell the cops on you unless you are ever mean to me again if i decide to live past tmrw.*

CRIMSON & CLOVER

CHAPTER 27

The Rosemont had no signage, leather couches, a long line for the bathroom, and a mirrored dance hall that led to a patio, and the ability to bring a man to your lips who could make you forget the past for a couple hours. What started as Wednesday nights, occasionally with Alexander, mostly with anyone, turned into whatever night was possible. Yes, I started fights. Occasionally with people from grad school, who offensively believed one of our nights possibly contained transcendence. I informed them that barely one writer in history had rendered a bar scene worth reading. They rendered dance scenes that read like they had danced exactly once and used the word *neon* as if neon were beautiful and symbolic. When I ranted, they thought I was joking, doing a bit, but beauty was not symbolic. Beauty kneecapped the delusion of existence—the accidental collision of the shortness of your own life and the endurance of the world—with a limited reach but nearly inexhaustible supply. I suspected these people believed that if they could create beauty somebody might love them. If you could not understand the consequences and seriousness of beauty, you should have no control of any world, real or imagined. Beauty demanded care and received destruction. If neon was beautiful it would have been assaulted and carried out of every bar on the backs of people willing to sacrifice their lives

for the chance to touch brilliance. Instead, neon winked lascivi-
ously on a wall, barely capable of crucifying the flies.

During the hangovers, I got up in the afternoon to smoke,
doubled over in pain, disgusted by how much time had passed
since those blissful early days with Moans in San Diego. I tortured
myself with longing. James advised me to take five ibuprofen and
jerk off. All I could see were the barber's eyes. To soothe myself, I
searched for guys who wanted to come over, never sending them
my address, but bringing the conversation as far as they could go.
I told them the subway stop. The intersection. Everything but
the number of my apartment. I wondered what would happen if
Moans came knocking on the door and saw the men fucking me.
I knew he had a room in an apartment in Park Slope. Two weeks
of silence since the day he left.

Visions filled the void.

Russ spiking my lungs with crystal.

Vincent lining me up for a picture.

The Barber drenched in tequila.

At night, when I closed my eyes to sleep, I felt the Barber's
fingers slide down my throat, his dick hanging off his body like a
hunting trophy. Sometimes he would be so drunk and high that
I couldn't bring any of him to life, so Vincent would get me high
and fuck me in front of him. Every time Vincent would thrust
into my ass, my lips touched the Barber's limp cock. He'd rattle it
at my mouth, or slap it against my cheeks, like the world's worst
balloon animal. This wasn't the life I had wanted to live, but it
was the life I got. Vincent would eventually leave us. The Barber
owned me for the night. He would try to pull me open and stuff
his flesh inside me, cutting my insides with his nails, and he'd tell
me not to move as I straddled him on the couch, my arms over

his shoulders, his mouth at my neck. When I gasped, I got him hard. He pushed my chest back and kneed me to the floor, my head next to the glass coffee table. He put his weight on top of me, the chain against my cheek as he rocked his hips, his breath rotting near my ear. The blank television caught some streetlight from the window. The rug scratched my cheek with dog hair. I could feel that he was going to cum. Then I'd be done. He had a hand on each elbow, his knees between mine. He was not strong. He whispered, *Jack, you're not sixteen. Jack, how old are you? Jack, are you fifteen? Are you fourteen? Have you ever been raped?*

He came inside me and it dribbled out. Hours had passed of my own failures to get him off. Hard work. If only I had distracted him, drunk his liquor so he would have had less, I could have ended it earlier. He told me to clean off his dick with my mouth, and I did, and then he passed out on the couch long enough for me to shower, all while Vincent slept soundly in the other room. The man told me to lie beside him. I would corpse myself in his arms.

Days passed like this. Visions over visions. The decade between then and now like nothing at all. I skipped class. I ignored James. I finally texted Alexander that I couldn't be alone.

I waited on the steps of the public library in the West Village for Alexander. Alexander approached unevenly, zagging across the sidewalk, fiddling with a wide gray scarf. It wasn't that cold for a November night, and Alexander had the strange look of preparing himself for worse weather, for what hadn't yet come but would surely arrive soon. He had pointed leather shoes that had recently been shined. When he stopped in front of me he said, "I have had more than one drink, but I have fostered an elite tolerance to vodka." He offered me his hand to pull me up, then stared at the space next to me and sat beside me. Alexander dusted a leaf off his shoe. "I ran out of time. I was going to get you flowers." He handed me two bottles of airplane-sized vodka. "Instead, I have these."

"This isn't a date," I said, and I downed them.

"White lilies. The funeral kind. You aren't bringing good news."

"Are you cool?"

"Says the guy with neck tattoos."

"Are you good? Are you going to be sick?"

"I'm great."

I didn't want to drag him across the city like this. His face was flushed, his hair falling into bangs, and his hands were red. He saw me look at him and smiled with big teeth. Alexander reached under his collar and retrieved a cross necklace and kissed it before he started to laugh and let it hang in front of his sweater, relieved to show the pendant, and rested his head briefly on my shoulder before he lay back on the steps and placed his hands behind his head.

"I missed you," I said.

"That's very sweet of you to say." He was looking at the sky. "Do you mean it?"

"Yes and no."

"I have been feeling sick after hanging, like I would have gotten in trouble, or that I had misstepped, and I am not a person who does wrong. I feel like I don't have advice, and I cannot advise you to not hurt yourself. My advice is do what you must, but I see now that is hurting you. I realize you have to do what you have to, but I don't want to be the one to agree that you should be hurting."

"Are you cold?" I asked. He was shivering.

"I have a jacket."

"No, you don't."

"I must have left it at the bar."

"Want to go get it?"

"Perhaps," Alexander said. "Let's hear what I've been summoned for."

"We can do this another time."

"I'm happy you texted. I've been thinking. I don't think I want to see the priest." Alexander raised his chin. "The stars are out in Manhattan tonight. Can I say something crass? I hope he kills himself. I think about it a lot, that our firm gets news that the man has hanged himself. It's always hanging, too. I cannot picture another method. Maybe it's because one of the clients hanged himself, and I think he deserves the same fate." Alexander laughed hopelessly and stood up. He slipped his hands into his pockets and swayed. He seemed as if he wanted permission to continue to speak, and I nodded so he would continue. "I have looked at the suffering of others at some distance for a good portion of my life, and this fucked-up law has twisted my mind. When the client killed himself, I thought, maybe the church will understand and give up fighting the case, but it didn't." Alexander was speaking while shaking his head slowly, his lips staying parted between sentences. "I have thought maybe I should hang myself in the office or the church or the court. Truthfully, I have thought about shooting him in the middle of the courtroom. One of the clients was informed that he could pursue a criminal case against the priest, too, since he was *forcibly raped*. That's the term, and it's a frightening idea because there was very little force involved in what this man did to me. So my only recourse would be a civil case. I thought, How *lucky* you were to have been hurt like that."

"I need my evidence, too. I'm sorry."

"There's also no statute of limitations on *forcible rape,* by the way. Some lucky boys got it harder than others and not only have the chance at reparations, but to put their priests in prison, where they won't last a month." Alexander faced the street. "All my life I have been a kind man. Seeing all these cases has changed me."

"I crushed the man's foot," I said. "I stepped on him so fucking hard his nails cut into my skin. I literally bled over him."

"Did it help?"

"I don't know yet." I stood beside Alexander and watched the French restaurant across the street. The outside seating area had vines covering a trellis. The black silhouettes of waiters lingered to pour wine, bending over slightly, with one hand bent behind their backs. I turned to Alexander and said, "I didn't think I had the chance."

"If you did?"

"Do you want the truth? If I could have punched the man in the face I would have. I don't know if I'm that type of person and that's what stopped me, or if it was that we were in public and I was ashamed, or if it was that we were both naked and I didn't have the guts, but I went home and stared at my foot all night. You read my file, Alexander. Tell me."

"Do you hate yourself for leaving out the stuff that would have sent him to jail? When you went to the police?"

"What do you mean?"

"You could still have a case, if you go back and tell them that you left out certain details. The child porn, for one. They won't blame you. And if you have evidence, they will have to do something. They want guys like that in jail, for better or worse. Lucky you, too. Lucky everyone. I hate myself for not joining the suit."

"Fuck," I said, falling into a crouch. "Fuck!"

"Fuck indeed."

"I don't have the evidence. That shit was taken of me. From me. That's on some fucking sicko's computer. That shit is gone."

"You're screaming."

"I'm not."

"Look across the street," Alexander said. "They're watching."

The people at the restaurant across the street had eyes on me. Alexander flicked his hand for me to follow him. He blew into his hands to warm them and said, "Let's go get my jacket."

"I don't know what to do."

"I have another confession," Alexander said. "If you can kick a man to his knees, if you can crush a man's foot and threaten him, you can find a way to get what you need. The confession? You are almost there, and I believe in you."

"I don't think anyone has ever said that to me."

"You terrify me, too."

"That I have heard."

"For different reasons."

"I don't think that's true."

"You haven't betrayed me. You have never scared me. You terrify me because I would love to do what you have done, but I never will, and I'm jealous of the consequences of your actions already. Let's go."

I followed him silently across the dark green streets of the West Village, hardly able to look above the ground. Every so often we would pass a woman walking her dog or a fluorescent smoke shop and I would feel my chest burn. This was not what I wanted to spend my life doing. To storm out of my home and hate every stranger. To commiserate with another broken man. To have a price set on my past. Alexander turned around to check if I was still following, and he pointed at a bar on the corner. He went inside and grabbed his coat and then took my hand and pulled me into a run down the block, his coat flailing behind him, until we were in the dark under an overhang. Alexander placed one hand on my shoulder and the other on my back and we kissed against the brick wall. I could feel his cold nose against my cheek. I slipped my hand under his belt and grabbed his body. We took a second to breathe and took off again down the street, running for blocks until we arrived at an apartment entrance. He took out his keys and let me inside. We walked up a flight of steps to a studio in the Village where all the lights were out. He threw his coat on the couch and didn't turn on a single light. We made out on the way to his bed. I toed off my shoes and he pried his feet out of his. I took off my shirt and he tossed his sweater to the floor. He sucked my neck, and I undid his belt and took off his pants. With his ankles on my shoulders, I removed his briefs and pushed back his thighs to eat his ass. I got naked and he squirted lube into his hand that he rubbed over my dick. I entered him slowly until I was fully inside and fucked him with the backs of his knees against my elbows, kissing him as he placed one hand on my neck and the other on my ass. His necklace jingled with every thrust into him. I turned him over and fucked him with his face under his pillows and my chin on his neck. He grunted and pushed his ass against my dick, leveraging himself onto his knees, as I grabbed his shoulders and slammed into him. I came inside him as a single line of light from between the curtains fell across his face. Our foreheads touched as he busted. We kissed a few times and I rolled beside him. We breathed next to each other for a minute. Alexander pulled the curtains shut and when the room was completely dark a night-light turned on.

Days later, I was in Matan's office, recounting what happened. His sleeves were pushed up, exposing his thick wrists and the large hands he held so delicately. I never saw him leave a fingerprint on anything. I never heard him type. I didn't think of him as graceful—just skilled at tracelessness, gentility, civilization. I wanted to see the bitch fight or even just wring the neck of the mason jar he used as a water glass. Instead, he barely touched it, sliding two fingers over the ridged top and lifting it to his mouth without any effort. The glass settled silently.

"I could have averted all of this," I said with disgust. "If I had not been so afraid."

"Could you have truly?" Matan asked. "You're the one who said you have changed."

"I'll save you some time here. I am angry at myself. At the dumb bastard in the hot seat."

"Do—"

"Hold on, I can take this to the end, too. I should offer my younger self compassion. Okay. Young Dylan couldn't use all the right words. He was afraid of the officer. He couldn't bring himself to tell everything. He did as much as he could. Be gentle with him. *Good boy, good job, Young Dylan.* And yes, I'm here now, so not everything was lost, but time was wasted. And as someone who has wasted a lot of time, you start to realize it's not a great feeling to look back and see how long this all took."

"Let's do an experiment. What if you didn't waste time?"

"Then time doesn't feel that great."

"What if it doesn't?"

"I can use my Matan voice. Everything I did got me here."

"You've already begun to change, but none of this matters without belief."

"Convert me, then."

"Let's say it was impossible for you to understand what happened as it was happening, and the years following weren't about understanding but about escape and survival. You escaped. You survived. You used the skills you learned and your instincts to move you through a life you didn't understand. Maybe you weren't able to get what you needed from the police, but I would say you probably didn't know what you needed then. It's probably why you weren't able to tell them everything. Is it possible that your instincts led you to this moment, where you know what you want, and now, after a long, painful time, you might be able to get it?"

"It took me a while to get there, if that's the case."

"And what if that's the case?"

"Well, that's obviously the case." I stared at him. "I don't want to live like this forever. Some days I feel like I have no control over my life at all. You know how unfair that is?"

"It's unfair. It's, to put it as you would, fucked-up." Matan took a deep breath, resettled his hands. "There is science behind all of this. Think about that. There is a way to manage this and lessen everything you're feeling. Every week you come in and you work hard. I will say that it might get harder before it gets better because now you are starting to feel it, recognize it, see how what happened infected your everyday life. That's terrible. I wish I could take it all away."

"I wish there were a pill I could take to make this better."

Matan smiled and waited for me to say more, but I didn't. I looked around the small room. I thought about mentioning Alexander, but I didn't need his help understanding that I didn't want to see him again.

"What are your plans for the weekend? Who are you seeing? Are you going to be alone? Do you think it would be a good idea to let a couple people keep you company?"

"Of course," I said, and left the building. The window, too, I felt I was leaving. I did not need it, and that made every second just the more painful. This was not a year of my life that would end. This was the extension of everything that had already come before it. I doubted I could wait a week to get what evidence I needed. I could only blame myself for lateness now. And knowing that, I started to feel absent. The late November sky was blue, and the light was pale, and a wind drew across the city, taking me closer and closer to where I wanted to go: The Rosemont. I danced. I did a bit of coke. I had a bathroom fuck. I was not alone until the end of the night, when I settled beneath the blankets and tried to imagine a normal life. This was not my world—this was only another place to which I'd escaped. It didn't matter that the man didn't recognize my face. I had a buzz cut and grew a beard. I was the costume that contained the secret. Time meant nothing. I woke up another day. Still waiting for the set designers to part the curtains on this divorced apartment and reveal the one true stage of my life: a locked room in Vincent's house. I waited for the chorus of men who had blown me apart to clap and whistle, saying, *ENCORE. ENCORE. ENCORE.*

CHAPTER 28

I tried to prepare myself to visit Russ. Getting Russ to confess meant touching the world of Vincent—the world of fire and crystal and blood. Even though Vincent no longer lived in New York, I believed in my ability to force his return. I didn't know how to be near it without being consumed. In my idle daydreams I encountered a feeling of fearing truth and avoiding destiny. You will go there, and you must go there soon, or the life you have wanted to live will cease to exist. The pressure toppled all private moments of calm. Every step signaled moving closer or falling back. The bodega was closer, the park was farther. The L was closer, the G was farther, and it didn't even connect to Manhattan, which provided extra safety. Therapy was farther south, but it was easier to go to where I had grown up from there. James kept telling me to take my time, and I knew he didn't understand, even as he said he would come visit. I had just broken up with my husband, and I was living alone for the first time in a decade. But I only had three more stipend checks coming while I lived at this address, where Moans agreed to split the rent until the end of December. After that, I had a month between checks, and I really should have been saving to prepare for my loneliness, made worse by the fact that I hadn't been speaking to Alexander. We had a friendship forged from loneliness, and now that ours no longer overlapped, what had made us friends now separated us.

My sheer window curtains became silver screens, where the shadows of people walking on the street were apparitions of youth. I shut off the television. Sleep would not come. I opened my computer and decided to find somebody to keep me company in the dark. A man named Rian offered to get me high. He announced, without cue, that he was full-blooded and first-generation Irish. I invited him over and trembled while I cleaned out. Better to invite the right man over and control the future than leave it up to chance. I couldn't rid my body of the old instinct for tremors, but I pushed through the routine. Fill the enema with water, empty my ass, repeat until the water comes out clear. My body went cold, and I brought back some warmth to it in the shower. I used the downstairs TV for ambient light and played white noise by the front door. Rian would arrive soon, and I threw on some ripped jeans. In the yellow hallway, with my face to the glass, I watched the cars drive down my street. Rian parked across the street and bounced toward me, his backpack slung over his shoulder. He had thin brown hair, brown eyes, and a natural friendliness. I let him inside, and we walked downstairs, passing the windows, when Rian said, "Mind if I?," as he used dusty books to push the curtains to the walls. Rian sat on the edge of the bed, unlaced his boots, and pulled them off with a grunt. He folded his shirt over the chair in front of my desk, chuckling over a note I pinned to the board: EVERYTHING IS EXILE.

"You look better than your pictures," Rian said. "You're not frigid. The pictures seemed a little cold."

"Want to make a bet?"

"What about me?" Rian said, smiling as if for a school portrait.

He had a decaying handsomeness. You got the sense that each time you saw him, you'd want to remember him from his last appearance. He answered another question that I didn't ask, gesturing at his hunched shoulders. "Landscaping. The outdoor life. You'd never know how much work goes into some tiny little flowers."

"I'm not so good with plants."

"No need to announce such a thing when each one you have is dying." Rian chuckled at a money tree wilting over the stairwell. "If the truth is what'll be told here tonight . . . What do I do? All terraforming. Our land doesn't support much besides the ideas of future high-rises. It makes me sick. I turn decrepit and dying sections of the city into brand-new places for life. You hear that? The big L? Life. So I've got a minor God complex? We all could use a bit. In the old country, they had a thousand gods. Not a jack-of-all-trades. I know who I'm going to for advice." He was roaming around my room, picking up books and cups, trinkets that he promptly set down. "Sometimes I cruise the revived parks. All men wander off the path to the darkness I myself set into the landscape. Luckless one night, I was down, suicidal in my own creation, until some bushes rustled. I thought it was another man. I unlatched my belt to signal—*ding*—but it scared a fox that darted off, and I nearly tripped chasing the thing trying to get a look at what had returned to some nature I myself had restored. That's when I knew what I'd been doing with my time." He took a giant breath. "You got porn on that thing?"

"A fox?"

"Porno," he said.

I handed him the clicker. He browsed the internet and picked a scene. We sat side by side on the bed, watching the opening of a

California adventure. Two men rode the gondola down from the icy mountains to the Palm Springs basin.

"I've been lost in that desert," I said.

"What was it like, Mr. Mystery?"

"Hot."

Rian lifted his backpack onto the bed and retrieved a pipe, a halved plastic straw, a little sparkling bag, and a torch lighter. He plugged the straw with one finger and poured the crystals into the straw, which he then upended into the bulb of the pipe. The crystals didn't reflect the light; they swallowed it. Rian asked me to hold the pipe while he packed the rest up in its case, grabbed a paper towel, and ran it under the water in the bathroom. He set the towel down on the desk. I got absolutely hard holding that pipe like a bomb. I gazed at a power unknown to me. My life? That rickety old thing? It was only what precipitated this very moment, where I would torch crystals. I held the pipe an inch from my lips, while Rian pulled the trigger, shooting a flame that caressed the pipe as the drugs slowly melted into an amber liquid, the bottom of the glass browning. The pipe filled with dense white smoke. Gently, Rian pinched the tube and pushed it against my lips.

"Slow slips," Rian said, his cheek pressed to mine, "to let the pipe refill and not burn out the goods." I did as he said. "Keep going. Keep going. Keep going." His gentle lips parted, staring at the pipe, the lighter blazing evenly, and his eyes flicked over to mine. "One more and blow it into my mouth."

I shotgunned Rian, who inhaled and exhaled a column of smoke, opaque and long and effortless, as if life had turned his intestines to ash and all he was doing was letting it out.

"You're blowing real clouds."

Rian rocked the pipe to prevent the liquid from hardening. He leaned over my cock and blew the smoke over it. What a baptism. The high obliterated everything. Even that moment had fallen from my hands, and I was in the next second, and that too fell behind me. Rian scooted up, his dick growing hard against my ass, and I pulled the trigger, aiming right below the glass. I carried the smoke and locked my lips with his, taking us all the way to where we needed to go. A great laziness overcame my body with a swift steady beating of my weird heart. Rian kissed me and placed me on my back, spreading my knees so he could suck my dick. He fucked my throat. Sweat dripped off us, pooling on the bedsheets. Rian flipped me on my knees, my head in my arms, as he ate me out until I was wet enough. He reminded me of an exceptional life-altering pleasure, occasionally disrupted by a painless torrent of an ecstatic inner rain. Rian came inside me. He could have cum a hundred times and I'd never know. I was only riding a feeling to the end. I knew this sensation wouldn't last. Only as long as the pipe allowed, and you know damn well we huffed that fucker dry. We were in a fantasy, the yuck and muck of pure consciousness. As the great sages say: higher than a motherfucker.

What came from the pipe could ruin a whole life. And it wasn't beautiful. Each source of light had a blinding corona. I had not seen such radiancy before, but I'd paid little attention. How many years had I been ignorant? A very long time. I chose to be aware of the moment of transformation: I chose the pipe, I fucked who I wanted, I was the one who asked Rian to take me all the way. Only then could I see why the men chose this as the vehicle for destruction. I bled in the room with Rian, blood dripping like rubies to the floor. I might fall to my knees and gather what I lost in my arms. Those men from my childhood had to have seen that, too. The high could convince you that no matter the violence a reason persisted for chasing it. I understood why they used it on me. What a convincing delusion. If you accused me of worshiping my own demise, I couldn't say you were wrong.

Hours fled.

Days.

Rian said we'd only tell the truth, but I think if I asked how long he'd been high he would have lied to me. I knew the answer anyway. I wasn't special to him. This was only another body on the route. He ran his fingers along my tattoos and said, "I know what happened when you were younger. It's all over your body. It's all over your face."

"No," I said. "No."

"You're not the first to erase the past."

"Why are you telling me this?"

"I don't know. I was trying to say something."

"Say it," I whispered.

"I am not going to do it to you."

"I didn't think so."

"I would like to get to know you," Rian said.

"Come back later."

"Drink your electrolytes."

"Are you cool to leave?"

"The only way God made this in six days was on needles of pure crystal. They love me out there. You should see me. It's my element. Sometimes I feel like a god, or like I could have been." Rian kissed me again, already repeating himself. "Not anymore. Nobody thinks this thing I call my body is a god. Promise you'll see me later?"

"Yes," I said.

I spent the day thinking about Rian. You've seen a person like him. You see them all the time. He carries loads of metal in an orange vest. He loved you once, long ago, but he drank himself away from you. You went to high school with him and now he carries kegs of beer from the basement to the bar. You see him at the streetlight, both hands on the wheel, staring straight into the darkness before suddenly catching your eye with a wink. You have seen pictures of him in a hospital dying, open-mouthed and dry-lipped, or maybe even dead. He wasn't your type, but he went to town on you. You know who I'm talking about. He was there, too, pruning the garden before you woke up. He knew what happened to you, and he helped you forget about it. If you think there is a limit to how high you can get, you are wrong. You know, at this very moment, there is a probe circling Jupiter's moons, and eventually it will move beyond that, until we lose contact. I read about it much later, but I thought: There is always something farther out, something people don't know about yet. Many know far more than I ever will. That's where the trouble gets me. When all of this started I'd been very naive. Vincent had taken advantage of that, but there is nothing wrong, in the right circumstance, in letting another person guide your hand. I wouldn't want to control the spacecraft. Would you? How many days had gone by? I never paid attention to the time then. Now all I do is track what I'm losing, where I was and how I got there. I wear a watch. I like the skinny dance of the second hand, grinding all over the hours.

CHAPTER 29

Rian showed up after a few days of work, coming from a retirement party for some cop who had been on the force for twenty-five years (*twenty-five years!*) and was getting a good pension (*for the rest of his life—for yonks, for nada*). He loosened the tie of a dress shirt, wearing stiff jeans and shoes scuffed only on the lower edges so if you looked down they appeared unmarked. I told Rian that he was handsome with his hair slicked to the side. He stroked his shaved jaw and shook his wrist until his silver watch appeared. He seemed sad and calm. I hoped he couldn't see my face. I realized this was what he'd look like in his coffin.

Rian stared at himself longer than I could handle. He spoke about pilgrimages home, childhood loves with boxers (*aye a punch a punch it's not that bad*), the cop who'd kept him out of jail purely because Rian had always acted like a good boy. Rian lectured me. He told me he knew more about me than I could imagine. I kept my distance on the other side of the bed. Rian didn't believe he had too much longer to live on this planet. He said it wasn't the track marks, or the drugs, or the labor, or the poverty, or the feelings that occasionally broke through the surface.

"I love the world too much," Rian said. "That's the curse right there."

"I don't know about that," I said, even though I fully believed he did.

"Do you know what my father said before he died?" Rian was nearly naked now, rifling through his bag for the drugs. "*Rian, be good and save.* Financial advice." He laughed. "That's how he parted with the world. With me! I was still in high school. What do you think I did with my money? It wasn't saved. I'll tell you that."

Rian mixed half a dose of GHB into fruit punch, which he warned would taste like turpentine. It was worse. He gave me juice to wash it down. We smoked a little. No crazy thunderheads from our lips. Only small gentle clouds. Forgettable things. I didn't know if we'd even fuck. We talked on the bed for a while when the drug suddenly lifted me into a gasping sensitivity. If he didn't fuck me right then and there, I'd die. The high didn't last too long. I took a few breaths and had a glass of water. I wanted to keep going, but Rian had work. He kissed me goodbye, leaving in a plain white undershirt. So much for the suit. He walked to the car, a wave hit me, and I braced myself against the frame of the front door. I took the sight of the moon like a sucker punch. Do you know what the moon felt like? A reason to stay alive. I should have stopped right then, but I bungled the message from the universe.

On my phone I had a notification from some guy in Park Slope who asked me to be his party boy. I took a dizzying car to his place. The bare trees were bound with white winter lights. He met me outside to walk his dog. Nothing bad could happen if the long-haired stranger could care for a dog. He was twitchy, and we needed to be silent. In the elevator he said neighbors had complained about the noise. When the elevator let us out on his floor, he unlocked the door to an expensive loft, where he gave me a cup filled with ice and walked me upstairs to a room controlled by his voice. He told the lights to turn red, and the room turned red. He had encyclopedias along the wall, a dog bed, and a series of computers that made me think he worked in security. It was late, nearly four in the morning, and he put his dog in the other room while I got undressed. He asked if I minded if he tied my hands. I didn't mind. He hunkered over me, sweating heavily, and told me I was going to take a nail, an entire rock of crystal meth, as pure a shot as can be taken without shooting up. I told him I could handle it. He inserted a long tube into my mouth and told me to inhale when he tapped me. He sparked the pipe and blew a long dark smoke down the line, like watching fluid flush down an IV. Into my lungs rushed the white smoke. My heart, that bloodied humper, wanted out. I don't know how long I was there. When I was thirsty, he lifted a cup of ice water to my lips.

He left the room to care for the dog. When he came back, he opened a steel door revealing saws and clamps and devices that pretty much spelled the end of my life. I wasn't too worried. Enough people wanted me dead already. One more couldn't hurt. He kneeled in front of a safe and retrieved a vial of clear liquid and crystal meth. When he closed the door shut, I knew I was safe. He asked if I wanted a hit of G, and I told him, like I told Rian, that I was a lightweight and I had taken it earlier that night. The guy sat beside me, rubbed my back as my hands were still chained behind me, and he told me I could watch him deliver the proper dosage. He was a professional. He showed me the dose and told me to suckle the dropper. The guy went over to his computer while the room spun. I became extremely warm. I caught a glimpse of him doubled over, speaking to himself, butt-naked, and I knew I had to get out.

I was starting to overdose in chains through a fit of ecstasy. I rolled onto my back and pulled my knees to my chest and slipped my legs beneath my tied wrists. I sat on the bench and undid the binds. The man was still cracked, and I had to squeeze by him to get my clothes. His eyes spun like lottery balls. He flipped his soaking-wet hair and told me he might have overdone it. We called it a night. Every few seconds, my mind flushed like I'd cum, and the room blurred, accompanied by a warm and tingling rush. Not to mention the fucking lights throwing jabs that knocked out my vision. They were boxing a bitch whose mind was exploding every couple of steps, coupled with a terrible remix of a heartbeat. It wasn't a fair fight. I got dressed and called a car and told the driver he needed to hurry. My head was rolling, I was moaning, and the driver asked if I was okay. Obviously not. Just get me home. I got my keys and entered my apartment. I undressed and filled up multiple water bottles to drink. I couldn't text or form words right. Each whirling blast in my head killed some tender connective tissue. The sun was coming through the windows. I threw up dark red liquid into the sink while I shit in the toilet, trembling. Eventually, I woke up after having unknowingly passed out.

I tried to ride out the withdrawal. My bones were cold, and I treated my heart like my mother treated me in high school—better not to think of the truancy. Those beats were supposed to show up on time, but I looked the other way when they didn't. Randomly my heart beat so hard that my vision darkened, like the end of a

Looney Tunes episode. *That's fucking all folks!* I called James, who didn't pick up. I called again and again. When he finally picked up, James said, "What's wrong?"

"I need your help," I said.

"Where the fuck have you been all week?"

"If I tell you, please don't judge me."

"Which drug?"

"Crystal," I whispered. "And I overdosed on G last night."

"I can be down tomorrow," James said, and I heard him typing on his computer, probably already searching for the ticket. "I can get on a bus tonight."

"I have therapy tomorrow. You can come the day after. I appreciate this, James. I am scaring myself."

"Are you sure?"

"I'm sure," I said, and I told James I had to go back to sleep. Sleep was a rollicking fear of a heart attack. I turned on the shower to steam out the drugs, followed by splashing cold water over my head. I tried to drink meal replacements. Eventually, the next day arrived. James texted in the morning to make sure I was alive. Unpleasantly, I was. I took the worst subway ride of my human life to the Center. Everyone knew I was tweaking. Nobody stood close. I was one of those people who revealed themselves plainly, shaking in sunglasses on a bright train. I pulled myself up the station steps to the street with both hands. At each one, I had to wait to catch my breath. I was late without attempting to be. I simply couldn't move faster.

CHAPTER 30

Matan sat in his armchair, leaning back, deciding whether to speak or wait for my confession. He had one of those placid faces whose surface registered even the slightest disturbance. He never appeared angry or annoyed, only various levels of concerned. However, he normally didn't hold back. If he wanted to tell me he was scared, he told me. Now some threshold had been breached, and what common response he might have offered had I simply looked unwell he held in his throat, leaving his lips slightly parted. This was a face in wait. It didn't help that he only wore blue or white. No room for variation. I was still having trouble catching my breath. I told him I would speak, and I took another moment of silence before I tried to get out what I needed to say. I appreciated that he let me take my time. I loved him for it.

"Here's what I learned," I said. "What happened to me happened to me. That means, for the rest of my life, I will be that person. And each person I meet, I will either have to lie to or tell the truth, and then they'll think of me as that person. And it's not fair. If you do the math, I got thirteen years where I wasn't what I am now, and now I've had almost fourteen years of being this thing."

"What thing?"

"I should have said *things*. A child whore. Somebody bought and sold. You can't ever really be unsold. There's no refund. No mint-condition Dylan. What I have to offer now is a divorced, insane former child whore on his way to becoming a crackhead." I waited for a second to catch my breath. "I was gonna say *faggot* too, for emphasis."

"Shame is powerful," Matan said.

"Over the last two weeks, I have done crystal meth more times than I can count." Matan was going to say something but I cut him off. "And this week, I overdosed on G. I was in and out of consciousness for hours. It hurt. It was physically painful."

Matan took a deep breath and asked me to do the same. He was gentle in his movements, speaking in a low voice that didn't irritate me. The pipe in his office clanged and I jumped. He waited a minute for me to resettle. I told him James was coming down tomorrow, that he was going to stay for a couple weeks and keep me company.

"Let's acknowledge the fact that you asked for help," Matan said.

"I'm not so gone that I can't see what's happening here."

"I'm going to be direct. You need to stop using, immediately. Can you hear that?"

"Obviously."

"But I'm trying to talk to the adult Dylan who escaped and saved his own life. You are not fourteen anymore. Do you hear me? You are free. Even now, the door is unlocked, and if you want to leave you can leave. Do you hear me?"

"I hate this," I said, and I started to cry, which through my headache felt like pushing stones through my eyes. "You know how stupid it feels to have to be reminded of your age? I think if you brought me to a neurologist right now, maybe not right this very moment, but if you brought me to the doctor they would tell you to give up because Dylan is too far gone and he's too damaged. They wouldn't even lock me away in the ward. They'd just lethally inject me right then and there, like a sick old dog. Drop me at the pet cemetery and throw the box wherever they put unclaimed dead dogs."

"That's quite a feeling."

"I stopped myself from continuing. I had more."

"You sound like you feel very lonely, and you sound angry at what happened to you, and you also sound, despite the drug abuse, like you are asking for help." Matan scratched his brow and adjusted his navy sweater. "I need you to tell me if you are going to hurt yourself, or if you really want to stop."

"I want to stop. I did stop. I knew I had to see you today."

"When is James coming?"

"Tomorrow morning," I said, and pledged that if I was going to party again I would call him. I believed Matan cared for me, and I felt ashamed. Everything I did was to feel better. What else did we say? How come ten years passed without the smoke? Crystal's great and the sky is beautiful, isn't it? Obviously I confessed to everything he asked. I was transparent after wearing myself down. I didn't deny that I had re-created a scene from my youth, and I didn't know what I wanted from it. He approached the question from different angles, but I couldn't reveal something I didn't know. That's the truth. I was searching for something I couldn't name. The session ended. Slowly he stood and opened the door for me. I caught eyes with other therapists in the hall and cradled a cigarette until I cycled through the revolving doors to the street.

Outside Cipriani, I called James. I was embarrassed that I couldn't handle the unknown and didn't know a way out. I was sorry for interrupting James' life. While I was on the phone, Rian started texting me, asking if I wanted to hang. I didn't respond. I ignored his texts. I didn't tell James either, who was trying to impress the seriousness of the situation upon me, which was like explaining a joke to a comedian. I understood the stakes. I knew the material. I simply disagreed with the approach. Rian wanted to hang out. We didn't have to party, he said. *Hey, Did I do something?* He said, *Just tell me if it's over. It's okay. We have a connection. We have something.* I felt I owed him. He bought the drugs, the drinks, the supplies, and what did I do in return? I gave him the spectacle, the work I had been trained for.

"If I'm coming," James had said, "you cannot get high before I come. Can you do that? Will you promise me that?"

"Yes," I had said.

And I believed I could.

Instead, I invited Rian over. He wanted to know if I'd been avoiding him, treading lightly in my apartment. I was only busy, I said. To make up for it, I told him something: "You were right about one thing. What you said happened did happen. That thing. This guy would come over when I was a kid and get me as high as possible until I was barely human. I think I've been trying to figure out why or how, and I got some answers, but there's one I'm missing."

"I'm not going to rape you," Rian said, as if that were even a question.

"No," I said. "I want you to get me as high as you can. You decide. I want you to fuck me up to a point of no return. Would you do that for me?"

"If you promise me something." Rian sensed an ending, he let it be known. "If you are going to disappear, promise you will tell me first? Promise me."

"I swear," I said, but I knew it was a lie, and he filled my lungs with smoke I couldn't exhale in one breath, like a steamboat, releasing and releasing, covering the ceiling, the television, up the vents and out the windows, a curtain rising against the world. He took a hit and opened my jaw, and we passed the smoke back and forth for minutes until it was just air, the elements. I used to wonder how a person like me gets high on that dark shit, but have you ever gasped for air? Some gasp their whole lives, some get kicked right back into the water. It's not what you think of life, but it's what some of us know life to be.

Rian left.

Hours passed on the bed, alone.

I tried to stand and my vision blackened. *That's all, folks!*

CHAPTER 31

I wish I could tell you I remembered waking up, that I had a moment where I realized what was happening, but my body understood something that I am now incapable of describing, a moment of loss so analogous to death that I only register an absence. But I woke up. I gripped the stairs and pulled myself to the shower, to knock myself into feeling right with frigid water. The cold ripped out my breath by the root. I sat on the ledge and turned off the water, wrapping myself in a towel as I moved unsteadily to the couch.

My arms were numb; my heart thrashed.

If I tried to stand, stars veiled and blurred my eyes.

I knew I had gone too far.

I called 911 and said, "I think I overdosed."

"Where are you now?" I got the impression she didn't believe me from the accusation in her tone: If you overdosed then how are you talking? I answered some of her questions. I was worried that if I admitted the drugs I had taken I'd go to jail. She dispatched an ambulance. I thanked her and returned my attention to the terrible transformation of my apartment. A corona grew around every light, and it seemed impossible not to worship the world I was leaving. What had before been a lightbulb I installed incorrectly now seemed like a judge interpreting the laws of the world I

229

had lived beneath ignorantly, the arbiter through which light was filtered to capture this temporary sensual paradise.

The lightbulb said, *You fucking idiot.*

To stay awake I returned to the cold shower. What emerged from the silver pipe? A cool stampede of longing—under that pressure, I could barely take a breath. I grabbed a jacket and waited on the street. If I collapsed the ambulance would find me. I heard the siren and the ambulance approached me slowly as I waved. They didn't hurry. Two paramedics exited the vehicle and examined me as if I didn't meet the requirements for the ride—you need to be *this* dead for saving. The driver wished he'd stayed home, and the paramedic helped me into the back. I strapped into the side seat, watching my home diminish through the double windows.

"What did you take?" the medic asked.

"I don't know," I said.

"What does that mean?"

"I didn't ask."

He chewed the end of his pen and tapped the page.

"It didn't come up." The driver ignored me, and I really had to piss. "I just took it."

"Can you approximate your symptoms?"

"My heart's whacked and I'm gonna collapse." I didn't tell him his flashlight was loaded with a diamond bullet. No sense worked how it was meant to, and I didn't know how much further my sight could be deranged. "And something's wrong with my eyes."

"What type of drug was it?"

"Some kind of amphetamine."

"Was it meth? Crack? Speed? Angel dust? Did you mix substances?"

"I'm sorry," I said. "I can't believe I did this."

"It's okay, man. There's help out there. How long has this been going on?"

"Isn't the help supposed to be in here?"

"Overall," he said. "How long have you been using it overall?"

"Two weeks?"

"There are programs you can enter."

"I'm already in one."

"For how long?"

"Months."

"Do you have a sponsor?"

"It's not a drug program."

"What kind, then?"

"I'm sorry I did what I did," I said, my voice cracking. "I can't believe myself. I am so ashamed. I don't think you can understand a single word I'm saying."

"Are you hallucinating at all?"

"No." I covered my face with my hands. "I'm just not prepared."

On the speed bumps, my heart electrocuted my arms and legs, and blood drained from my head. I could barely hold myself up. I looked at my phone. It was useless. I voice-dialed Alexander.

"You," Alexander said.

"I'm going to the hospital," I said.

"What happened?"

"I don't want to die alone."

"I'll be there. Which hospital?"

"Brooklyn in Fort Greene."

I hung up. My heart trampled my chest. Each bump in the road sent my eyes rolling back, if there were any bumps in the road at all. My stomach kept dropping, and I couldn't hold on. I didn't have the power to scream. I was silently ending. The paramedic started talking about recovery programs. He spoke like someone who never received bad news. I wanted him to tell me I was fine, but we arrived at the emergency room. He helped me down and they both checked in with the nurses. I needed to piss so badly, and halfway through taking a piss the door opened and the driver leaned his head in to observe. He had to have thought I was pulling out the pipe in the bathroom. They walked me to a chair and returned to their ambulance for another emergency.

In the waiting room, the security guard watched over me. Some time passed. Alexander found me sitting across from the vending machine, where a man threatened to beat it empty before actually giving it a punch. He rubbed my back and told me he was sorry for disappearing, and that he didn't think I would die. Alexander viewed the vending machine brawl and walked to the security guard. He pointed at me, but I couldn't hear what he said. Within moments, I was brought to a room behind glass where a long-haired nurse took my blood pressure and then walked us through a corridor with people sitting in chairs, judging us to see if we would get ahead of them in line. Some wore hospital gowns, others suits, school uniforms, looks of pure hatred. The nurse brought me to a room where I was asked to piss in a cup, and then they ran an EKG, fixing sticky nodes to my chest that tingled. The machine printed out what looked like sheet music, and the tech called for a doctor to give me the test again. Just to be certain that I was having a heart attack. Another nurse arrived to check the results and ordered me to sit back down beside Alexander while he got someone else. Whoever was in charge was missing. If you're looking to become an atheist, an emergency room is a good place to start. I was trying to tell Alexander something, but my vision went, and I no longer had the ability to speak. Alexander pulled a nurse over who placed me on a gurney, seemingly disgusted that I was holding a cup of my own piss like a bouquet. He took it from me, set it down, and Alexander followed us to a skinny ward, holding my jacket and his own belongings. A deep pain in my heart started to grow and I asked him to find a nurse in the empty hallway to take me away.

"Take my phone," I said, and he held it gently. "Text James and Moans. Tell them what happened."

"What would you like me to convey?"

"The truth."

"What sort of truth?"

"The truth-truth."

"I hear you." Alexander looked terrified. "I'll do that."

"If I die, tell Moans I love him. Tell James I love him."

"Heard."

"You know what I want to say to you too?"

"I do," Alexander said.

Alexander watched the TV above me while my body fell into chaos. You wish there were more to moments like this. But there is not. There is the erasure of automation, the feeling that you have to force yourself to breathe, to stay awake, to not let go of something that you felt you never had to think twice about: staying alive.

CHAPTER 32

I woke up in a different bed with James at my feet. Alexander placed his hand on my leg then left. When I got my bearings in the Emergency Department, James was bringing food from the vending machine to the bed and stealing cereal from the nurses' station.

"Is Moans coming?"

"No," James said. "He's not coming."

"Does he know?"

"He knows."

"Why isn't he coming?"

"He doesn't want to watch you die."

"Am I dying?"

"Not anymore."

"What was Alexander watching on TV?"

"There's no TV," James said.

"What is it?"

"It shows your vitals."

"How do they look?" I asked, and James didn't say shit. He rubbed my leg and demanded to see the cardiologist, who spoke to James instead of me, as though he were my translator. They administered medication to open my arteries. James rubbed my shoulders, whispered into my ear, as the medication took a

234

flamethrower to those great chambers of being, and I screamed until my veins opened. When my heart rested, James fell asleep, head back, jerking suddenly to consciousness, saying, "I feel like I traveled across the ocean," and that he was going to go back to my place to rest a little. I stayed awake as my wide-open veins prepared for some yet-unknown passage.

CHAPTER 33

After the shift change, the loudspeaker said: *Code STEMI.* My phone was dead, and a nurse gave me magnesium and zinc, things crystal drained from your system. The little cups looked like baby food and the nurse watched me swallow to make sure I got the medicine down. Another Code STEMI was announced, and the ER door burst open with a man gurgling purple blood, reaching over his gurney to grab hold of anything. A nurse ran for a saline drip, morphine, words I didn't understand. The next casualty, a woman barely conscious with a stomach wound, losing blood as a nurse I hated gently pressed gauze to the opening, took the empty space next to me. Her gurney pressed against the curtain. To save her life they trached her throat. One moment she had a voice, the next she groaned. They floated her onto a bed of painkillers. Doctors ordered blood, trying to fill her leaking machine. They performed little procedures right there, with a bloodstained curtain separating us, all while the nurses in the opposite corner of the ER attempted to persuade a naked woman to shower because her clothes were contaminated. Security was summoned to keep this woman trapped in the bathroom. Between the contaminated woman, the dying man, and the woman whose procedures played out across the curtain in silhouettes, I knew I needed to leave. Through the curtain, a shadow man leaned over the body with a scalpel, telling her they were going to make sure she could breathe. The sounds these shadows made could haunt your dreams forever. When the nurses left the room, they didn't look convinced this woman would live. Every patient in the hospital screamed. A surgery was performed in the hallway just outside the doors.

I unhooked my heart monitor, and one of my nurses came over to convince me to keep it on.

"I have PTSD. I'm supposed to stay calm, and this is only making it worse. I need to get out of here, otherwise I'm going to lose it." The nurse started walking away when I said, "And I need you to knock me out with something that's going to keep me calm. Everyone around here is dying, if you haven't figured it out."

"They can hear you," the nurse said.

"My heart's gonna blow next."

The nurse attended to some other screamer. If you were outside the doors, you would hear one terrible voice. The child and the newborn and the stroked-out grandfather, the attending and the ultrasound whisperer and the woman who would not shower, the loudspeaker or the voice of God, even the unutterable voice that rang through my interior, all had one mode of existence: the pain of being was unimaginable and yet here they were—imagined. I could not stand to be among them anymore. I wanted my home. I signed the papers to leave against medical advice. Legally they had to hold me for twenty-four hours—cardiac watch, they called it—but the cardiologist said he would call with the final results. He never did.

James returned with a bag of clothes for me to change into, surprised that I was sitting in the chair waiting for him. I grabbed his hand—I barely had strength to walk—and we took a cab home.

James had emptied the house of anything potentially related to drugs. I wasn't going to touch them again. I hadn't meant to get here. I would never get this close again.

I regained my strength slowly. How important is the heart? It's not a metaphor, I'll tell you that. James went with me everywhere. To the bodega and the cardiologist, outside to smoke and down the stairs to the bed, where he slept beside me at night. A problem occurred where if I walked too fast I got light-headed and fell over. James caught me, most of the time. The cardiologist had told me to sit when I felt light-headed, but it was difficult to tell the difference between exhaustion and collapse. As the days passed this happened less and less.

A week later, James and I went out for lunch and walked around SoHo to buy a pair of shoes I wanted but couldn't really afford. James had to slow down to keep pace. I thought I deserved a little gift for staying alive, a pair of iridescent sneakers, which normally I would have bought with Moans, who still hadn't spoken to me, nor I to him.

I was sitting on a bench in the back of the store staring at the shoes, a little out of breath, when the look on my face scared James. He kneeled, asking quietly if I was going to collapse. I shook my head and tapped my heels. I took a benzo and put my old shoes in the new box and paid for something I wished Moans could see. James and I smoked on the stoop of the Howard Street shop and I said, "I'm going to text him."

"Who?"

"Moans."

"He didn't come to the hospital. What if you died?" James dropped his cigarette and tamped it out. "If he was in your position, what would you have done?"

"I'd have teleported to his bedside. God would have bent the laws of physics to put me there."

"But he didn't do that for you."

"I ended our marriage."

"You need time alone."

"I'm not alone now."

"Single, I mean," James said, like a diagnosis. He stood and offered me a hand. "Don't you remember the past few months?"

"Do you think I don't know why I'm here? I need to get out of the house and find the guy we went to. That's what I need. Whether I text Moans has nothing to do with shit."

"Learn from your mistakes."

"I'm going to text him," I said, and I sent Moans a message that said: *What's up, Mr. Moans?* James and I walked silently to the train. He'd become very tense and obsessed with his phone. On the subway, I waved in front of his face and he said, "All you do is betray me," which came as a surprise. I thought he was joking, making a joke of his own frustration since I didn't listen to him.

"What did I do now?"

"I asked one thing. Don't do drugs before I come down. And what did you do?"

"That was a setup."

"A setup?"

"I asked you to help me. What did you think I needed help with?"

"I set a boundary and you crossed it."

"A bullshit boundary," I said. A dog licked the floor. His owner pulled the leash. I wasn't loud. We could have been talking about the weather. I didn't have the energy to fight. I didn't know why James was mad. "You set me up to fail."

"Why did you do it?"

"I felt like I owed it to him."

"You owed *him*?"

"Something kicked in and I felt like I didn't have a choice."

"A stranger? Over me?"

"Do you want me to tell the truth?"

"And Alexander? I still don't get it. You said that he had fallen off. Always another guy. There is always another guy. And then there's me."

We arrived at the Bedford–Nostrand stop and left the subway to walk back to my apartment. I carried the shoebox in my hand. James no longer waited. As soon as we entered the apartment, he began to pack his bag. I didn't stop him. I knew he would say more. He left to call his mother and returned to say, "I need to leave for my own sanity. It's extremely difficult to hear that you chose a stranger over me when I was very clear with what I needed from you. I dropped everything for you. Do you understand that? I was on a bus for six hours wondering if you would still be alive when I got there. Can your mind even comprehend what that is like?" James grabbed his bag. "I stayed for as long as I could without losing it. You're better. I can leave you in an okay condition."

"Why are you so mad?"

"Do you remember when I was on the other side of that hotel door in San Diego? For years I never thought I was good enough because you chose somebody who wasn't me. And you have done it again. It hurts."

"We didn't have chemistry," I said. "And the stakes were different."

"Does that mean what you did was okay?"

I thought about telling James what he wanted to hear. I was tired enough not to want the heart of things beating a mess of the two of us. That's why he waited. James wanted to put down his bag, but I could not live like that anymore. I said, "We were eighteen. I was a year younger than you, too. Was what I did okay? Yes. I was escaping, and you weren't going to be the one to help me get away. That's the truth. You didn't do anything wrong, but you were not meant for me."

"No man is ever going to save you, Dylan," James said, and he left the apartment to go home. I didn't follow him. I didn't text him. I wasn't sorry. I showered and got into bed and slept. I walked slowly around my neighborhood. Every time my heart chopped at my chest I took a benzo and talked myself down from feeling like I was going to die. This was what recovery looked like, a man in the street looking at the world and walking home. Chest pains. Glittering sights. The cords on the cardiologist's table and the slick swishing of an ultrasound. A doctor who tells you that you are on the way. An ex-husband who finally responds: *Want to come over?*

CHAPTER 34

Moans waited for me outside his apartment with the dogs on leashes. When they saw me, they wailed and pulled, leaping and twisting and raving. Moans dropped the leashes and they ran to me, crying the whole way down the street, flipping onto their backs at my feet. I crouched and ran my fingers through their fur as they whimpered. I believed they knew what happened. They cried as if they had never expected to see me again. I picked them up and carried them to Moans, who led me up to his apartment. When we reached the door, I grabbed Moans' hand and put it against my chest. Moans recoiled. My shirt was twitching as that dramatic organ pounded. Moans looked half-afraid, half-disgusted, and he said, "I remember that feeling."

"It's terrifying."

"But you're fine?" Moans closed the door and I followed him into his small room, where he sat on the bed in a navy windbreaker and ripped black jeans. He had been working out, had let his hair grow, and seemed to be waiting for me to confess something. I was waiting for the same from him.

"So what is going on?" I asked.

"Aren't you the one who should be answering that?"

"I want to know something."

"That makes two of us."

"Why didn't you come to the hospital?" I sat on a leather armchair at the foot of the bed. "I don't understand."

"Why didn't I?" Moans asked. "Why didn't you want me there?"

"I wanted you there."

"That's not what James said." Moans crossed his arms and leaned against the wall. "I was told you didn't want me to cause you more stress."

"I asked for you. I waited to see your face."

"That's not what I heard."

"What did you hear?"

"The stress of the breakup made you snap."

"What are you talking about?"

Moans reached for his phone and pulled up his conversation with James. After James had told him where I was and what was happening, James wrote: *I don't think it's a good idea that you come. I'm almost at the hospital. The stress of you moving out hit him very hard. I'll keep you updated. He is with the guy you met at the bar. I think they're together.*

Moans wrote, *Just don't. Let me know if he's going to survive. I don't want to be surprised.*

Will do. I'm sorry.

And that was the end.

I said, "I never said that."

"Are you sure?"

"I didn't have my phone. I asked Alexander to tell James to get you there. I was shocked when you didn't come." I moved to the bed and sat cross-legged in front of Moans, and he uncrossed his arms. "I told him to let you know how much I loved you."

"Why should I believe you?"

"What do you believe?" I asked, and Moans patted the

empty spot beside him. I took off my shirt and offered him a benzo from my pocket. We each took one. Moans turned on the television, and we fell asleep with our backs pressed against each other, our lungs inflating and deflating in unison. We slept all day and night.

The next morning, we walked the dogs as a couple a final time. Moans took a few drags of my cigarette and teared up. I had no idea what was coming. "But I want to say something. I don't like to think of you like this, but I want you to know I know the truth." He started to cry and choked on my name. "Dylan, you were attacked hundreds of times. You were"—What a sob!—"fucking drugged—" What trembling. What power the truth had over the body. It caused devastation, a turbulence breaking him apart at the center of his being. I could not tell you if the truth freed him or destroyed him. Only time would clarify. I did not reach out to help him as he shambled in front of me. You cannot rescue somebody from the truth without submerging them further in a lie. It was up to Moans to push through the moment and rectify his inner world with the history that surrounded us. "—and sold like meat. Like meat. You were treated—in a way you never deserved—to be treated and I'm sorry—that it's taken me so long to say—that shit out loud but—I wanted you to hear it—from me while I still resemble somebody you loved." Moans crouched and rested his elbows on his knees, his head hanging down as he wiped his eyes on his sleeves. He purged a final sob that toppled him, planting both palms on the concrete. Moans stared at the ground. At what, I could not see. He took a deep breath and stood up. "Not what you were expecting?"

Moans offered me his hand, and I held it. We walked through the iron gates of his building down to a park. Moans took the leashes. The dogs sensed life in the woods and pulled him off the path into the wooded area, where he was obscured by the fronds, in a toothy yellow light. Before he disappeared, Moans turned around, his expression tense, and he grinned, ear to ear, just like when he had been above me the first time we fucked, staring down at me naked and full of love. Years vanished from his face, for an instant, no longer than the barking of our dogs, and the mask he wore in the world was gone, and Moans let me see him then as he must have been as a child in the Big Sur jungles, or as I had seen him as he was falling in love with me. I told him I loved him, and he nodded. Moans said, "One day, not now, maybe you can tell me why I wasn't the one." The dogs ran him into the woods, branches cracking beneath his feet. I listened for the last of his voice and heard the cicadas, followed by the wind. I didn't think the separation would last forever. That's what I told myself as I walked home. I realized my mistake as I reached Nostrand Avenue. I should have told him what I knew of his future, right then, as he embarked on his time without me. He was always going to be great. What I wanted was for him to comfort me, but I should have comforted him. Moans, if you're reading this, I have faith in your future. I look for you in the streets. I know you're thriving, even if you are still taking the strange path through the woods, slicing your hands on thorns and losing your way in the dark. I knew this then, and I know this now. I had no control.

All that night Moans drove me cross-country in my dreams, carrying maps I'd stolen from rest stops, stopping every now and then to walk in a field of darkness, hand in hand, lured by the blue stitches of wounded stars. You have no idea how sorry and how happy I am that we ended.

CHAPTER 35

I shaved my face and trimmed my chest hair. I wore a black hat, black jeans, white sneakers, and an old blue flannel that I still had from when I was a teenager that I knew Vincent had photographed me in when he would post me on Craigslist. I costumed myself as best I could.

I wanted so badly to take a couple of pills. I couldn't act strange; no desire could exist other than the one: sex. Russ needed to feel like I might want to fuck him, and I thought I was capable of exuding that. The problem became whether he would desire me. Thirteen years changed a whole face. He might simply apologize and pretend he had been mistaken. He might say that he now lived like a saint. I took an Ativan and placed another in my pocket, for safekeeping and a lucky charm. I practiced recording from my phone. I set the button to record, placed the phone upside down in my back pocket with the microphone sticking out, and talked to myself, checking to see how it sounded. Make sure to ask him about Vincent, I reminded myself. I was not remotely prepared, and I was prepared as I ever could be. I imagined myself succeeding unless he put his hands on me, and then I hoped, if I had any good sense, that I would kill him.

I called a car and rode to Mount Vernon. I paid cash. A warm breeze helped shut the car door after the driver let me out. I walked down Third, where the stone border of the house made it seem like the ruins of a great wall, and it continued to the next house and the one after that. They took unusual steps for privacy, tall hedges, clusters of emaciated trees, and metal fences. The street angled slightly up a hill, and I couldn't see Russ' house. My gut contracted as I tried to walk down the street like I lived there, smiling at a woman bowing to her hydrangeas who rose from the dirt with fistfuls of weeds. She ripped the plants to pieces and buried them in the dirt. She dumped bags of food in the holes she dug.

The closer I got the more each house resembled a one-room schoolhouse, a little square with a pyramid on top, painted to match the trees. Boughs of ivy extended into the street over yellow fire hydrants. The parked cars radiated heat beneath phone lines that hung between street poles. I arrived at the lamp whose orange light I'd passed through last year to knock on his door. A strange question passed through me: Who was looking at the house? Was it me then, or was it me now? I trembled at what such a home contained. A bee flew by my head and landed on a wilting sunflower. I reached into my pocket to take the other pill. Thank God.

I walked up his driveway, past his car, and entered his screened porch. There were a few stacked lounge chairs, dirt and plant food, a children's sand bucket with a yellow shovel. I didn't think he had a family, but I didn't know much about him. He worked a job in the city, and I remember that he had framed pictures on his nightstand. I wondered if his parents were alive, if Russ was short for Russell, if it was a family name, if he had siblings, if there was a person he would call if he got into trouble. I imagined his face with the prison phone linking his ear to his lips.

Russ grunted in the backyard. I followed the driveway to the end. The answer to what this man did with his days appeared in the form of evergreens. He had five trees with burlap wrapped around their roots, and he was planting them. With his back to me, I pressed Record on my phone and placed it in my back pocket. I didn't let him know I was there, at first, because I had to take stock of how beautifully he'd cultivated this land—truly. Small trees ringed the yard. The kind that lived all year, that sprung no flowers, but whose dark green leaves would outlive us. Beneath these plants red mulch darkened from a hose bubbling at the grass's edge, bruising it almost purple, a high contrast to the grass and the stone path to four benches with a firepit in the center. Russ dug into the far corner, blue gardening gloves covering his hands, where a lone Japanese maple caught the afternoon sun. Almost all the leaves were gone. He held a wooden shovel, which he slammed forcefully into the ground, stepping on the handle to leverage a stone from its place. He placed the shovel down and wiped his brow with his forearm, his face streaked with dirt. He straightened as much as he could. Russ' brittle gray hair was glistening down to his scruffy jowls. He looked like an old starving bloodhound.

I said, "Need a little help?"

Russ was startled, turning quickly, squinting. His look stirred my guts. To greet him, no matter how fragile or ugly he seemed, was to crash into his glacial eyes, all the more powerful by how little light hit them directly. One moment, they carried no color, and the next, blue light. I had the urge to turn away and was simultaneously captured. I had to look around at his wilting daffodils and upturned stones to free my legs of their temporary paralysis.

Russ said, "These things have been here longer than I have." If he recognized me as the bearded crybaby who'd appeared on his porch late one night the previous summer, he didn't show it.

"It's wild. This garden." I moved closer, until we were both in the center of his garden, encircled by rhododendrons. I ran my fingers up my neck and said, "I was driving home and thought it would be nice to drop in on an old friend."

Russ scratched his head, mouth agape, showing the bottom row of short teeth.

"It's Dylan," I said. "Vincent's boy."

Russ peeled off his gloves and slapped them against his palm. His eyes widened. "Dylan! What a surprise."

"I don't think I'd ever seen your backyard."

"I have all that leftover energy. I get the jitters. You know how it is." Russ checked beyond me, checking his neighbors' yards, and he resembled a crackhead in the sense of planting evergreens so close to winter. I was sure he got high and then drove to a nursery, taking whatever was left to be planted. "Help me with this one." He pointed at the next stone in the path and handed me the shovel. "I'm sick of tripping on these."

Russ stepped back and held out his hand, offering me space in front of him. I took my place, and he gave me directions I didn't need. I wanted to keep an eye on him, but he was standing right behind me. I took the shovel from his hand and stomped on the blade. I pressed down the handle, flipping over the stone. The bottom was damp, and in the dirt black beetles curled into themselves.

"Put it with the rest," Russ said, and I placed the stone with the other discarded pieces.

I began to sweat and touched my hands.

"I could use a break and some water." Russ pointed at the door. "What about you?"

"I'm not really dressed for gardening."

"No." Russ sized me up. "Not for gardening."

Russ walked through the back door. I followed him. Directly to the left was the living room with a couch by the window and a television on the wall. Russ didn't walk to the kitchen. Up the steps to the second floor to a bedroom, where he took off his shirt and retrieved the black case from his nightstand. The room was hardly bigger than the bed with its light blue sheets and brown nightstands. He placed the case with its pipe and crystal next to him and leaned back.

"I remember this room," I said.

"Oh, yes," Russ said. "What a wild time."

"Wild."

"Do you think about it?"

"I can still feel your dick."

"If you say that, you know what's going to happen." He adjusted his crotch, undoing the top button on his jeans. "You want to see if your memory is right?"

"I do." Russ unzipped the case, but I said, "Not yet."

I walked from the threshold to the edge of the bed, where I kneeled and leaned my arms against the bed, my elbows by his feet. The rings around his eyes were dark. He reached above him and turned the blinds. The room went dark. Russ said, "Call me Dad."

"Yes, Dad," I said.

"Do you want to party?"

"Not yet."

"Dad."

"Not yet, Dad."

"Be honest," Russ said, his dick growing hard against his jeans. "How old were you the first time I had sex with you?"

"How old do you think?"

"Sixteen."

"Nope." I shook my head and unbuttoned my shirt completely. Russ pulled down his pants.

"Fourteen," Russ said.

"Yes, sir. Just a boy, and is that the same black case, Dad?"

"Yes. Do you need to be tortured?"

"If you want to torture me, Dad."

"I loved hurting you and you loved it." Russ took out the pipe and held it by his dick. "I liked abusing you."

"Did I look younger when we were together?"

"Oh yeah," Russ said. "Did Vincent pimp you out often?"

"Yes, Dad. What did he pimp me out for?"

"Drugs. Money. Fun."

"He pimped me out to a whole bunch of guys."

"I know," Russ said, sitting up. "I told you to call me Dad. You'd do whatever he wanted."

"I don't remember a lot of the guys. It was easy when he always got me so high. I was too fucked-up. Let's talk more about us, Dad."

"Say, 'Please hurt me, Dad.'"

"Please hurt me, Dad."

"Does Vincent know you are here? He would love to know how he ruined you. Vincent would love to see you on your knees."

"What was your favorite thing?"

"How docile you were."

"Tell me everything you did to fourteen-year-old Dylan, Dad."

"You would do anything sexual for me." Russ got on his knees, erect and above me. He spit on my face, but I didn't budge. I thanked him. He continued: "You hated it. Who cares. Dad ran the show. Dad was in charge. You said whatever, but Dad did what he needed to do. Your purpose in life was to be tortured. It still is. I can see how badly you want it."

"Is that why you liked to tie me up and get me high on crystal, Dad?"

"I pissed up your ass. Did you shave?"

"If he pimped me out, I had to have no hair on me whatsoever."

"Now. Did you shave?"

"No, Dad."

"Bad." Russ reached for my face, and I winced, as his palm still covered most of my face. Once, his hands were so big that he only needed one palm to hold me down, and I believed that time would have changed this. I was wrong. He pressed down lightly on my chin. "Did he video you a lot, too?"

"I don't remember, but I wonder if he has old pics. I wonder what I looked like."

"I know. I probably still have a few. You don't look the same. I can tell what you've been up to. We corrupted you. And now you can't get enough."

"Is that what you wanted, Dad?"

"Did Vincent tell you I liked him better than you to humiliate you?"

"He told me I needed to do a better job, Dad."

"I always wondered how you liked sex like that so young."

"That was all Vincent."

"Would he torture you, too? Did he fuck you to hurt you? Did he make you beg? I used to secretly video us and give it to Vincent to sell. I heard he hit you hard."

"If I didn't clean out properly for Dad, yes."

"You were made for torture," Russ said, as he grabbed the pipe and towered over me. I met his eyes. I could tell he was done talking because he was moving his dick closer to my face. The door wasn't locked. I wasn't fourteen anymore. For a moment, I thought about staying. I went to grab the pipe and smash it across his face, but I was honestly too afraid. I wasn't trying to spare myself a worse future, although I wish I could have told you that I had that sense about me. This was not my job. I didn't need to serve him. I didn't need to hurt him. I could outrun him. Or scream. The door was not locked, and I rose to my feet, stumbling back a couple of steps, and then walked out of his bedroom, down the stairs, passing each and every picture of his friends and family, his diploma and childhood portraits, floral paintings and Gauguin prints, and emerged from his house. I ended the recording and ran away, past his evergreens and the composting woman and the town where I never wanted to return, until I found a place to call a car to the police station. I needed enough to implicate him and Vincent, and the police could get the rest.

CHAPTER 36

A man in an apron smoked a cigarette outside the police department. Somewhere nearby a brick oven was burning. The man nodded while wiping his hands clean. Inside, I approached the bulletproof glass and asked for Detective Threader. It had been four years, but Threader never struck me as the kind of person to retire. I told the desk cop I had evidence to turn over. Then, I closed my eyes and didn't think at all.

When I heard the doors open, I saw Detective Threader come toward me in a suit, looking slightly confused at my presence. We shook hands. He brought me into the interview room, which was a small gray room with a table and two rolling chairs. I felt sure I had finally gotten the evidence I needed to get to Vincent, and I felt like a different person inside that room.

"It's been a long time," Detective Threader said. "How have you been?"

"You're still here."

"It's my job."

"It's only been four years, but it feels like much longer."

"That's what everyone says to the police."

"Do you remember at the end of the case you made a joke about me wearing a wire?"

"It wasn't a joke."

"What do you mean?"

"I wasn't joking. We were trying to see if you'd be able to, but you didn't seem like you were in the right mindset." Detective Threader leaned back when he finished talking, and then he leaned over the table, putting his palms down as if they were a hand of cards. "What about it?"

"I recorded one of the guys," I said, and I placed my phone on the table and pressed Play. As I listened to the recording, I started to shake and silently cry. Everything hit me at once. I wiped my tears on my shirt as the detective switched between staring at me and my phone. When it was finished, Detective Threader said, "Do you know how much guts it takes to do what you did?"

"No," I said. "I did what had to be done."

"This piece of shit implicated the one you wanted. It is enough to investigate, but we need to talk to somebody else." Detective Threader reached out for my hand again, and then lifted his palms apologetically. Nobody else was in the office. The empty chairs sat beneath gray desks. The heat kicked on, and he lifted his fingers to the button at his collar. "I will tell you something. There are cases that you think about and cases you forget. I remember your case now, but I don't think about it. It hurt not to get these guys back then, but so much worse happens around here. Every day. And then you have the backlog in your mind. I am not numb to anything, but I look at the world from the perspective that it seems unreal and is real too."

"You sound like me."

"I have seen some of what you've seen, even if it hasn't happened to me."

"I hate being here," I said, looking around the office. "I didn't want this to be my life, and yet here I am in a police station. I am so tired. I can't believe what happened. Today, I mean. The old stuff I can't believe on other days."

"Life is a motherfucker, and some days are just a bitch."

"I think that's true."

"Sometimes, buddy."

"And other times?"

"I wish to God I never got born."

CHAPTER 37

Matan always referred to trauma as "unbearable aloneness in the face of violence." This time that did not apply. Detective Threader forwarded the recording to the FBI, and the next week I took an Uber to the FBI building. The car dropped me off at a green intersection, three rows of pines, and black iron gates. The early December day returned us briefly to the end of summer. You get days like that in New York, not the endless summer of San Diego, but days so out of place you might forget it will ever get cold again. Your parents will text you and tell you it's seventy-eight degrees in December like it never happened before, that they are at the beach, and ask you what you are doing with the great weather. You forget this weather happens every year. If you're lucky, the surprise will remind you of better days, like it does for me: endless summers of freedom. The detective waited in the parking lot, holding a manila envelope, handsome and tan, wearing a polo and khakis. Behind him, the FBI building was a gray square with opaque windows. Truly pristine grass—the kind untouched by man, mirage-like— led to a small man-made pond, aflutter with gnats and dragonflies and swooping birds. Some people think beauty is noble and sway wholeheartedly at the disguise.

"It still takes a minute to recognize you," Detective Threader said.

"It's me," I said.

"You didn't have all that ink."

"You get addicted, and then you're me."

"Did the ones on your hand hurt?"

"A little."

The detective scanned me, wondering which of these tattoos linked, if any, back to the time when we first met. He ran his hand along his forearm and told me he wanted one there, and then on the other side of his arm, and then on his bicep. He looked like he was scratching a full-body rash. "There's the liaison. Don't worry, buddy. You're in good hands now."

The liaison opened the gate with his pass.

We entered the building able to breathe easily, as we walked past a metal detector in a gray-painted lobby, where a single security guard watched us turn to a corner room. Temporarily hung on the wall were portraits of the president, vice president, attorney general, and FBI director. One face blended into the next. I could imagine the day next year when the janitor rolled his roving garbage can to this spot, where he'd drop each portrait into the garbage with a flick of the wrist. The second any photograph was hung, the moment was already gone. People held on to their lives more the less it was documented. I tried to greet each moment as plainly as it came. I was living in the present and failing, and I tried to let shit go. Maybe I was becoming successful after some practice, or failing less obviously. It was hard to tell. You think you're ready to tell your story, and then you're facing a portrait of the president, thinking to yourself, *I won't ever be a great monk*, and you realize you're never going to be prepared. I could barely explain the present moment, if it existed at all. Once it happens, it's already gone, and a new present arrives, and so on and so on. That's how I felt waiting for the interview room to be unlocked.

Twenty-seven years before this I was born. Fourteen years after that, I met Vincent. Thirteen years after that I was attempting to ensure the safety of anyone who chanced upon all those men. But the present moment? It's your breath, whoever encounters this story, since mine has long passed. Now, I am far away from that very moment, if I am even alive. There's a chance my present has ceased. If that's the case—if I'm gone—I had two hopes: to map a way of healing from a form of violence I never totally understood, if it's understandable at all, and to provide a guide on how a person in the present of their lives might speak the unspeakable. Language failed me for many years. All I did was run and scream. That might be my legacy, too. Anything can go in any direction.

Finally, the special agent for crimes against children arrived and unlocked the door to a small gray room. There was a table and four chairs, and I sat in the corner closest to the wall. We drank our water and stupidly considered the empty cups. Threader stacked our cups inside each other and crushed them into a ball. He moved his chair back, whereas I nearly leaned my elbows against the desk, and crossed his arms. I sat across from the liaison between the FBI and the police. Threader broke his posture to place his manila envelope on the table in front of the special agent, who had parted long dark hair, a cerulean shirt, and two phones.

"Hi, Dylan," the special agent said, leaning over the surface like a writer, hunched and interested, hoping for information, her hair falling all over her shoulders and arms. "My name is Special Agent Qian, and I work with the FBI on their Safe Streets team. Part of that team is the Violent Crimes Against Children division, which is my specialty. I work many of these cases. I hear you declined to pursue a CVA case. Is that true?"

"I want to tell you that I still have time to figure it out, but I don't want the money. It's a great law because I had time to think, but it's a bullshit law because I don't know what money is gonna solve."

"You may change your mind."

"Knowing me, that'll be years after it's possible to do anything."

"You're lucky to have her," Detective Threader said.

"To start, can I have your information?"

I handed her my ID.

"Great, and I want to say, however you want to start, if you want to start now with the confession, which, by the way, you did good work. I was joking that you could join the FBI. I have seen many victims attempt to get a confession and you were able to get some good stuff."

"I was terrified I wouldn't get it right. I needed him to talk about Vincent. That's honestly all I want. I never would have met Russ if it weren't for him."

"You're a smart guy," the liaison said, without any inflection of meaning. It didn't matter if he meant it. It seemed rehearsed, as if he had said this many times before, in other circumstances, in order to receive something in return.

"I'm not that smart, but I needed that confession." My eyes welled up, and I shook it off. "I needed that."

"Are you ready?"

"Yes," I said.

CHAPTER 38

Matan had nothing in his office other than an analog clock. We would be taking a couple weeks' break for the holidays. I realized I knew little about Matan. I noticed his wedding ring, and I was sorry I couldn't ask him more about himself. Today he wore loafers that made me doubt he lived in the city. He was gay, but never understood my references, and he liked to laugh. I imagined him as a wonderful party guest. I also knew that if we met in real life that he would not like me, though he probably would have liked Moans.

"Since what happened started, it has been thirteen years, but since I escaped it's been ten years. Some days it feels like no time has passed at all, and other days I feel like I'm still fourteen."

"Can we stay in the feeling together?"

"I can try," I said. I smiled and told Matan, "I have been doing one thing."

"What?"

"Counting down the months until the window ends. Eight, bitch."

"You said that Vincent carved the wedding date into the window, and that when you were raped"—I squinted, still, it unnerved me, the word—"you counted the days until you no longer had to perform the tasks he asked of you."

"That's true," I said, "but I don't get the connection."

Matan saw me check the time, and asked if now would be a good time to end. I told him I'd think about what he said, and we could pick it up on Friday. You think because some shit resembles other shit that I can understand the meaning? That wasn't totally true. I understood exactly what he meant, but I couldn't express the meaning in words. Near the end of the session, Matan said he had business matters to bring up, and asked if we could change the subject. Matan seemed excited, calm but hurried. He adjusted himself in his seat and rolled his shoulders. If the bitch had a trumpet, he'd have blown it. I thought, for a moment, that he was going to tell me we were finished with therapy.

"In the spring, I'm going on paternity leave," Matan said. "We are having a baby."

"Congratulations," I said.

"Thank you. That means for five months I won't be in the office. During that time, we can try to arrange you to be able to speak with someone else. When I get back, we can return to our sessions or discuss what you need at that time." Matan took a long drink of water, and then he set down his water and asked, "How do you feel about that?"

"I'm happy for you."

"No other feelings?"

"To be honest, I've been thinking about taking a break from therapy. I thought you were going to say we were done, like it did what it needed to do, so it was over. But I'm relieved it's not that."

"We are not done, and we still have months of meetings before I go on leave."

"Are you excited?"

"I'm thrilled," Matan said, and he smiled in a way that broke himself open, that showed the gleaming-white teeth, all in order. He didn't smoke. I think he had been wanting to tell me about his child and had waited because I had not wanted to know about him. I have lost trust in people in seconds, often when they revealed themselves in the briefest inconsequential flashes, and I never wanted the opportunity for ammunition to fall into my hands. Matan sensed this, too, which is why he'd waited until that moment to give me a glimpse of his life. I was happy for him. I believed he would make a great, unstylish father. Matan would let as little harm come to his child as possible.

THE WINDOW

CHAPTER 39

After all that, the window ended and just disappeared. Matan had a child. Moans took the dogs west again. I never destroyed my heart. I graduated from school. The pizza shop I worked at closed down, and another one opened, and every other shitty thing you hear about New York continued to happen. Williamsburg is the new Village (except the people who live there know they are assholes), and I tell stories to my boyfriend about the places that used to be where something else exists now. The phrases of New York continue to be *Fuck out of here*, and more importantly, *Do you remember when?* I miss California, but I rarely consider leaving anymore, except for some lonely hours when I misremember my youth as a period of freedom that I didn't really have. I never miss Moans. We made our peace, and I think that's why occasionally I fantasize about getting absolutely pummeled by a stranger: I only long for what torments me. Imagination remains the sole inheritor to my past. It is the only part of me that still has such proximity. People lie and say they live in Bushwick when they really live in Bed-Stuy, which looks more like Carroll Gardens every passing month. People move to Brooklyn, and the next day start screaming about gentrification. It's a rite of passage to pretend you have lived here longer than you really have, and then to leave the next year because the city doesn't care about you. Next time you're in Brooklyn, go to Happyfun Hideaway and find the drunkest person at the bar: they won't be here next year. I could tell you more about Manhattan, but I care less about it every day. It's a college town, for all I know. More important: I gave up my years of bottoming and turned into a top, which is the gift of dealing with your trauma: you will get rock hard again, and I wished Matan would have told me that from the start.

Today, I light a cigarette in the morning and slowly walk around my neighborhood. My goal remains to stay alive, in case I have to give a victim's impact statement at the trial. The men would rest behind desks in their suits, staring at the scuffed floor. I think about what I will say. The trouble with the statement: Nothing would change their minds. The men who annihilated me care nothing for my troubles, and I laugh at the idea that I would ever tell them that they had ruined my life. If you could cover the mouth of a child as you raped them, an adult berating you with the sadness of life isn't going to trip any wires. I have ideas of placing a stethoscope to my heart and forcing them to listen to the beating. It's true. I want to punish them more than justice. The men would never change. People like that don't. As much as I want the gavel slammed on them, for my sake, I want to give the boys in their future as good a chance as any at escaping the pipe and binds. I wasn't trying to save anybody.

I no longer kept my life a secret. I went to rehab for the trauma, and a man liked every single picture I had ever posted of myself. Every day, a couple more hearts. I didn't see any of this until after I got out. The man I woke up next to today was trying to get my attention, and he did. He's very handsome, and we like to video each other when we fuck and show other people. What I'm saying: we have fun.

Why did I waste time and money to go to a rehab if I didn't need it? I hadn't realized how far I had come from my own youth, partially due to the accelerating nature of loss and the toll of my mistakes. Surrounded by strangers who could barely utter their own histories, I witnessed the start of a new era. I told the story in groups and in individual sessions. I could talk about everything. I made a fucking map of it on day one. The therapists told me I didn't need the rehab. It takes time for the mind to catch up. I flew back home to Brooklyn, where I went on a date with the man. We got drinks at The Rosemont, where he fingered me on the patio in front of everyone, took off my shoes to lick my feet, and gave me hickeys on the floor after we fell off our chairs. The boyfriend is the type of person who dares you, and he hadn't realized I was the person to say yes. He knows what happened to me. Similar events happened to him. As I moved through the years, men frequently told me stories of their own youths, and every so often I would see Alexander at Nowhere or Unter or somewhere else in the dark of night, when the blue lights beam down on the face of a stranger who had once been a friend. We make eyes and nod and dance away from each other. I don't wish Alexander the best. I dream of his life in ruins. I want to say he prays for the same, for the truth to strike his life and let him touch the world as he knows it, not as he pretends it to be. I don't think he ever told anyone. I never saw his name in the cases. And then I hope peace settles over him. If it hasn't already. I don't know.

I toss my cigarette in the sewer and return to bed, where my boyfriend sleeps with a pillow over his face. Maybe we will waste the day, my boyfriend and I, by day drinking and sucking each other off in the bathrooms of cash-only bars. He's street-smart, hung, and a little bit of a fool. I'm lucky.

I carry a plastic bag that holds a shirt from the Vincent era, a shirt from one of the pictures the FBI found. The shirt no longer fits. The blue-and-black flannel is Bible-paper thin, ragged, with the old scent of a thrift store and the candles that once burned in Vincent's room. I don't know why I kept it so long. (It is harder to let go of what happened than I thought. For so long, I took so much meaning from terror. I am afraid of such a loss. Who will I be if I am not bound to an altar with a knife at my throat?) When I ask my boyfriend to breathe in the scent, he tells me that it's time for the shirt to go, which I know. It's ugly. I know. It's old. I know.

So instead of lazing around, two years after the window finally closed, I decide to celebrate the anniversary. Another false mark in an alternative history to which I belong, as do many others I will never meet. I rent a scooter in East Williamsburg, and we each wear a blue helmet. I sit up front and my boyfriend sits behind me, his arms wrapped around my waist. He doesn't like to ride the scooters. He has nightmares of a fiery crash that ends his life prematurely. Tonight, as the falling sun reddens the sky, he rides for me, all the way down to Riis Beach. As we push beyond the boundaries, my phone vibrates as we break the permitted zones. You're not supposed to leave the city, but I don't care. Nobody rides these scooters anyway. I'll be banned after this, and it won't affect my life at all. What a great feeling to have mistakes that cost you nothing. The wind blows over Marine Parkway Bridge and the silhouettes of stragglers blend into the dark blue night. We hit the peninsula and slide into the quiet beach. I don't want the cops to catch us. I drive slow and act normal. The last streaks of light break with the waves. Darkness settles as we park the bike and waste a few minutes on the boardwalk, hearing the water and broken glass of the abandoned building above the beach. First it had been a tuberculosis hospital, then a planned HIV ward, then an old-age home before the city shut it down. Now it's a cruising ground that is soon to be dirt. One good storm and the hospital will be rubble.

I take out the shrooms and leave my bag on the bench. We remove our shoes and walk onto the cold sand. We bury the shrooms. We don't need them, and my boyfriend makes a face like they should be saved. They can't. They're already gone in someone else's future. Fate, baby, do your work. I want to remember this, I tell him. Close to the water, the hard sand cracks beneath our feet. My boyfriend stays beside me. He does not talk, nor persuade me against the idea. I ask him to hold the shirt while I light the edges. He cups a hand around the flame. I take the old flannel and light a sleeve on fire. Up the wind comes black curls, a bright orange climbing flame, and I walk farther into the water, as the shirt, engulfed in a long-ago fire, in a fire I did not ignite, in a fire I would end, starts to burn my hand. An ocean breeze drags across the fire and stings my eyes. My boyfriend gasps. I am barely singed. I laugh at how stupid a death this would be, to consider an offering to my youth and end up a victim—a sacrifice, just like the sick old Greeks had imagined the word. I laugh like a boy who was once in trouble, and from this laugh, with a cradle of flames to my face, I scream what is due to any great effigy and pitch the flames into the air. I look at my boyfriend, whose face is illuminated briefly, as the burning tatters stream into the ocean like great tears, plunged into an irresistible coldness. I look for all of you. I look back at the city, where you are waiting for someone to burn their hands in your honor. I look back at my boyfriend, who I can tell is still afraid of what happened to him. Do you know I scream for you? I want you to see what it looks like to let go. I want you to hold my hand in the water. We trudge against the tide back to the beach and collapse into a shivering, sea-dark stupor, staring at the moon that had for so many years brightened those nights I had wished to not be alive in Vincent's bedroom. The end of its light meant the end of my trouble because the men would go home. I held my knees as my boyfriend cupped my palm. I touch my hand where it hurts. A thousand boys were keeping secrets. What should I tell you? This is only a moment of suffering, and it is passing already. What follows gets only the briefest grip on your life before it passes away. Should I tell you what will become of me? But wait, you people, the moment of telling—it is already gone.

ACKNOWLEDGMENTS

Thank you to John Freeman, Katie Kitamura, Nathan Englander, Chris Parris-Lamb, Sarah Bolling, Tim O'Connell, Maria Mendez, and Jon Karp. To Deborah Landau and NYU. The New School. The S&S team. The Corporation of Yaddo. The Crime Victims Treatment Center. Yuval Moses. Scott Korb. Albert Mobilio. Lindsey Hoover. Jane Pritchard. Joana Sozio Pinheiro Guimarães. Raven Leilani. Cleo Qian. Kyle Carrero Lopez. Breyon Gindin. Arya Roshanian. Edan Lepucki. August Thompson. Asiya Gaildon. Parker Tarun. Cosima Diamond. Sam Lee. Elizabeth Nicholas. Carl-David Parson. Matt DiCiero. Sam Glatt. Dylan Leggio. Mikki Janower. Asafe Pereira. Vincent Napoli. My family: Gail. Marc. Shelley. Kelsey. Karen. Steve. My husband: Richard.

ABOUT THE TYPE

This book was set in Adobe Garamond and Pontiac Inline. Designed by Robert Slimbach, Adobe Garamond is a digital and contemporary interpretation of the original Garamond typefaces. It is a classic type in the world of desktop typography and design. Less is known about Pontiac Inline, but it is a layered Art Deco font designed by Fanny Coulez and Julien Saurin in Paris.

Printed and bound by BPG-USA, Fairfield, PA
Designed by Wendy Blum

ABOUT THE AUTHOR

Kyle Dillon Hertz received an MFA in fiction at New York University, where he was the Writer in the Public Schools Fellow. He lives in Brooklyn.